For Sue,
      Take time to
read the books.

Marilyn Pilegums

ON THE STRENGTH OF WINGS

ON THE STRENGTH OF WINGS

Marthayn Pelegrimas

Five Star • Waterville, Maine

Five Star First Edition Women's Fiction Series.

Published in 2001 in conjunction with Marthayn Pelegrimas.

Cover art by Scott Osia.

Set in 11 pt. Plantin.

Printed in the United States on permanent paper.

Library of Congress Cataloging-in-Publication Data

Pelegrimas, Marthayn, 1948–
    On the strength of wings / Marthayn Pelegrimas.
        p. cm. — (Five Star first edition women's fiction series)
    ISBN 0-7862-3378-8 (hc : alk. paper)
    1. Overland journeys to the Pacific—Fiction.
  2. Women pioneers—Fiction. I. Title. II. Series.
  PS3566.E36 O5 2001
  813'.54—dc21   2001033062

With heartfelt thanks and admiration to Jan.
We've made the journey together
because we *wanted* to,
not because we *had* to.

PROLOGUE

I was born knowing.

Answers and the warmth that only comes from true wisdom filled my heart close to bursting. And common sense. When the good Lord was handing out level heads, he put mine atop two of the squarest shoulders he had ever made. Pettiness and jealousy only serve to eat up what time we do have. I've always known the important pieces that make up a lifetime.

Mother's favorite story, concerning her middle child, serves as an example of how I have always conducted myself. She takes great pride not only in her three offspring, but also in her ability to remember and recount our family history. It's always the same: she starts off by including everyone seated around the table where she has inevitably settled after a holiday meal. The big dining room is warmed by all the bodies gathered as well as heat from the fire in the kitchen. We're usually so full of ham or turkey or mincemeat pie that we haven't got the energy to move.

"Remember?" she asks. Then polls random faces for verification. "You remember, don't you Harold? Remember, Margaret?" Two nods are all the steam she needs to continue. "When Mae would come over to visit Abigail, how she goaded little Abby to play her game."

"Aunt Martha . . ." Mae smiles and nudges the nearest person. She's past being embarrassed and is known for having a wonderful sense of humor. ". . . now you know that

7

we've all heard this story hundreds of times. Maybe you could think of another tale to entertain us with?"

But I always intercede on Mother's behalf. "Oh, no, Mae; we want to hear it again. Especially the ending. Stop interrupting."

Mother continues, "Mae would sit out on the porch and ask 'Why is the sun so bright? When will the rain water the flowers again? Why do flowers need rain anyway? Don't you wonder about all these things, Abigail? Aren't you the least bit curious?' Every question found its way to her tongue and she buzzed all day long asking her whys and whens. I dare say she drove us all frantic with her constant asking.

"But Abigail would just rock in that little chair of hers, out on the lawn. Never answered when she was asked, over and over, if she was curious or why she was not curious about anything Mae chose to wonder about. No, she just rocked, back and forth, while Mae chattered on. You were always a tranquil child, Abigail. Nothing ever seemed to agitate you.

"Well, about the time Mae asked her twentieth question, I believe it was, 'Do you think God knows how many leaves are on that tree?' Abby stood up and slowly started toward Mae. She walked with such purpose, all the while her little feet kept catching in her skirts. She would fall to her knees, straighten up, walk a few more steps, get caught again. I remember watching from the parlor window.

"When she finally had climbed all ten of the steps, she sat herself down, straightened her skirt and calmly, with great deliberation, struck Mae. Not a playful slap. No, she made a fist and brought it squarely down on poor Mae's head.

"I waited for my niece to let out with a cry of some sort. But Mae just sat staring at Abby with an expression of shock on her face."

The room always fills with laughter when Mother comes

8

to this part of the story. My elder brother, Robert, adds his commentary.

"And still she maintains her ladylike demeanor, our Abigail. But one well-placed fist, most times as not, gets her point across more efficiently than volumes of words."

"Now wait," Mother continues, "she did add a few words after Mae made quite sure she wasn't hurt and wailed, 'What ever possessed you to hit me?' Abby looked straight ahead and replied, 'You are a silly girl and I am tired of your silly questions.' Then she stood again, marched back to her chair, and sat herself down as pretty as you please."

Each time Mother finishes her story, all the relatives laugh at my spunk and I am again reminded of my five-year-old frustration. For I always thought of myself as being caught in quite a predicament. My soul yearning to impart its wisdom, express itself, all the while surrounded by a family subscribing to the doctrine that a child was to be seen and not heard. Patted on the head, tickled under the chin, talked *at,* but never with.

Father was the only grown-up who seemed to sense my uneasiness. But he hasn't been home in years. Right after Charles suffered his second bout with influenza and was displaying early symptoms of consumption, Father gained employment with a large import firm abroad. My parents' marriage seemed to have improved with each mile that separated them. But still, I often wonder if having a father in residence would have helped me feel less peculiar.

By the time I was ten, I understood that if I stayed to myself, relied on my good sense and divine knowledge, I found contentment. It was my experience, however, that a wise child made for a sullen child. And while I appreciated each new day, I appeared distant. Mother called Robert, my elder brother, her charming man. My younger brother, Charles, was Mother's sickly boy. And I, Abigail Lavinia, was Mrs. Belshaw's quiet child.

When I turned sixteen, it was enough that I knew the quiet demeanor housed a wise soul. There was no longer the need to fight to be heard. Wisdom I had been born with was not only there to guide and comfort me but was my very fabric.

I have known all of this without question.

PART ONE

BALTIMORE: 1847

CHAPTER ONE

The women in my family, as far back as I can recall, have always chosen practical men.

Father's mother, Granny Sarah, was a seamstress. She specialized in outfitting members of touring dance and circus troupes. Her spangled costumes and feathered flounces made her as popular as the entertainers themselves. Where one row of lace sufficed, Granny stitched in three. She worked and dreamed on an exaggerated scale. Red was her preferred color not only for her famous costumes but for her own clothing as well.

New work required that she order yards of silks and satins. And it was during one of her trips to a specialty shop in New York that she met the new clerk, Ezra Belshaw, a young man of sixteen. Ezra had just arrived in town to learn the business of shop keeping. His parents, recently killed in a terrible fire, had left him not only freshly orphaned but without home or sustenance.

Ezra was a sad, withdrawn boy. Until he met the vivacious Sarah. With each order she came to place or pick up, the boy fell more in love.

Coincidentally, the very day that young Mr. Belshaw gathered courage enough to ask Miss Sarah to dinner, the petite woman arrived quite upset having just fended off the advances of a drunken actor during one of his fittings. So you can imagine how charming the naive clerk seemed in comparison when he stuttered an invitation.

And it was at that precise moment, Granny explained, "That I saw Ezra for the true gentleman he was. I realized I had been blinded by all the glitter. Before me stood the genuine article."

They were married on Grandpa's seventeenth birthday and my father, their only son, was born a year later.

Granny Mary, my mother's mother, studied at a conservatory in England. First the violin then the cello then the harp. She practiced the classics until her fingers bled. Born into a family of musicians, she grew up knowing and caring solely about her precious music.

But when it came time to choose a husband, she married Thomas Meeker, the owner of the theater in which she gave her farewell performance. A man seventeen years her senior who filled in her life with the "real world." Thomas took his new bride on her first picnic, he taught her to manage the household money, bake bread and put up preserves.

They had three children, all girls: Wilma, Freida and Martha. Thomas taught, the gifted yet inept, Mary, how to bathe, feed and diaper her babies. She gained ten pounds with each child and when she wedged her dusty violin under her double chin, she smiled at what a wonderful life the practical, hardworking theater owner had given her.

Aunt Wilma, the eldest sister, married into a family of blacksmiths. Conversations around the table in their large kitchen were set to the rhythm of Chalmer's hammering out back. Metal beating metal kept time almost like a primitive clock.

And while it was gossiped among the cousins that Wilma kept a tintype of a world renown thespian beneath her quilts, she never conveyed her discontentment to a soul.

The middle sister, Aunt Frieda, married Uncle Harold because he was an inspector for the railroad. While it's a known truth in our ancestral history that Frieda was smitten with Wilfred Johnson, a charming piano teacher who gave lessons from his parlor, it would have been unthinkable for Frieda to marry an artist of any caliber when a reliable suitor waited just around the tracks in Maryland.

The baby sister, my mother, Martha, possessed the highest degree of artistic temperament. While Frieda played the piano and Wilma molded little statues from clay, Mother set up her easel and mixed jars of colors. Her still life paintings and seascapes filled every closet in grandmother's house. Her most recent family portraits line the hallways in her own home. She writes poetry as well as short stories. Several have appeared in the "Ladies' Home Companion." She designs our clothes and does all the stitching herself. But she, like her sisters before her, chose a practical man.

I am told my father was an enterprising boy. He set his sights on becoming a wealthy man by the time he was twenty-five. His cradle was set up in the smallest room in the white house attached to Grandpa Ezra's store. Father's playground was the worn wooden planks of the store and his playmates were the salesmen who called daily to sell Grandpa new merchandise. While other children were learning their ABCs, Father was learning credits and debits. He was an eager learner and born of such an outgoing mother as Grandma Sarah that he won over many friends due mostly to his affable personality. And those who were not susceptible to his wit and charm were won over by his handsome looks. He had it all. His plan was right on schedule . . . until he met my mother.

Martha Meeker was an aspiring writer and artist when she met and fell instantly in love with Dalton Belshaw. It had been her great desire to travel abroad, to live among other artists. But the desire to be with her new-found love suddenly became the only thing she wanted.

It was immediate for the both of them. He had to have her. She had to be his. They were married a week after that initial meeting.

The men in my family talk often of the balance within their households. "Find yourselves creative, lively women," Uncle Harold constantly advises my brothers. "They fill your heart with passion and your life with excitement. It's the man who must make a solid and sturdy home, but it's the woman who fills it with beauty and music."

My brothers listen and agree. Everyone happily agrees.

Except me.

For over the years I have sensed the discontentment deep within the females surrounding me. It seems only reasonable, I suppose, that such a creative bunch would tire, occasionally, of their uncreative husbands. When I hear Aunt Frieda play a waltz, I wonder if she secretly plays it for her absent teacher. And I also wonder, would it have been so terrible if my aunts, or mother, or even grandmothers had trusted more in their own talents?

Therefore, due mainly to my inborn wisdom, I have grown, deliberately, into a practical woman. And, due to my observation, I have chosen a husband with similar interests and ideals. And these instincts and insights have left me, like the other women surrounding me, married to a practical man.

CHAPTER TWO

My husband, Samuel, was born on the twentieth day of April, in the year eighteen hundred twenty-seven. His entrance into the world brought exceptional joy to his parents. Lenore Gray had been told by several doctors that she was unable to have children due to her delicate nature. And her husband, George, feared that if the doctors were correct, Baltimore would be minus a master ship builder produced by the Gray family for the first time in seventy-five years.

But fate not only smiled at the anxious couple, it laughed. Four children, two boys and two girls, followed their older brother, Samuel, in four consecutive years.

Even before any of the youngsters were old enough to understand, their father introduced them to the sea. It was the belief of the senior Mister Gray that respect and love of the water should be considered more important than walking or speaking. This introduction was followed by lessons in navigation and sailing. As each child graduated from playthings to primers, they were educated in the reading of building plans. When coordination matured, tools were handed out along with warnings on the use and care of each piece. I must admire Mr. Gray's progressive thinking, for his girls were equally instructed with his boys.

How often Samuel has reminisced about his unique childhood:

"The shipyard was the best place for a boy to be. Excitement hung in the air and clung to our clothes. Father's office

17

in front of the warehouse always smelled of fresh wood. I can't remember a time when he was free of the shavings or sawdust: in his hair, on his lapels. His whiskers were spiced with sunshine and bay water.

"Outside, the air was filled with the pungency of fish and oysters being loaded on great ships along with bales of tobacco. Voices laced with foreign accents shouted to be heard above peddlers and bells and ships' horns. It was a noisy playground for my brothers and sisters and me.

"My father knew everyone. From the builders, to the captains, to the merchants. He remembered each name. They all respected him and, in turn, respected his wife and children. Our house overran with their gifts from distant ports of call."

Now, it was my mother's habit to walk along the shore in search of the perfect subject and lighting for one of her masterpieces. She would study and stare, impressed by the many shades of blue the water offered up. Recalling a specific wave or cloud later when she brought it to life on canvas. How I begged to accompany her. For although our walks were leisurely and we were not far from the house, it felt as though we roamed a foreign land.

It was on one of these trips that I saw the five Gray children scampering, playing hide and go seek amongst the great ropes and carts and commotion that the seaport held. I had never seen any of these faces in my schoolroom for we lived within the city while they lived on the edge.

I remember peeking at the tallest boy, who appeared to be close to my age, and thinking he had the most wonderful grin. Mother later teased that I would grow up to be a terrible flirt if I did not watch myself. Of course I denied being guilty of any such thing. But my pulse still quickens when I remember Samuel with my ten-year-old heart.

My Uncle Harold traveled our state extensively. His duties for the railroad necessitated that he ride the lines and inspect the great engines. He was hard working and dedicated to a profession he loved. At the groundbreaking ceremony for the Baltimore and Ohio, he had even given a short but eloquent speech.

It was due to these travels that Uncle Harold became acquainted with George Gray. And it was my gentle uncle who brought the news to our table that the entire Gray family had been lost at sea.

I remember Mother served stew that night. I was passing the bread to Aunt Frieda. She took the bottom slice then nudged her husband. "Tell what you heard today."

Uncle Harold looked down at his plate. "It's so sad. Such a sad, sad shame."

"What is?" Father put down his cup. "Tell us."

"The Gray family. You've heard of them?"

"The ship builders? The ones with a shop down on Lancaster Street?" Father stroked his beard.

"Yes, they've been there for years. I've had several conversations with George, myself. Very nice man." Uncle Harold had a difficult time getting to the point.

I continued eating my dinner. This was grown-up talk.

"They have five children. Well-behaved, bright youngsters. Maybe you've seen them by the docks? They're always helping their father." Aunt Frieda touched the pearl button at her throat as she spoke.

Mother smiled, remembering my infatuation. "Abby and I have seen them on occasion."

Uncle Harold still couldn't bring himself to tell us the story; he was a soft-hearted man, so Aunt Frieda continued.

"They decided to take the children to England. Mr. Gray thought it would be a great adventure, having the whole family on the maiden voyage of one of his very own designs."

Uncle Harold set down his fork and folded his hands together above his plate. "They are lost. No sight of the ship nor its passengers. Families of the crew are waiting for word. They are three weeks late in their arrival."

"What if they encountered a storm? Or somehow got off course?" Father raised his heavy eyebrows in question. "Things like that are common, aren't they?"

"I would think so. But still there is concern for their safety. Up and down the line, I hear stories."

My heart and spirit dropped thinking I had lost my love without ever having really known him.

Before another three weeks passed, however, our family was to learn that wreckage of the *Baltimore Lady* had been spotted and several bodies recovered from the sea.

When I accompanied Mother on her next excursion to the docks, that wise old voice inside my head counseled my sorrow. I held my mother's hand tightly and allowed myself to be guided through the streets. The same streets that had once felt his footsteps. But I could not bring myself to look at the cold water.

We finally came to a quiet spot. As I lifted my face to the sun, I caught sight of Samuel Gray sitting on a large rock, bare feet dangling in the wetness. You can imagine what shock we experienced at the sight of the sad boy. I half thought we were watching a ghost. Mother waved as we approached.

After a few minutes of awkward introductions, Samuel told us that he had been left behind by his family due to his propensity toward sea sickness. His father had grudgingly left his eldest son in the care of a family friend.

As he told us his story, my mother knelt to touch his shoulder. He seemed grateful for the sign of affection and smiled up at her kindness. I was too overcome to offer any sympathy. The very idea of being left on my own, with no family, was a devastating notion I did not care to consider.

CHAPTER THREE

I can still remember the memorial service for Samuel's family. Two large wreaths of greenery tied in black ribbons were tossed into the sea. Then four small bouquets were thrown into the choppy water and left to trail behind the wreaths as the dark water swirled. A prayer was said by Reverend Turner, and we all sang our grief in a hymn. It was a chilly day in late autumn.

Things were solemn around the shipyard for several months afterwards. The loss of the children set a more sedate mood. Laughter and adventure seemed to be missing when I next walked the docks with Mother. The men discussed business and the ladies kept their heads bowed as if not wanting to disturb the sacred ground. I heard the comment made, often, around our table as well as in the streets, that George Gray would be greatly missed. Mrs. Gray was also commended for her gentle manner. And the children. Tongues were clicked and eyes lowered to study the pattern of stitching on the tablecloth whenever the poor little ones were mentioned.

The large building that had once housed the Gray Family Ship Building business was now abandoned and locked. Outstanding debts owed by the firm were paid off from the public sale of inventory and the family home. Too young to manage on his own, Samuel was sent north to live with his godfather, also in the business of building great ships. The few dollars remaining after the sale of all his worldly effects were put in a trust to cover the youngster's food, clothing and education.

Three years passed without so much as a glimpse of the orphan. Of course, I wondered about him daily. But the distance of more than thirty miles and the fact that my family had no occasion to travel to Havre de Grace, meant that Samuel and I were not destined to meet again until I was almost fourteen.

Just as he had appeared that day on the rocks dipping his feet in the water, Samuel appeared on the porch of the Allan house. A black monstrosity, the edifice had stood in our neighborhood for too many years.

"Hello," he called from the widow's walk, three stories above me.

"Hello," I answered, sure I was seeing an apparition. "What are you doing up there?"

"My godfather's thinking of buying the place."

"You'll be moving back from Havre de Grace then?" The sun shone so brightly that day. I like to think it helped burn that precious memory deep into my brain. I held my hands like a visor protecting my eyes from the brilliant glare.

Samuel stopped his pacing and leaned over so far I thought he would fall. "Yes. Will you be glad?"

What an odd question for him to ask me. And yet, without one moment's hesitation I shouted, "Yes!"

"We shall be neighbors then as well as classmates. Provided my godfather decides to buy."

"It's a very . . . old house," I said, trying to be kind.

"And ugly, too. So ugly, I can't help but like it." He seemed happy, filled with anticipation. I wondered if his disposition was always so positive.

Suddenly I wanted to see the world from the top of that big old house. It had always seemed like a sort of looming monster. Now it was very important that I conquer my small fear. "Can I come up there? Have a look? Do you think it would be all right with your godfather?"

Samuel shrugged. "I don't see why not. He's downstairs talking with the bank man. Just come inside, I'll meet you on the big staircase." Before I could answer, he disappeared.

I raced up the steep steps and pulled opened the heavy door. The foyer smelled of damp wood and dust. There was no one in sight and I walked, pretty as you please, across the wooden floor, up the grand staircase and found Samuel waiting for me on the landing. He grabbed my hand and yanked me after him for the rest of the climb and into a small bedroom. We stepped through an open window and I found myself on top of the house.

The wind blew a greeting and some errant leaves fluttered across my shoe tops. I suddenly realized I had never been so high before. I held tightly to the wrought-iron railing. Samuel skipped across the gritty surface while I stared straight ahead, afraid to look down or upward.

I could hear his shoes scuff as he shouted to me. "Look, over there. You can see the water and the ships. I can even see my father's old warehouse. Look!"

"I can't. I feel as though I'm going to topple right over the edge."

He didn't laugh or snicker as I expected. He just spoke to me in a calm voice. "You're not going to fall. I won't let you." Stopping abruptly, he stood by me. Just stood by my side for a few minutes until I regained my balance. Even at that young age I remember wanting to hug him. The wind blew his scent into my face and I was immediately aware of a sparrow in an oak, close enough to touch.

My eyes slowly lowered their gaze and I could see the great ships as well as a few smaller boats sitting on top of the glistening water. Seagulls glided by as if suspended on silver strings. And clouds drifted so close to the water it looked as though they were sailing too.

"It's beautiful." I could not offer any other words.

"Isn't it." He stood for one peaceful moment and then ran in the opposite direction and started to climb over the railing.

Horrified, I screamed, "What are you doing?"

"There's something stuck on the gable. I saw it before you came up. Looks like a kite; no telling how long it's been there." He struggled, lowering himself over the ironwork, onto the slope. One hand gripped the rusty metal for support while the other reached for the tattered square of paper.

Fear for my own safety drained as a new terror made me race across the roof and lean over the edge to cover Samuel's hand with my own. My knees shook as I tried screaming my fear but even stronger than my fear, was my surprise at how thrilling I found his daringness. My lips froze open in silence as I watched his progress. I distinctly remember my toes growing cold and then completely numb as I stood frozen there. I also remember how anger battled with the excitement that slowly gained ground within the pit of my stomach.

"Maybe, if you reach over and lean down, I can hold onto you instead of the railing. Maybe then . . ."

I was edging up, tight against the wrought iron, in spite of the terror and anger and excitement. His instructions came from a place I believed instinctively. My skirt, my favorite skirt, the one I begged Mother to stitch with green thread, was getting soiled as I ground it into the dirty railing and grabbed Samuel's hand.

He grunted and reached and for that moment, retrieving the broken toy was all we thought of. The most important thing to both of us had become the challenge rather than the kite itself. The sun warmed my face and I knew I was smiling.

Then the silence that accompanied our concentration was suddenly broken.

"Young man! What are you doing up there?" It was my

mother's voice and she yelled up to Samuel as he reached. "Get down from there this instant before you break your neck!"

I ducked down, just enough to obscure my mother's view. Still holding tight to Samuel, I whispered, "Hurry up!"

Making one last attempt, he caught the kite with his free hand and held it up for me to see.

Heavy footsteps sounded from behind me.

"You! Little girl! What in the world do you think you're doing?"

Unable to turn around, I continued helping Samuel over the wrought iron. When he was standing safe and brushing the dirt from his trousers, I still kept my back to the grown-up for fear of the scolding I would receive.

"Uncle Nathan!" Samuel held up his tattered treasure. "Look what I . . ."

"You risk your life for a piece of trash? What were you thinking, Samuel? How many times have we talked about you being more responsible?"

It was as if the words never found their target. Samuel just smiled and inspected the kite. His godfather slapped his leg in annoyance and tension hung over the three of us like a black cloud ready to explode with thunder.

Finally, realizing that Samuel had no intention of introducing me, I slowly turned. "I'm Abigail. I live next door."

"Then that was your mother? The woman screaming from the yard?"

"It was all my fault, Uncle. I brought Abigail up here and then I saw the kite and decided to retrieve it and . . ."

The grown-up in the black suit smiled, just slightly. "I'm sorry our first meeting has been so uncomfortable, Abigail. It was very kind of you to keep my godson company while I attended to business."

"My pleasure." I offered a smile in return.

"Are you going to buy the house? Are we going to live here?" Samuel had dropped the kite, his interest now shifted. "Are we?"

"I'm afraid so," Uncle Nathan laughed.

The boy ran toward his godfather who caught him up in his thin arms. The two hugged playfully and I felt like an intruder watching the affection that came so easily.

CHAPTER FOUR

The first thread had now been strung. And each day wove another string into the pattern that was to become familiar where my relationship with Samuel was concerned: Samuel always reaching for something beyond his grasp and I continually bending and stretching to help him get what he desperately desired. Only, after the struggle, Samuel lost interest almost instantly. I, on the other hand, would cry with fear and frustration along the way, only to later discover I had enjoyed the adventure.

Mr. Miller, Samuel's godfather, or Uncle Nathan as he preferred to be called, bought the Allan house. Within a week's time the bachelor and his charge were settled inside the oppressive fortress. My mother often took pity upon the two and invited them to share a meal with us.

Samuel never complained about the dreary house or his uncle's preoccupation with women and the business of setting up shop in the shipyard as well as within his own home. Instead he held the gentleman in great regard and spoke often of wanting to grow up in his image. As Miller Ship Building Ltd. flourished, Samuel absorbed details and techniques taught by his uncle, handed down from his father.

Samuel quickly reacquainted himself with old friends as well as making new ones. He was, on most occasions, a well-liked, charming, intelligent young man. But he could be so serious my mother often remarked that, "the poor child assumes the demeanor of an adult three times his age." And spoiled. Not that he got into any serious trouble, just accustomed to having his own way without encountering contradiction in any form.

I remember well one particular winter, two years after Samuel's return. Each time that the sun dared to melt away a few inches of crusty snow, the sky would turn gray and lay down another layer upon the earth. Week after week each house and yard was blanketed in white. And the more the flakes accumulated, the more resolute Samuel became to navigate the hills outside of town. It was all he talked of for days.

"Come on, Abby," he begged. "It'll be fun. Just you and me and Johnny Pengra and Lizzy." Lizzy Hopkins was my best friend; we'd known each other since the first grade. Johnny was Samuel's best friend. Their fondness for one another existed before and thrived after the death of Samuel's family.

"I don't know." I did know that my mother would have a fit if I traipsed out into the woods at night as Samuel planned. The nighttime always held particular fascination for the boy as did daring into unknown territory.

"It must get very tiring being so perfect all the time. Is there no adventure alive in your heart? I thought you were my . . . girl. Come on, it will be our special secret." Within a minute's time he had made me re-evaluate my character, my spirit and my devotion. Then while I took another minute to recuperate, he smiled and held my hand. He should have sought a patent for that technique. It never failed.

"I'll ask Lizzy after class later."

"Now. Ask her now. I'll go with you." He hummed as he pulled me along.

The night was so still. The kind of stillness that causes the

29

inside of your ears to vibrate. The moon was brighter than a hundred candles. The four of us took turns pulling the sled, a row boat-looking affair Samuel had fashioned from scraps in his uncle's shop.

How brave we were. There in the cold night, the moon reflecting our childish smiles and hundreds of stars guiding us deeper into the patchy woods. Samuel held my hand and I could feel his warmth through my mitten. My toes tingled from the cold but I never let on that I was uncomfortable.

One minute we were laughing and the very next we were standing on top of a steep drop off. Coming from the sloped side, along the path, the climb hadn't registered as being a high one. As I gazed over the sparkling snow, I rubbed my ears then hugged myself to chase away the chill and fear.

"You get on first, Abby. Then Lizzy, then you, Johnny. I'll hold it steady then push off and jump on back last."

"But," I interrupted, "the trail bends to the left. If we go over here, we'll run smack into that tree."

"No, we won't. Get on, come on, it's cold out here." Samuel patiently held the sled and waited for me to climb inside.

"Lizzy, what do you think?" I grabbed her sleeve. Pointing to the bottom of the slope, I asked again, "Don't you think we'll end up over there?"

Lizzy was a whiner and wailed, "Look, Samuel says we'll be okay, he should know, he . . . builds things. Now come on, my nose feels like it's going to fall right off."

"Johnny," I crunched through the snow to ask his opinion. "Can't you see that the path will lead us right into the base of that huge tree?"

"I guess so." Johnny wasn't a whiner, he was an agreer.

"John! You don't trust me?" Samuel raised his voice.

"Sure I do."

"Then come on, all of you, get in the sled."

It was three to one. I was out-voted, out-numbered and more than anything else, hated being a spoiled sport. Silently I climbed inside the home-made sled and held onto its rough edges. Lizzy climbed in back of me and put her legs on either side of mine. Johnny jumped in next and hugged onto Lizzy. Samuel pushed us off then leapt in behind Johnny.

All I could feel was the frigid air blast across my face and all I could hear was the wooosh of the sled across the snow. We sailed past the trees and over the cold ground.

I had been wrong. We were going to land safely at the bottom and as Samuel yelled for us to lean to the right, the sled maneuvered itself beautifully. The snow shimmered while my excitement came out in cloudy streams from my mouth and nose.

But abruptly the sled and its four passengers jerked to the left. Abruptly we were whisking along a collision course. The ancient oak waited at the bottom of the hill to hug us and hold on tight. I turned to yell at our navigator, craning my neck to look at him.

The space behind Johnny was vacant. Samuel lay on his back, in a pile of snow, waving his arms.

"Jump! Get off!" he screamed from a distance.

Lizzy stood up and dove over the side, causing the sled to tip over. All Johnny and I could do was roll and watch the sled crash into the tree.

"I knew it!" I yelled. Anger flushed my face as I brushed snow and dirt from my coat. "I knew it!"

"You certainly did." Samuel's voice was soft. He shrugged a little and then smiled.

"We could have been killed," Lizzy whined.

"Then why didn't you listen to me?" I asked her.

"I just thought that Samuel knew what was best. He is a boy and boys know about things like this."

"But you can see for yourself that the ground is uneven and sways to the left. You can see it with your own eyes, Lizzy."

"Sure can," Johnny agreed.

"Well, we better get home before my uncle misses me. Want me to get into trouble?"

I couldn't believe he was serious. "You were the one who insisted we come out here. And you were the one who said we'd be fine in the sled. And you were the only one who wanted to come out here in the dark at night."

"If none of you wanted to come with me, then why are you here?"

I stared into his confused face for a long moment. And then I turned and started for home.

"Aren't you going to wait for us?" Samuel shouted to my back.

"No."

Later that night I realized he'd done it again. He'd woven another intricate pattern into our history.

I started to laugh at the thought of us all heading for that tree. I shook with fear and then laughed some more. I vowed Samuel Gray would never con me into doing something I felt in my heart was wrong. I promised myself to be true to my own dreams and not borrow his.

And half-way between his twentieth and my nineteenth birthday, I married Samuel and vowed to love, honor and obey him forever.

CHAPTER FIVE

Before my wedding took place, the issue of where Samuel and I should reside became the main topic of conversation around my table, as well as throughout the entire town of Baltimore. My brother Robert was the most vocal, echoing the town's sentiments on a daily basis.

"First of all that house is too big for one woman to care for, let alone a young, inexperienced girl. I know Mrs. Carlson comes in twice a week, but I also happen to know that she plans to give her notice by month's end. Once she leaves, what will you do then? Secondly, should you be able to keep up with the house and your new husband, there is the matter of a full-grown man—Mr. Miller, living under the same roof. Thirdly, the talk. People say Nathan Miller brings his women home. For dinner and . . . breakfast. If you live in that house, with all sorts of women coming and going at ungodly hours, people will think you're a part of it, that you condone such behavior. Do you want them to think such things about you? Do you?" Then slowly and ever so deliberately, he would cross his arms, stare down at me and tap his foot.

I focused on the adam's apple bobbing as he swallowed down his vexation. It made his appearance even more reminiscent of Washington Irving's gawky schoolmaster, Ichabod Crane. I knew the girls that patronized our store whispered about his good looks, but all I could see when looking at my older brother was a tall, slender man with too much hair and too much nose.

Mother would usually burst out laughing long before Robert finished his last objection. But on this morning she did not laugh or even smile.

"Enough, Robert. I'm sure we appreciate your concern for Abigail. But really, the two years seniority granted you by birth does not give you authority to dictate her life." Mother had to look up at Robert's adam's apple, too. "I have listened to you vocalize your opinion but not once have I heard you ask your sister what she intends to do or what she would like to do. Am I mistaken? Have you asked Abigail about any of this?"

Robert sat down limply, resting his hands loosely in his lap. "No. I just thought she would want to move into her own home when she married."

"Well, I did ask Abby what she wanted to do before I offered advice. For you see, I, too, care about your sister and would never let my daughter venture into harm's way." Mother remained standing and looked down now at her elder son. "You don't think I would ever abandon my own daughter do you? Or any of my children for that matter?"

"No, ma'am, I did not mean to infer that you would."

I jumped to my own defense now that Mother had opened the gate. "You've known Samuel and his uncle for nearly as many years as I. You know they are both honorable men. Why you should hear the plans they have for fixing the house up in any arrangement that would please me. They've just never seen much cause for fussing with decorating until now. They have both made it clear that I am to think of the Allan place as my own and would welcome me as well as my belongings in their residence."

"Of course they would," my brother agreed. "I never said you wouldn't be wanted next door."

"And I told Abby that we would all pitch in when Mrs.

Carlson leaves, until she is able to manage things on her own."

"I could stop by after I close out the accounts and help with . . ."

I interrupted my brother's offer. "But, should you have asked, I would have told you how very much I hate that old house. I could never feel at home there and have already asked Mother if Samuel and I may live here until we are able to find something smaller, more cozy, of our own."

"You want to stay here?" Robert was confused.

"My room should suit us quite well. Temporarily."

Mother took pity on poor Robert and put a hand on his shoulder. "I also feel Abigail should reside in the home of her husband. But this is a peculiar situation, I suppose. What with Mr. Miller living there also, running his business from the front parlor. You're quite right about people coming and going, business people that is. The house would be quite a consuming place to run properly. And regarding what is proper and what is not, there is to be no more talk about Nathan Miller's private affairs." Mother thumped my brother's forehead with her knuckle.

"Your father taught you to be responsible, industrious and honest. I have nurtured your talents and taught you to cherish those gifts. Imagine my disappointment when this morning I look at my elder son and instead of seeing the dashing businessman who not only balances books but recites and sings like an angel, I see an opinionated, self-righteous prude of a man."

I had intended to lay into Robert again. It has always been my opinion that as younger sister, it is my birth right to prod Robert, especially when he is struggling. But this time I saw the blue in his eyes turn a cold gray at the thought of disappointing his adored mother.

"I'm sorry. Abigail, I am truly sorry."

"That's better." Mother gave Robert an embrace and motioned for me to do the same.

I cannot say that incident put an end to my brother's lectures on proper conduct nor his concern regarding public opinion. But it did soften his heart a little and instigated a more thoughtful demeanor.

Father arrived home in November, a week before the Thanksgiving holiday. Having been acquainted with Samuel for nearly as many years as I had, he was overjoyed with my choice of bridegroom. Father also considered Nathan Miller to be a kind and honorable gentleman. Even our plans to live under Father's roof until Samuel and I could find our own home was agreeable. I suspected but never expressed my thoughts that Father was relieved I would not be living with a middle-aged bachelor, but he would never let Mother know of his provincial attitude.

Samuel and I were finally married on a cold day in January when there was a slow period at the warehouse. Robert was the best man, Charles was an usher. Mother designed and hand-made my wedding gown as well as her own outfit. Father looked dashing in his new suit when he walked me down the aisle. My aunts, uncles, cousins and friends smiled and cried and danced with happiness for me and for my new husband. Uncle Nathan was elegant in a black waistcoat he had shipped in from England especially for the occasion. His present to us was the remainder of the trust fund set up for Samuel from his parents' estate. He had added his own money to hire a carriage that took us to the Mount Vernon Hotel for our honeymoon night. And when we signed the registration, we were informed that he had booked our room for two nights. A bottle of champagne in a silver bucket was waiting for us.

Samuel threw his bag on a chair and gathered me into his arms once we were behind our hotel door. "You are the most beautiful bride there ever was." He whispered in my ear and then kissed my neck. "How my mother would have loved you. Almost as much as I. And my father . . ." his voice trailed off.

"I would have loved them, too. They gave you to me, after all." My emotions had never been so close to the surface before. I wanted to laugh one moment and run in terror the next. The happiest day of my life was turning out to be also the most frightening. And yet, there was such yearning for this man that I blushed.

Lizzy and I had joined our limited knowledge of men and women to figure out, step by step, what went where. Father told me: "The most valuable thing a man has is his pride. Don't ever make him feel foolish." Aunt Wilma warned: "You must never say no to your husband." Mother patted my arm and said: "Don't worry, your body will know what to do."

Telling myself to remain calm, I climbed into bed that night in my lace nightgown, ready to experience love. Never did I anticipate that Samuel had not asked his uncle for advice or bothered to seek out one of his married friends for guidance.

"I don't know what to do. I'm sorry, Abby." He had shaved before coming to bed and was still damp on the edge of each ear lobe.

I kissed the water away. "It's better that we learn together, from one another."

We settled into the big bed and pulled the white lace comforter over us. I snuggled my head into the crook of his arm.

"Do you mind if we just sleep tonight? Would you be terribly disappointed? I'm so tired. Getting married was a harder job than I thought it would be." He laughed almost to himself and I could feel the warmth from his mouth tickle my hair like a feather.

"We have our whole life to get to know each other's body. It's fine if we just caress."

The relief that flooded through us both gave way to sleep and such peace I had never known.

CHAPTER SIX

A maid brought breakfast up to our room the next morning. Samuel and I sat across from each other with the meal spread out between us. I was wearing the dressing gown Mother had special ordered from New York. The cream colored satin complimented my fair complexion and my hair looked like spun gold against the fabric. On the breast pocket I had stitched my married initials in pale blue. At the time I had thought it was such an extravagance. But now as I reached to pour my husband's coffee from the silver pot I felt confident and so womanly.

"You look beautiful." Samuel buttered a piece of toast, never taking his eyes off me.

"Thank you, I feel beautiful today."

As I stared into my coffee, watching sugar dissolve from the teaspoon, I could hear Samuel push his chair back from the table and walk around to me. When I looked up he was kneeling at my left side. "It feels right, doesn't it? You and me? Here, together? You're not sorry are you?" He took my hand and waited for my answers to his many questions.

"I'm right where I want to be, Samuel. Here with you. On our honeymoon. I'll never be sorry I married you. Never."

His eyes got all glassy with tears and he slowly stood up. Removing the napkin from my lap, he led me to bed. My fancy dressing gown ended up in a heap on the floor and our breakfast was stone cold by the time we had exhausted one another.

The day ran into early evening and we laughed each time

our stomachs growled. The eggs and bacon had gotten hard and cold. The coffee looked like mud but we managed to eat the soft middle of the bread. Time away from the rumpled, warm sheets of our canopied bed soon gave us both an appetite for something besides the day-old bread.

Our room was soon dark. Being winter, the evening came earlier. At one point, we discussed getting dressed and hurrying down to the dining room for a late dinner. But Samuel's kisses were all I craved that night.

When the maid arrived with our breakfast that second morning, Samuel and I could not help but notice the amusement expressed on her face. Evidence that yesterday's breakfast had not been touched and the disheveled appearance of our room and ourselves must have given her answers as to why we had not eaten. Such a tactful woman she was to never say a word but clear away the untouched plates and reset the table with hot food. When she finally left, we raced to the table and plopped into our chairs, quite the opposite of how we'd seated ourselves the previous day.

We gobbled up the wonderful breakfast of hot cakes and ham, moaning pleasure between chewing and stuffing more food into our mouths. I remember the butter was pressed with the hotel's insignia and fashioned in perfect pats.

Our two days at the Mount Vernon were running out. The realization slowed down our chewing. We finished eating and silently dressed in separate sections of the large room. Collecting our belongings, we checked out of the hotel and into our temporary residence on Chester Street by six o clock that evening.

As I unpacked my clothes, I wondered how to begin. Should I be doing something differently now?

When I last stepped across the threshold of this familiar

bedroom, two days before, I had been Abigail Belshaw. A nineteen-year-old virgin, daughter of Martha and Dalton Belshaw, sister of Robert and Charles. Educated, well read, an honest and generous person. When I crossed back over that same threshold, I was Abigail Gray, nineteen-year-old wife. Same daughter, same sister, same person inside. I wondered what I was supposed to do differently now.

Samuel had gone directly next door to see his uncle and gather a few belongings. As I opened the bottom drawer of my bureau I found it empty. Opening and closing several other drawers, I was startled when I noticed Charles staring at me from the doorway.

"Mother made room for Samuel's things and Mr. Miller moved a big armload in yesterday."

I opened the chifferobe to find several unfamiliar shirts and trousers hung up neatly next to my dresses. A brush and shaving kit were arranged on my dresser top. I was surprised at the rush of resentment that hurried through me at the sight of his things crowding my own. Granny Sarah's bed looked too small suddenly and I wondered how I would sleep comfortably again.

"They should have waited until we were home," I grumbled.

"Why would you even want to live here when there's a whole big house just next door? A house that you can lord over and fuss about."

"It wouldn't be like that. Uncle Nathan does business there. You've been in the parlor. Every corner is filled with bundles of paper, little pieces of wood and metal, ropes. He has clients coming in and out at all times of the day . . ."

Charles interrupted, ". . . and night. He had a most unusual visitor last night; I could see her from my window. Well, some of her. It was dark and she was all wrapped up in this

41

shiny black garment."

Samuel rushed into the room, his arms loaded with shirts. He dropped them onto the bed, kissed my cheek, said hello to Charles and dashed off again.

I stopped what I was doing and started putting the shirts away before wrinkles set in. "You have to stop spying on people, Charles."

"You're such a stodgy girl. Honestly, don't you have any curiosity in your soul?" He walked into my room and plopped himself down on the bed. "Besides, I wasn't hurting her nor Mr. Miller, not even myself. I was merely looking out the window, for God's sake."

"Lower your voice. I don't want Samuel thinking he married into a family of spies."

As if on cue, Samuel rushed in again and deposited two large crates of books at the foot of my . . . our bed.

"How much more are you going to try and cram into this room?" I was irritated, watching my living space being taken over by strange books and stiff shirts.

"We're living here because of your wishes, my love." He hugged me around the waist. "And I only live to make you happy."

He was out the door again and I was left wondering if he had intended his statement to be one of fact or sarcasm.

Charles stood up and waited until he heard the front door slam. Then he turned to me and lowered his voice to imitate Samuel. "I only live to make you happy. My love. My sweet, sweet love." Then he hugged me around the waist so hard I thought I would surely pass out.

"Stop it!" I pushed him to let me go. The past several years had restored some of Charles' health and he now had a thirty-pound advantage over me. He swung me around the room smug with his strength and my helplessness. I realized fighting would be futile and waited for him to grow tired. After three full spins he dropped me to the carpet.

I grabbed my brother's ankles and was wrestling him to the floor when Samuel walked in. "This is the last of it, for now." A brown leather valise was deposited next to me.

Starting my new life wasn't something I had to worry about any longer. Rather than wait for me to start it up, it had begun on its own.

CHAPTER SEVEN

While I was still struggling, adjusting to all the changes marriage had brought about in my life, Uncle Nathan died. It was at this time that I learned about change. How it rarely comes in gradual doses, but abrupt rushes. Frightening everyone by its suddenness. Its immediacy.

Samuel and I had been living in Father's house for almost a month when Nathan became ill. At first the doctor was sure it was just the influenza. He prescribed bed rest, warmth to sweat out the virus and as much liquid as we could manage to pour down our patient's throat.

Mrs. Carlson had given her notice as threatened, leaving Mother and me to take turns staying with Uncle, seeing that he was comfortable, had food and medicine inside of him. We kept the fire going strong in Uncle's bedroom and covered him with three heavy quilts. Mother made her special barley soup and I added a few teaspoons of brandy to his tea when he coaxed enough. He kept insisting he was fine, that we were not to fuss so over him.

Samuel, now a full partner in the shipbuilding firm, spent his time between the warehouse and parlor, meeting with workmen, suppliers and customers. Charles ran errands after his classes; Robert brought medicinal aids after closing the store in town. Father had intended to stay in Maryland for the entire year once he'd crossed the ocean to attend my wedding. But business dictated that he divide his time between districts and he was in Boston when Uncle first took ill.

On the fourth day, Nathan awoke burning with fever. When Samuel helped his uncle change into a dry nightshirt, he saw a rash had formed on his chest and stomach. We summoned Dr. Stanberry again.

The diagnosis was changed immediately from influenza to measles. The doctor said he would order the house quarantined and we were told to separate ourselves from Nathan and hire a nurse to care for him so as not to contaminate the entire family.

Samuel was outraged and told us, "It was Uncle Nathan who cared for me when I had the measles. I'll not abandon him now nor leave his care to a stranger. Tomorrow I will move my things into his room and tend to him myself."

We all tried reasoning with him. I feared he might have a relapse if exposed to the disease a second time. Mother told Samuel he was a husband now and must consider the wishes of his wife. Dr. Stanberry said we weren't doing anyone any good, least of all the patient, by arguing and Uncle Nathan's care should be left to a professional. Robert took me aside and told me he knew for a fact that the nurse being suggested was Dr. Stanberry's daughter and she needed the employment.

The anxiety sweeping through the room must have aroused Uncle Nathan for suddenly he sat up, motioning and shouting, "Samuel, come here. Come to me, boy, I must tell you something. It's most urgent."

Mother and Robert and I stood off in the corner so as not to intrude on the privacy Uncle Nathan apparently wanted to share with his godson. I watched the two men embrace then turned to check the fire. That was when I heard Samuel whimper.

"Don't go. Please, Uncle, don't leave me."

I knew Nathan Miller was gone without even turning to face the scene. Mother and Robert crossed the wooden floor to comfort Samuel; I heard their footsteps. Stabbing at the log with an ornate poker, I squeezed my eyes shut. Waiting. My back turned to my husband.

Sadness started filling me from the bottom up. First my toes went cold then icy sorrow worked its way up my legs, into my knees and stabbed my stomach. Like a windowpane frosting over with winter moisture, I was laced with frozen fear.

What was Samuel going to do without his beloved godfather? How was I to comfort him when my arms were locked at my sides and my head gripped by the frigid reality that Uncle Nathan was gone forever?

Granny Mary and Grandfather Ezra had both died before I had even been born. My other grandparents, great aunts and uncles had been so old when I was young, I never got to know any of them. As they each passed out of my life, I was as unaffected by their deaths as I had been by their lives.

But Nathan Miller was someone I had loved, admired. From the day of our first meeting on the roof of this very house, I had liked the elegant gentleman with the curly black hair. Had talked with him almost on a daily basis over the past five years. The thought of never seeing him again was unbearable.

"Abigail, your husband needs you," I heard Mother say.

Replacing the poker, I wrapped my shawl tighter around myself and turned to see my new husband crying uncontrollably into his Uncle's sleeve. Flames flickered light on the ceiling and across the large, richly paneled room. I walked toward the bed as if in a trance. Pieces of my broken heart floated upward to my throat making words impossible.

Uncle Nathan was laid out in the front parlor of his home,

in front of the tapestry curtains a merchant had brought over for him from England. He was dressed in his naval uniform complete with hat and gloves. In a glass case, Uncle Nathan's medals were displayed against a burgundy background. Samuel had fashioned the casket with the help of several workmen at the warehouse. It was made of cherry wood and its finish held the light in an amber glow.

When Nathan Miller's death became public record, friends started arriving to pay their respects. Within a day's time, the line snaked out the front door and past my family's house. Seeing so many faces, I wondered if half of them came out of curiosity rather than compassion. The newspaper had run a story detailing Nathan Miller's life, featuring his move to Baltimore to care for his godson. Samuel had always ignited sad memories in that portion of the population who still remembered the Gray family's tragic demise. Now beset by another turn of bad luck, I wondered if some of the mourners came solely to see how Samuel was holding up against another heartless twist of fate.

The weather turned remarkably mild, the sun even shined on the house now draped in black. I marveled at how life continued, undisturbed, outside our front door while inside everything had changed. I had changed. I felt guilty for not remembering my grandparents better, sad that my yet-to-be-born children would never know their Uncle Nathan. Through all of it, Samuel remained even tempered. Until the photographer arrived to take Uncle Nathan's final picture on the last day of the wake.

All the visitors were gone. I hurried to set new tapers in the pewter holders at either end of the casket. Samuel followed behind me lighting the wicks. He was annoyed that one candle in particular wouldn't catch and cursed each time it extinguished.

"We don't have to do this," I told my husband. "I think it's strange myself to remember him that way. I prefer to have my memories."

"Memories constitute most of my life. I need something substantial to hold in my hand as proof he existed. You know the only likeness I have of my father and mother, all of them, is the portrait in my old room upstairs. I need to have this now."

He had never spoken to me of these feelings before. I listened and told him I understood.

The photographer set up his tripod. There was no posing, no primping, no hair to be smoothed. Samuel and I stood out of the way. When the powder flashed, I cried.

CHAPTER EIGHT

Once again Samuel packed his shirts and books, but this time he returned them to the house next door from where they had come originally. I followed with my bags. It seemed the most practical solution to our old and new problems. We could begin our married life separate from my family. Samuel would be able to go through Uncle Nathan's papers easily. I would have only the two of us to care for and we would both have more room in which to live.

The master bedroom had always belonged to Samuel. At first the extra space had been cluttered with toys. Fearing Samuel might get hurt exploring the attic and cellar of the old house, Nathan had given it to his godson as a playroom. Later it served as a study and bedroom combined. Now we rearranged furniture and hung paintings brought from my own room, trying to turn the large area back into a master bedroom.

Each morning when I awoke, staring at the unfamiliar ceiling, it took me several moments to remember where I lived. It was most disconcerting. Sometimes my heart filled with panic, I wanted to grab my belongings and run. I never told Samuel my feelings. He needed the comfort of familiarity now and as I worked diligently to get us settled, I reassured myself that soon I would feel at home.

The first few weeks were consumed with unraveling Nathan's affairs in the hopes of being able to tie up countless loose ends. In the beginning I tried helping, but Samuel

49

needed to deal with the business of it all and I was ignorant when it came to the particulars. After trying to assist and ending up with only frustration for my efforts, we came up with a plan. Samuel would deal with the tangible: contracts, bills and money. I would deal with the intangible: errands, organizing and managing.

On one particularly hectic day, Robert decided he could be spared at the store and offered to take me to Chesapeake Heights to pick up the last photographs of Uncle Nathan. Classes had let out early that day and Charles wanted to accompany us to the studio on West Baltimore Street. Samuel had been buried beneath piles of agreements and plans down at his godfather's warehouse.

When we reached the storefront, Robert told Charles to stay with me while he tended to the carriage. I told him I was in no hurry and suggested we stay together. But Robert was determined to have his way and insisted we get out, right there in front of the studio. Knowing he would call me silly if I told him the truth, that I did not want to be reminded of Uncle Nathan's death, let alone see photographs of him in a casket, I stepped down.

Charles was anxious to see the inside of the shop but I made excuses. I told him we had to wait for Robert, that I wanted to look at the portraits in the window, that it was such a nice day I needed more time to enjoy it. As usual, my younger brother was oblivious to my discomfort.

I continued staring at strangers displayed behind the glass while they stared back out at me. All of sudden, Charles grabbed my arm and swung me around to face the street.

"See that woman over there? In the shiny coat?" He was excited and I told him not to point. "She's the one I saw coming out of Mr. Miller's house that night. Remember?"

Charles got even more excited when the woman caught

sight of us and started across the street. "Oh, Lord, she's coming over here." He could barely contain himself.

I tried not to stare but couldn't help noticing she was wearing a stylish satin coat with black velvet trim around the cuffs, hem and collar. Her hat sat forward on her head, dipping slightly over her right eye. The same velvet trim had been woven through the band and trailed down the back of her long hair in spiral curls. I remember thinking how pale her skin seemed in comparison to the darkness of her outfit and hair.

"Excuse me," she said in a timid voice. "Is your name Abigail Gray? And are you married to Samuel?"

I was glad for any distraction that would delay my entrance into the shop. "Yes, I'm Abigail and yes, I am married to Samuel."

"I thought that was you. I'm Sarah Franklin."

"You're a friend of my husband's?" I could see Charles shifting back and forth out of the corner of my eye.

"No, I was a friend of his godfather, Nathan Miller."

Before I could respond, Charles stuck his hand out. "I'm Charles, Abigail's brother."

Miss Franklin shook his hand. "Glad to meet you."

Charles dug his hand into a pocket, embarrassed. "Glad to meet you, too."

"You'll have to excuse my manners, I'm a little preoccupied today. You said you were a friend of Nathan's?"

She smiled at the mention of his name. "Yes, for quite some time."

"I wasn't aware of the situation," I stumbled, searching for something more to say but coming up with nothing.

"No, I don't suppose he would have told you he was seeing an engaged woman."

I wondered where Robert was and smiled an uncomfortable smile. "No, I don't suppose." Trying to change the subject I asked, "I'm curious, Miss Franklin, if we have never met, how did you recognize me?"

"I attended the wake and then the funeral. But had I not seen you either place, I would have recognized you solely from Nathan's descriptions. He was so fond of you all."

A quiet moment hung between us. We were each missing Uncle Nathan.

As if waking from a daydream, Miss Franklin suddenly stood a little straighter and said, "Well now, I came over to introduce myself for a reason, and if I'm prying just tell me to mind my own business."

"What is it?"

"I was curious if Samuel was going to proceed with his godfather's plans?"

Assuming she was referring to Miller Ship Building, Ltd. I asked, "Plans for the business?"

"Yes, the plans for expansion. He always talked about going out west. I'm sure he must have told you."

Charles and I responded at the same moment with the same word, "West?"

She laughed at our surprise. "He was so in love with the adventure of it all. He was a man obsessed. How could you not have known? I am truly surprised."

So was I.

Robert was approaching and I wanted the chance to tell Samuel about Sarah Franklin myself without explaining everything to my older brother first.

"Miss Franklin, excuse me for being abrupt, I am in a bit of a rush today but I do want Samuel to meet you. He will be so interested to hear about Nathan's plans. Would you be free to dine with us? Next week? I hope Wednesday is all right. Shall we say six o'clock?"

"I'd like that. Wednesday's fine. Charles, it was nice meeting you." She shook his hand again. "And Mrs. Gray, it was a real pleasure." She walked back across the street, and I hurried into the shop before Robert could question me.

The studio was partitioned off by a dark green curtain. The waiting area had several wooden chairs lined up against the far wall, a small counter with a cash register and tray filled with business cards took up one corner. I could hear voices behind the curtain and assumed Mr. Perry, the photographer, was at work. We each took a seat and waited.

"Who was that woman?" Robert asked.

"A friend of Nathan's."

The answer satisfied him and he settled back into his chair. I have always been amazed at how little explanation men really want to hear. A simple yes or no is usually all they require.

A flash went off on the other side of the curtain lighting up the ceiling. I could hear what seemed to be a group of subjects sighing and moving about. Mr. Perry stuck his head into our side of the room.

"Can I help you?"

Robert stood and said, "We're here to pick up some portraits you did of Mr. Nathan Miller."

"Last week. It was a wake," I added.

"Right there, next to the register. Take a look and I'll be with you in a minute." His head disappeared behind the curtain again.

I walked to the counter and saw a large, brown envelope labeled "Miller." I wondered how Mr. Perry knew we would be in this afternoon. No prior arrangements had been made with him concerning the time of our visit or the day.

Handing the envelope to Robert, I asked him to check the

contents. He studied the photographs for a few minutes with Charles peering over his shoulder. Finally he said they were fine and returned them to me.

Another flash lit up the room. After a minute or so, Mr. Perry opened the curtain and walked to the register. "Is everything satisfactory?"

"Fine." I started to open my handbag then stopped to ask, "How did you know we were coming this afternoon?"

"Oh, I had no idea."

"Then why were the photographs ready and on the counter waiting for us?" I tried not sounding too suspicious.

"Because of the other woman, the one who arrived just before you. In fact, I'm surprised you didn't run into her. She said she was Mr. Miller's fiancée and wanted to buy a copy of the photograph."

I must have looked surprised.

Robert said, "I didn't know Nathan was engaged."

"She only wanted the one; I hope that was all right. There are four others left, if you want more . . ."

"No, that's quite enough," I assured him. "Thank you."

"Was she wearing a shiny black coat?" Charles asked. "And was she pretty, with long black hair?"

"Yes," the photographer smiled slightly. Holding up a ledger book, he pointed to the last entry. "Her name was Sarah Franklin."

CHAPTER NINE

Samuel did not find the idea of his godfather keeping company with Sarah Franklin in the least surprising. It had been an accepted part of his childhood that Nathan Miller "entertained" quite often. Nor did he find it intriguing as to the identity of Miss Franklin's fiancé. What my husband did find astonishing was the obsession Miss Franklin had spoken of.

"Why in the world would Uncle want to leave Baltimore? He loved it here."

"How long had he been living in Havre de Grace when you were sent to live with him?" I asked.

"I don't know."

"Did he come here because of you and your family's business, or because he wanted to make a change in his life? For his own reasons." I waited while he thought a moment.

"I never asked."

I tried offering Samuel a few excuses. "You were young when you were sent to him; you'd just lost your family; it was all so tragic and upsetting."

"At first, I suppose, all you say was true. But later on he loved me as completely as my own father would have." Samuel looked ashamed. "Uncle gave me a good life. How could I have been so disinterested in his?"

"Maybe Miss Franklin can answer some of our questions on Wednesday. I've invited her for dinner." The prospect of meeting the mysterious woman seemed to cheer Samuel a bit.

Mother had recently hired Clairise, a Negro maid, and

volunteered her services to us for the evening. When Sarah Franklin arrived for dinner, we were ready. The chandelier was lit in the dining room and the table was set with Uncle's best English china. After answering the door, Clairise served sherry then left the three of us in the library.

"At last, I get to meet the wonderful godson Nathan spoke of so often. He couldn't have been more proud of you, not even if you had been his true son." Miss Franklin settled comfortably on the settee and arranged the folds of her purple skirt.

Samuel sat next to the attractive woman and eagerly started to question her. "How long did you know my godfather, Miss Franklin?"

"I hope you don't mind my husband's enthusiasm." I sat down in a chair across from them.

Miss Franklin shook her head. "Oh no, I love talking about Nathan." She looked into her glass. "We met about two years ago, at The Relay House. I had gone to the resort for my health and the scenery. Nathan was there for a rest. He was having a bad time of it with his business. But then, you knew about his financial matters better than I."

Samuel looked sad. "No, it wasn't until this year that I became a partner. Before that, Uncle only instructed me in the actual building of the vessels."

"Oh, I see." Our guest seemed a little surprised then continued. "We got on from the start. He was interesting and funny. I sought him out in the dining room and for walks around the grounds. My three days were over far too soon."

"If I may?" I asked. "You mentioned you were engaged when we spoke last week."

Not one shade of embarrassment showed on her cheek. "I was newly widowed when I met Nathan. He respected my situation and was always the gentleman. And the twenty-seven-year-age difference between us gave the other guests cause to believe we were father and daughter, casting suspicion toward other more likely targets.

"My three days ended before Nathan's week was over. He asked me to visit his warehouse should I be in the area. I've wondered, many times, if he really believed I would accept his invitation."

"Why wouldn't he?" I asked.

"Because our meeting had more of an impact on my heart than it had on his. It was obvious to me. Besides, I was in mourning and not supposed to be having such desirous thoughts."

"Did you ever tell Uncle Nathan about your feelings for him?" Samuel asked.

"Not until much later." Miss Franklin paused a moment. "I waited a few weeks and then stopped by his warehouse one afternoon. He seemed genuinely glad to see me. He talked about you, Samuel; he told me about his best friend—your father. He was so full of plans for your future. And from that day on, we met, discreetly, almost once a week, every week for more than a year."

"I must have been about eighteen when this started," Samuel said thoughtfully. "I can't believe I was so unaware."

"Come now, Samuel, I'm sure you were very aware of how much Nathan enjoyed being in the company of women. Oh, he was dashing and so romantic. He never forgot my favorite flower or fragrance or color. Nor the favorites of many other women. And," she laughed, "he never got us confused. But when I finally summoned the courage to ask if he felt the same love for me that I felt for him, he kissed my forehead and admitted he did not."

My heart hurt for Miss Franklin. I looked to Samuel and knew that neither one of us knew what to say.

Sarah Franklin set her glass on the table. Pulling out the handkerchief tucked in her sleeve, she dabbed at a tear sliding down her cheek. "When he told me he did not love me, there was no harshness in his voice. He held my hands and said how fond he was of me, how he wished the years between us weren't so many. That if he had a first-love heart to give, he would give it to me."

"So you were never engaged to Nathan?" I asked.

"No. But I couldn't give up our weekly meetings, neither could he. All the while Nathan encouraged me to see other men. And soon I met a physician who asked me to marry him. I told Nathan, hoping, I suppose, that he would become jealous, confess his love. But he only wished me his best."

"I'm sure my godfather missed you very much," Samuel said.

Sarah took a sip of her sherry. "We never actually stopped seeing each other. I managed to convince him that no one would be hurt if we remained friends. The truth is, I hadn't courage enough to give him up."

"That explains why my brother saw you leaving Nathan's house at such a late hour. He thought it seemed suspicious."

Clairise startled us when she announced dinner was ready and we stood to follow her into the dining room.

"You mentioned something about my uncle wanting to travel out west? You told Abby last week, I believe, that Uncle Nathan had been making plans?" Samuel offered Miss Franklin his arm.

"Why yes. I have a brochure in my bag. I can leave it with you, if you'd like. You'll find more papers in a box at the warehouse. Have you cleaned out the cabinet behind his desk yet?"

Samuel offered me his other arm and we started down the hallway. "No, I'm sorting through things here at the house first. There've been meetings with accountants, lawyers and employees. I worry I'm not doing a good job. There's so much I don't know."

"You'll manage," Miss Franklin said and then recited a verse I would never forget. "Ye fearful saints fresh courage take; The clouds ye so much dread, Are big with mercy, and shall break, In blessings on your head."

CHAPTER TEN

The very next morning after Sarah Franklin's visit, Samuel and I went to the warehouse. The workers had not arrived yet, it being only seven thirty, and without a word between us, we both headed directly toward Nathan's desk. The huge, old affair was more of a table sitting out from the wall in the back of the dusty work area. I had often wondered why Nathan hadn't enclosed his office, separated it from the crew and noise and mess. But he preferred being in the middle of all activities involved in his line of work. He loved the smell of fresh wood, the sound of hammering and sawing. He watched over draftsmen as well as deliveries. Sawdust was the carpet he found most appealing.

Behind the desk were several long tables, all connected, stretching the length of the entire back wall. Except for the corner nearest the desk. This space was occupied by a tall wooden cabinet with four drawers. Each drawer was adorned with a brass handle and small brass frame into which Nathan had inserted labels.

Samuel seemed unfamiliar with the contents of each drawer and stood reading the labels out loud while I silently read along with him. We started at the top, searching through papers in the drawer marked "plans." By the time we had finished rummaging through the bottom drawer, we still had not found a box of personal effects.

"He could have moved it since Sarah was last here. He could have even thrown all of it away." I hoped my ideas were wrong.

"No, Uncle never discarded anything. And I spent many hours last night thinking this situation through. I've come to the conclusion that he was trying to tell me about his plans before he died. Remember, Abby? How he told me it was urgent? Now I know he wanted to show me something. Miss Franklin spoke of his obsession. This has to be what he wanted me to see."

"I had always assumed he knew he was dying and simply wanted to tell you how much he loved you."

Samuel ignored my explanation and bent to replace errant papers into the bottom drawer. Seeing his concentration, I sat in the squeaky chair behind Nathan's desk. My feet accidentally toppled over several long paper tubes leaning beside the desk. Samuel stood and started admonishing me for my clumsiness. As he spoke he waved his arm and bumped a pile of papers resting atop the cabinet. As these toppled onto the floor we both were taken aback by the amusing situation and laughed.

I got up from my chair and was in the midst of retrieving the papers when I spotted a small box, wrapped in white paper, tied with a silver bow, on top of the cabinet. My sound of surprise caused Samuel to turn. He carefully picked up the box and brought it to the desk where we could both have a better look.

He turned it over in his hands. "There's a card. It's Uncle's handwriting; he addressed it to us both. Here, you read it." Samuel handed me the small white envelope. It had been sealed with red wax, pressed with Nathan Miller's initials. As I broke the seal, Samuel lowered himself into the chair. He was now suddenly weary.

I found a small wedding card offering congratulations in bold script. Inside was a personal message from Nathan, which I read out loud. "Dearest Samuel and Abigail, I know the practical side of life dictated my gift of currency on your wedding day. But now, please accept my gift of hope and a wonderful future. It took a little longer to wrap up. I apologize for the tardiness. May you always have a prosperous as well as exciting life together. Love, Uncle Nathan."

Before I could return the card to its envelope, Samuel was untying the package. His sadness seemed to have ended as abruptly as our laughter had. He tore into the box like it was a holiday package. I knew Nathan would have enjoyed his godson's reaction.

Wrapped in tissue paper, the first thing we found was a small model of a Conestoga wagon. Hand-painted in black letters were the words: Miller & Gray Ltd. along its side. Beneath that was a copy of "The Emigrants Guide to Oregon and California." It was evident Nathan had leafed through it more than once. Next there were letters from members of the Oregon Society. It seemed Nathan had been corresponding with two gentlemen concerning designs for a wagon. There were several maps and a poster announcing the public appearance of Lansford W. Hastings, author of the Guidebook. Samuel and I were both surprised to see an inscription along the bottom of the poster and knew that Nathan must have been in attendance the evening mentioned. After we had both looked at all the contents at least three times each, we packed everything back inside the box.

Before we could discuss our gift, we were interrupted by the arrival of Paul Laird, the head carpenter. He had hung up his coat and was tying on an apron when he noticed us in the back of the large room near the desk. "Mr. Gray? Mrs. Gray? Is that you?"

"Yes, Paul, sorry if we startled you," Samuel said.

The large man approached the desk. It was a chilly morning and he kept his knit cap on his bald head. "Is everything all right, sir?"

"Fine. Just some family business."

"I miss your godfather very much, sir. We all do. It was the suddenness of it that still has us upset. Such a pity, too. Considering all his plans to make the westward trek."

Laird had been with Nathan almost as long as Samuel had. The Englishman's reputation as a remarkable craftsman was one of the reasons Nathan's business flourished. When depression ravaged the country, Nathan could not meet his payroll for long periods of time. Workers left when the times were difficult, but Laird stayed. Considering the personalities of both men, their similar bachelor status, it was only natural they would become friends. But I could tell by Samuel's expression, he was hurt. Apparently, Nathan had confided in Laird instead of his own godson.

"Did he talk to you about his intentions? Did he show you the plans for his wagon design?" Samuel pushed the box across the desktop. "It appears he spent many months working on this. Have a look."

Laird made no attempt to pick up the box. "No need. It was I who assembled the tiny wagon and painted on the letters. It was my niece who wrapped the package in wedding paper upon your godfather's request when he first took ill." Laird stood in front of us smiling satisfaction at a job well done. He never thought, for one minute, that his actions had offended my husband. "Were you pleased with Mr. Miller's gift?"

"He never got the chance to give it to us. We found it this morning after a friend told us of its existence. We're still quite amazed by the whole thing," Samuel explained.

"Always thinking of your happiness he was, sir. Always planning for your future. I suppose once the shock of it all has a chance to settle, you'll be putting this place up for sale. And

I'd like to be the first to volunteer to go with you and the Mrs. All the way to Oregon, all the way to the grand and beautiful Pacific Ocean."

"Sell this place?" I repeated. "How will we make a living?" I was close to hysterics; I could hear the words shrieking from my throat and could do nothing to stop them.

"Calm down, Abigail." Samuel hugged me to him and I felt worse, embarrassed in front of Mr. Laird. "We have to go home and sort this through. We should talk this over with your father. He knows about business opportunities. And the lawyers, maybe there are documents in their possession that we should know about."

Mr. Laird followed us to the door, apologizing for upsetting me. "Mr. Miller had every detail planned. It's all there for you. You'll see. Nothing to be frightened of. From what I read, traveling west is like a glorious vacation. The entire trip takes only three months. Four months should there be bad weather. It's as easy as that."

CHAPTER ELEVEN

"As easy as that! Just pack up everything and move to some savage land! How can he be so casual about our lives? We have family here, acquaintances, lifelong friends. It certainly is not as easy as that to leave everything we know."

"Now, Abby, calm down. Nothing has been decided . . ."

"You mean to tell me you would even consider such a thing?" I wanted Samuel to reassure me we would never leave Baltimore. "That you could sell your family's business, take up residence in a rickety old wagon and never look back? Is that what you're telling me?"

He didn't answer right away but instead pursed his bottom lip. After a thoughtful moment he said, "Well . . . no. I'm telling you that Uncle was a thorough man. He sold his business in Havre de Grace and started again where my father worked. He took on the responsibility of raising a young boy, and he was quite successful in all ventures. It appears, from what I have seen thus far, that he was just as thorough in his investigation regarding this enterprise. It is, therefore, only fitting that we be exact in our review of his work. He was not a frivolous person. I have no immediate plans to sell the business and run blindly westward. However, I do have plans to read over the contents of that box and, after seeking a few unbiased opinions, I will decide what is best for us."

Home again, we now stood in the carriage house. I looked up into the determined eyes of a man I could not reason with. "I'll give you time enough to review your precious plans. I'll be next door visiting my mother. You can go wherever you please."

He sighed, "Suit yourself."

I found Mother in the parlor. Her easel set up, she was arranging apples in a blue glass bowl. While I told her about our trip to the warehouse, our discovery of the box and the papers contained therein, she never stopped fussing with the composition.

When I had finished she turned and clapped her hands together. "It all sounds very exciting."

"Exciting? What if Father asked you to suddenly pack up and leave your home, your friends?"

"He has. Many times."

"And go west?" I could not believe what she was saying.

"No, not west. To Europe."

"Well, that's entirely different. Europe is civilized."

Mother sat down. "Yes it is. But getting there would still involve the same process. Packing, selling the house, leaving behind my sisters and friends. And there would be new problems presenting themselves. Ones that you wouldn't encounter at the end of your trip. A new language to learn, new customs, new foods, why I couldn't even pick up a newspaper and read what was happening in my own city."

"So you can understand why I don't want to make this awful trip. You feel the same way."

"No, Abigail. I want to travel; I miss your father very much and want to be with him."

"Then why didn't you go when Father asked you?" I liked when Mother shared her thoughts with me but sometimes I did not like what those thoughts were.

"When your father was hired for the Paris position, Charles was too ill to travel. We decided it was best I stay here and care for you children. When Charles recovered, your father arranged for our passage but by then, you and Robert were in school and I didn't want to disrupt your studies. Soon after your eighth birthday, your father took an account in Boston and returned home. But those were hard times then and he was asked to return to Europe. That was when he demanded we return with him. But my mother fell ill and I was taking care of her. Your father finally gave up and sailed without us."

I remembered the arguments. "I always thought Father and you simply did not get along and found living apart more agreeable."

Mother looked sadly at her wedding band, rubbing the back of it with her thumb. "Hardly. Each year our responsibilities to each other slightly lessened while those to you, your brothers, my family, all seemed to increase. Now there seems no point in making a change."

She suddenly stood and picked up a brush. Her back to me, I was glad she couldn't see the guilt I surely had in my eyes. Unknowingly, I had kept her from being where she wanted to be. Had all those years filled with our private talks and teas and walks been lonely times for her? Had my hugs and kisses offered any comfort?

Trying to understand, I reasoned aloud. "Then we are living in this town, you and I, for very different reasons. I want to remain in my own home, surrounded by the familiar, simply for the love of it all. I freely choose to be here. The needs of others have forced you to reside here. How strange that we now find ourselves in the same place, but for such different reasons."

"No matter." She was now dabbing paint onto the canvas. "The way I see it, you have no legitimate reason not to follow your husband and every obligation to obey him. There are no children to consider, no sick family." She stopped her painting and turned to smile at me. "Think of it all as an exciting adventure."

We had arrived back at the beginning. As I heard my mother speak of "obeying" and "following" my husband, I felt as though the words came from the lips of a stranger. Just a few minutes before I had admired her independence, attributing it to generations of headstrong women in her family. And I had expected her advice to emphasize *my* happiness, *my* search.

I watched her turn the bowl of fruit around to catch the sun and knew that I now saw my mother in a different light. What I thought was her independence, I now knew was her loneliness. And I was sad for her.

But I still did not intend to leave my home.

CHAPTER TWELVE

Samuel and I successfully avoided each other for days. It is surprising how many places and activities offer refuge. Decorating our rooms in the big house required shopping expeditions. These I managed whenever Samuel decided to work from the office in our parlor. I dined with my family next door never bothering with what my husband ate or where he slept. Until one afternoon three days after discovering Nathan's wedding present, Samuel met me at the side door. I had stepped out to gather daffodils for the large table in our front hall.

He stood on the top step, arms stretched to block my way; I was startled by the shadow he cast. "You frightened me," I scolded. "Why are you home at this hour? I thought you were gone for the day."

He smiled down at me. "Is that any way for a wife to greet her husband? Here, love, let me take those." He stepped down and grabbed my bouquet into one of his large hands; with the other he took my hand and pulled me into the house. I was sure he had returned to apologize.

Deciding to make things easier for him, I smiled. "Thank you."

He closed the door and leaned against it, watching me divide flowers amongst several vases. Crossing his arms, he seemed content in my company. As I poured water into each arrangement, Samuel finally spoke. "I hate when you're angry with me, Abby. I truly hate it."

"It's not anger you've been feeling from me, Samuel. It's

confusion and most of all frustration. I've known you for the majority of years in my life. This is the first time I feel unable to reason with you."

He slowly walked over to me, stopping on the opposite side of the table. "Look at all you and I have been through in such a short period of time. First we are married. It was the most glorious day of my life."

I smiled at the memory and nodded a silent agreement.

"As we start a new life together, poor Uncle takes ill."

"An anxious time for all of us."

"Anxious? I was terrified. I was . . ." Samuel abruptly stopped speaking. I looked up from my work to see my husband's eyes brimming. He stared at me, fighting the urge to blink. When he finally gave in, the action sent large tears rolling down his smooth cheeks.

I started to speak but he held up a hand. "No, let me say this now and then I will never speak of any of it again." I pulled a chair to the table. How I yearned to hold my husband but instead, I sat down.

Samuel removed a handkerchief from his pocket. Drying his face, he cleared his throat. "My parents have been dead for many years now, as have my brothers and sisters. But a day never passes that I don't wonder about one or all of them. How severely would Father have punished me the day I broke the hallway window? Would my eldest brother, Josh, have teased me about loving you so much? Would he have challenged me for your hand? He was always the handsome one. What color dress would Mama have worn to our wedding? Some days I struggle with important decisions and wish my father or brothers could advise me. Other times something as insignificant as a leaf crunching beneath my shoe will make me ache to swoop up my baby sister, Sally, and swing her in my arms in the autumn sunshine. I had a wonderful childhood; we were a very close family." Samuel started pacing as he spoke.

"And then they were gone and I was sent to live with Uncle Nathan. I can't remember the first year or so. The gravity of my situation had not registered in my boyish brain. I was quite a lot for Uncle to handle, I'm afraid. But never once did he raise his voice or a hand to me. And when he at last decided we should move to Baltimore, I know it was to appease me. I see that now. But at the time I didn't care what the reason. I was back home. I was a selfish boy.

"Then, good things started to happen again. I met you, I helped Uncle with his business and managed to make friends as well. I had a grand life with him and grew to love and depend on my guardian very much. I review that life from an adult's perspective and appreciate how good it was."

Samuel stopped pacing and leaned against the table. "Then Uncle fell ill. And this time I thought, I am a man. I have a wife and people to help me; I can make Uncle better. Now is my chance to take care of him. But I failed."

In spite of myself I started to speak but Samuel cut me short.

"Once again I felt ashamed."

"Ashamed?" I was so taken by his admission that I could not contain myself. "What have you ever done to feel ashamed of?"

"Don't you see, Abby? I was too cowardly to accompany my family on that voyage. I wanted to remain at home. I let the worry of becoming seasick keep me from being with the people I loved most. I was unadventurous—afraid. I left them all to die without me; I broke up the family. I abandoned them. I betrayed them all.

"When Uncle Nathan took ill, I felt such dread. The more I tried not giving into my fear, the worse he got. He gave me back my life and how desperately I wanted to do the same for him."

"My dear husband." I stood. "You are not a doctor. It is not within your power to heal the sick."

"Emotions are not logical, Abigail. I will forever feel I should have been smarter or tried harder to make him well.

"But he is gone. We are left with only the plans and dreams he had for our future. And this time, dear wife, I will not be afraid. I will not let anything keep me from this adventure. I will not remain behind, fearful of what might happen, while others forge ahead of me. I will not. I cannot."

I understood every word and fear Samuel had expressed. It had never been necessary for me to lose my parents to understand the devastation he had suffered. And it certainly was not necessary for me to distance myself from my hometown to appreciate its beauty and charm.

I stared at the small patch of gray hairs hiding amongst the brown ones near the crown of his tilted head. He had avoided my eyes as he spoke of what he would and would not do. His voice had been steady recounting his fears and resolves. But while I understood heartfelt emotions, his anxieties were not my own. I harbored quite different fears. And I did not nor would I ever understand why I should have to atone for imagined sins that plagued him.

CHAPTER THIRTEEN

The men in my family gave Samuel practical advice and sound opinions. Uncle Chalmer thought the trip west would be, "a solid investment of time that could only result in large profits." The recession had not affected his blacksmith trade; in fact, he had been able to hire one additional man. The tightening of money had caused people to fix and make do rather than make extravagant purchases. My uncle encouraged Samuel to take the trip and use Nathan's notes as a guide. "With your business experience and good sense, you could patent a new design, make traveling by wagon more comfortable."

Had my uncle decided to make the trip himself, there is no doubt, at least in my mind, that he would have made money en route simply by virtue of his business. For it seemed to me that only one motive drove people west: greed. It certainly wasn't brains. And I seemed to be the only one who noticed that while Uncle Chalmer advised and pored over Nathan's papers alongside the other men, he saw no need to relocate himself or my aunt and cousins.

Father communicated his thoughts regarding our "gift" in a four-page letter. Mother brought the envelope containing his dove-gray stationery and laid out the pages for me to read. He stressed that the trip would, ". . . help make a man of Samuel and strengthen the bond between husband and wife." Mother pointed out that line for me.

But there was also doubt expressed when Father wrote, "For the life of me, I cannot understand why, if you are set on establishing a business, a ship building business at that, you don't travel to the west coast by sea, around the Horn. It would only seem the practical choice, albeit more expensive, considering Samuel has been knowledgeable about the sea since birth and all his business acquaintances are connected, to some degree, to the water. Why would he choose to travel across the country, subject my daughter to the possible threat of death or Indian attacks when a ship is easily available to him and the route already established?"

I agreed, in part, with Father. If we were forced to make this trip, the logical route would be by water. But fear is not a logical emotion and I defended my husband's choice of travel not divulging his fear of sailing. The defending was difficult since my heart did not, under any means of transportation, want to make the journey.

Uncle Harold knew it was only a matter of years before the railroad connected the small western towns to the larger eastern cities. "Dr. Hartwell Carver of Rochester and Dr. Samuel Barlow in Massachusetts have been publishing articles for over ten years now. They claim that a railroad stretching between New York and Yerba Buena, a Mexican city, would be inexpensive as well as practical. It's all just a matter of time. Read the *Westfield Intelligencer*." However, he went on to suggest we wait until "progress caught up to the foolhardy." He acknowledged the excitement of staking claims of both land and gold but since Samuel intended to do neither, what, he asked repeatedly, was the rush? Why not build up the business from our end and when the time was better, travel in comfort to the opposite coast? This opinion was approved by most members of my family.

But the loss of his godfather was still such a fresh wound. Samuel explained to me, in the privacy of our bedroom, that Nathan had planned to make the trip next year. A precise planner, all necessary preparations would take a full year to complete. And, by God, he would follow his beloved god-father's wishes . . . to the letter. It was the least he could do for the man who had given him everything. Samuel would not be swayed.

For the first time in my recollection, my brothers were in full agreement. Robert went on and on about the opportunity for opening a mercantile, the hunger for dry goods and, in time, he could possibly expand his operation to include a clothing store. He started to include himself in our plans until Lucy, his fiancée, delivered an ultimatum. "Civilization as a married man, or adventure as a bachelor." Robert decided to stay in Baltimore, at least until he was married.

Our dear Charles elaborated about the adventure. Samuel and he would talk about weaponry and "taming the new frontier." When he was forced to his bed on one of his frequent bad days, Charles read and reread the communications Samuel had continued with members of the Oregon Society.

While the others patted his shoulder and humored him, I had to admit he seemed the perfect candidate for such a journey. Young, enthusiastic, eager, he had all the qualities I lacked. And how comforting his presence would be for me. But I never voiced my opinion for I hated all the talk and commotion the infernal "trip" now wrought.

When I sat with the women, they chattered about the glamour of it all, the pageantry of the wagons, the beauty of the scenery I would see each day. They encouraged me to look upon the adventure as a new beginning. They talked about journals I must keep for the sake of my future children and grandchildren.

"How valuable an experience you will have. How lucky to be young enough to see and feel such beauty," Aunt Frieda said.

I would point out the "adventure" was one shaded with danger and hardship.

"You've always been such a serious child," Mother said one day. "I worry that you will never feel passion for anything. You seem void of curiosity."

"The moon in Kansas is the same as the Maryland moon," I said.

"If you believe that, if you cannot take into account the different colors in a prairie sky, shades you've never seen in the city, then I can't explain it."

When I asked her to come with us she said what her sisters said. "I've had my adventures. My place is here now. My family has always lived in Baltimore."

Why didn't she realize that mine had also? That I wasn't an artist and did not require nor need new colors on my palate to make life happy. I was content to take my days as they came and deal with what was in my sky above my own house.

Each for his or her own reason agreed that we should go, while each agreed they should stay.

I've always found it curious that those who push and poke another person to take action or speak up are the last to step forward or utter an original word.

CHAPTER FOURTEEN

Anger powered my trip to St. Louis as surely as the railroad, the stagecoach, and my own feet had. Each mile, each step fueled resentment toward my husband and the journey I now found myself forced to take. In the beginning I was included in family meetings, asked to accompany Samuel to the lawyer's office. But I have never been an actress of any degree and each time, my true feelings rose to the top and bubbled over into angry words.

After one particularly "fitful tantrum," as Samuel referred to it, I was banished from all meetings. From that day on I was privy to plans and conversations only from the opposite side of our dining room wall. I became the receiver of second-hand news from my brothers and mother and even neighbors.

As a staunch subscriber to the principle of laissez faire, I believed that if I ignored the whole silly idea, it might just go away. That with time, Samuel's guilt would lessen and his interest in the shipping yard and our marriage would consume the better part of his time.

How little I understood then the intensity of my husband's devotion to his godfather or his wish—no, desperate need—to make amends to his lost family. And with time I came to understand the reality of my situation: my life was to be offered up as a sacrifice to Samuel's guilt. Once the facts settled inside my soft brain, I was not an eager participant in any of the planning and I certainly was not going to contribute any excitement.

Mother never stopped objecting to the idea of my younger brother accompanying Samuel and me. But Charles alternated between threats of running off, without even a good-bye, and tirades about how he was after all, eighteen years of age. A man! One of the youngest graduates from the University.

Along the way, Samuel took up the fight with Charles and on several occasions I was the only person Mother would speak to. While I listened and agreed that such a journey might be harmful for someone of Charles' fragile nature, I was pleased at the prospect of company. My younger brother and I had always been close. It was with the sincerest of hearts that I promised Mother that I would be my brother's protector and nurse. I would guard his life better than my own.

When it was at last decided that Charles would make the trip, he suffered an episode and was in bed for days. Being a kind and honorable man, my husband delayed our departure by an entire week. My gratitude must surely have been evident although I never discussed the delay with him. But I understood the problems involved. My lack of enthusiasm did not mean I was ignorant nor did it mean I hadn't taken private moments to study guidebooks and maps. Father had taught his children that knowledge warded off fear.

Uncle Nathan had provided well for his godson in the will and selling the business, as originally planned, had been unnecessary. We had enough money to sustain us for the duration of our trip and, with careful management, extra to set up housekeeping once we reached our destination. Paul Laird was promoted as head of the operation in Baltimore. As such he was given access to the business accounts and an agreement was made between my husband and Mr. Laird that funds be wired to us periodically as we made our trip west.

That way, they reasoned, we would be less likely to lose our life's savings to whatever catastrophe might befall us. Oh, the plans the two of them had for expanding the business! And if things worked out, within a year's time, Miller Ship Building, Ltd. would be known coast to coast.

Samuel had promised a two-day vacation in St. Louis. I am sure he hoped to ease me into an agreeable mood. Taking the medicine in small doses would be less frightening to the patient, he must have thought. But I was pleased for the chance to see the great parks and architecture of the city I had read so much about. So I did not object when it was suggested but merely shrugged my shoulders when I was asked for my opinion.

Charles was excited about our vacation time, also. It would be the first time in over three weeks we could sleep without thought of rising early to catch a train or coach. A few days to enjoy a meal without the rush or discomfort of the road. And a bed of white linen in a grand hotel.

"I want to visit Lemp's Hall," Charles told Samuel. "They're famous for brewing lager beer; I want to sit on the bank of the Mississippi and have a glass. Doesn't that sound fine, Samuel?"

"I'm sorry," Samuel said. I remember how his eyes never turned toward either my brother or me. "Our vacation has been canceled. The week's delay we started with will have to be made up. You understand."

If Charles was disappointed at all, he never showed it in either his voice or mannerisms. "Of course. I have never used my illness as an excuse and I do not plan to start."

"As long as we're making this infernal trip, let's just keep going," I mumbled. "One large city is the same as another. And water, no matter if it's the Atlantic or Mississippi, is just a large amount of wetness."

79

"I knew you'd understand."

Samuel patted my hand and I withdrew it. Either he did not care to know my heart or chose to play along. I felt more homesick than I had since the start of the journey. My last glimpse of elegance passed by in a dusty blur as we rode into St. Louis and then right out again.

PART TWO

Council Bluffs, Iowa: 1848

CHAPTER FIFTEEN

Council Bluffs was called "the jumping off" place. I didn't have to ask or study to know this. Conversation around us, talk when we arrived, all concerned either the trip ahead or this jumping off place. How appropriate, I thought, the desperation such a phrase brought to mind. Frantic . . . jumping off a high place to an almost certain death.

When we finally arrived, that last week of March, in the year 1848, I remember the whole town seemed in motion. Half-constructed wagons lay around the town like giant carcasses picked clean of their canvas flesh. Brand new, completed wagons were being readied by hundreds of busy hands. And if they weren't building or fixing, the air buzzed with talk of provisions. Several men greeted us as Samuel helped me down from the wagon. One offered, for the sum of twenty-five cents, a list of supplies needed by travelers along with the stores where bargains could be found as well as prices for each item. He guaranteed it would save us time. My husband interrupted the man's sales pitch by producing his own list, provided him by correspondents of his wise uncle.

Cattle and horses were being auctioned at the end of one street while the other end was filled with large enclosures of oxen. Dirt and bargaining wafted through the air; loud voices shouted orders, dogs barked, blacksmiths hammered. I felt as though I had walked into a great circus arena; everywhere I looked there was frantic activity.

"Isn't it gloriously exciting?" Charles shouted.

"Yes!" Samuel agreed and smiled so broadly I thought his face would surely crack. "More exciting than I ever imagined. I counted forty wagons just on our way into town."

I fingered the tiny pearl button on my right glove. Since my opinion had not seemed important to my companions, I felt it unnecessary to offer one to the conversation.

Samuel unfolded the dirty sheet of instructions he had produced earlier. Creases had become stained into the sheet from Samuel's constant reading and returning the paper to his breast pocket. "The first thing we require are living quarters for our stay here."

"Which will be how long?" I asked, straightening my hat.

"A few weeks—possibly a month. Mrs. Coral Adams owns a boardinghouse; I've written her, reserving two rooms."

We had to wait for buggies to pass. So great was the commotion, we were unable to hear Samuel's words. After a minute or so, there was a break in traffic and my husband finished. "I'll run into the post office and get directions to Mrs. Adams' house and we'll take our things there." Before we could say anything, Samuel stepped up onto the wooden walk and Charles and I were left to wait.

"Must you be so disagreeable?" My brother asked the instant we were alone.

"Always remember, dear brother, that you chose to make this journey. I, on the other hand, was forced into leaving my home and traveling for weeks to this hellish spot. Now I must move into another woman's house and ready myself for an 'adventure' I never wanted to experience in the first place."

Charles plopped himself down on top of the largest of our bags. "You should have been an actress, Abigail. Such melodrama; such emotion."

"Such frustration! With both of you."

A small boy of perhaps seven years of age approached my

brother from an angle Charles could not see. As I stared at the child's weather-worn trousers and jacket, I was surprised at his boldness. Tugging on my brother's sleeve with his left hand while holding out his right, he introduced himself.

"My name's Decatur. What's yours?"

My brother had not seen the boy coming and was startled by the greeting. "I'm Charles. Glad to meet you, Decatur." He shook the small hand.

The child must have sensed my indifference and never acknowledged me.

"I'm going to California. My grandpa says there's gold there. Big pieces, just layin' around on the ground, waitin' to be picked. Are you goin' to California, too?"

"No, Oregon."

"Oh." The boy seemed disappointed. "Think we'll see some Indians? I hope so. And buffalo?"

Charles laughed at the questions. "I suppose we'll see all sorts of things and it sounds as though you're ready."

"I am! I even have my own rifle. Wanna see?"

A young woman, appearing close to my own age, approached in a hurried manner. She gathered up her faded skirt; I could see dirty boots underneath. Her dark brown hair was pulled straight back and tucked inside a faded red sunbonnet. Her small bag looked as though, at one time, it had matched the bonnet but now appeared brighter in comparison. It hung from her wrist by two white cords. Water puddling the street caused the woman to struggle to keep mud from her skirt as she ran and shouted.

"Deke! Where in the hell have you been?" The woman's accent was more pronounced than the boy's.

"Mama's havin' a conniption," Decatur observed.

The child amused me and I smiled as the woman stopped in front of us.

"How many times must I tell you not to wander off like that? I'm like to keel right over one day from all the worry you bring me." She grabbed his hand and quickly swatted the boy's backside.

"We just arrived; the boy was merely greeting us," Charles said.

Her anger was immediately replaced by embarrassment when the woman realized Charles and I were part of the situation.

"Oh, my gracious, I didn't notice you there. You must think me such a brash woman."

Decatur enjoyed his mother's discomfort. "This is Charles, Mama."

Charles smiled and touched his hat. "And this," he motioned to me, "is my sister, Abigail."

"Glad to make your acquaintance. I'm Velina Brown, mother of this here chatterbox. I hope he wasn't botherin' ya'll." She looked to me for some reaction.

"Oh no, my brother and your son were just comparing travel plans."

"We've been here since last year. I'm beginning to feel like this is my home now," she sighed. "But, hopefully, we'll be on our way soon and I'll get to be with my Pa."

"There's just the two of you making the journey?" I asked in disbelief.

"Goodness no! Why, I wouldn't know where to begin by myself. Besides, there aren't that many women makin' the trip let alone single ones. No, there's my husband, his three brothers, their families and my other children—fifteen of us altogether."

I envied this woman her family but not her responsibilities with children to take care of along the way.

"There's only three of us," Charles explained.

"And you're headin' to California? For land or gold?"

"Neither," I answered.

The woman stared at us, speechless. It was Decatur who finally said, "Well, then why are ya'll goin' out west for?"

Charles tried explaining the plans to the boy and his mother. Both shook their heads and giggled. I felt foolish while Charles defended our motives. Thankfully Samuel came out of the post office in time to rescue us.

"It's not far. We can walk there in a few minutes."

As my husband started gathering our bags, Charles stood to help. I picked up my hatbox and turned to introduce Mrs. Brown and her son but they abruptly turned and walked away.

CHAPTER SIXTEEN

Coral Adams was the most exotic woman I had ever seen. Her vibrant skin tones reminded me of the Portuguese sailors who manned the ships docking in our Maryland harbor. But when I looked closer, it seemed her complexion was the result of hours spent sunning rather than an inheritance from random ancestors. Her eyes were the brown of strong tea and seemed swollen with dark secrets. Thick hair was pulled back in one heavy braid that hung past her waist. When she spoke, her mouth moved slowly. Words came from her thin lips in an accent not so much foreign as it was unsure, as if pronunciation was something she concentrated on more than the words themselves. I tried not to stare at black markings dotting her chin but immediately was curious about our landlady and at the same time found her frightening.

"Your rooms are up the stairs, all the way in the back, across from . . . the other. You missed dinner. But come down to the kitchen after unpacking. I make something for you."

She walked away before we could thank her.

"Pleasant sort, I guess," Samuel whispered as we climbed the narrow shiny black stairs. It was evident many boot heels had kicked at the paint leaving it pock marked with a dark red color beneath.

At the top of the stairs was a threadbare runner. What patches that remained whole were woven with a floral pattern of pink roses and hideous green leaves. The walls were a ruby red and the solitary lamp flickered the long hallway with shadows. A tiny window at the very end of the passageway was covered with a heavy curtain discouraging the setting sun from brightening this area even a little. There appeared to be about eight doorways and we opened the ones at the end, marked with a brass number seven and eight.

Charles tossed his bag onto the single bed in the corner of the smallest room. "I'll wash off some of this dust and meet you downstairs."

Samuel and I closed the door on our temporary home and I hung up my coat. "I don't want to spoil your enthusiasm, but might I ask why you didn't book us rooms at the hotel? I noticed there were several right in the middle of town."

"Ahhh, a glimmer of interest?" He laughed and arranged our bags against the wall.

"I was simply wondering why we are to stay in this ugly place when there are perfectly good hotels."

"Come, sit by me." Samuel patted the purple quilt covering our bed.

I went to my husband and listened while he explained about the cost of a hotel for the many days we would be needing it in addition to the lack of storage space available in such living quarters. He had gotten Mrs. Adams' name from one of his correspondents who made note of the large back and front yards on her property. The gracious hostess offered the space to her tenants in addition to allowing her large barn to be rented out. It all made sense and I was impressed with Samuel's thoroughness.

"I know we don't have to be as careful with a penny as most, but that certainly is no reason to squander what we do have." Samuel ended his final sentence with a tender kiss.

"You have all the answers," I confessed, "but that woman. She's so strange."

"The tattoo was certainly a surprise."

"You mean you didn't know about her before you brought us to live under her roof?" I asked.

"I knew that she was reputable, that she was sympathetic to travelers and their needs. But, I admit, it never dawned on me to inquire if she had tattoos or what color her walls were painted." Samuel held my hand to his chest. "Abigail, darling, give this place a chance. Please. Just for one week. And, at the end of that week, if you hate it here so much you must leave or die," his melodrama made me smile, "then I will whisk you away to an expensive, tastefully decorated, albeit less convenient room. I promise on my life."

Having always taken pride in the fairness I was born with I was not about to act out of character, in spite of all the unfair situations I had recently fallen victim to. "All right. I'll make the best of it. I'll even help as much as I can. It'll distract me."

"That's my lovely Abigail."

As Samuel kissed me again I could taste the grime from the road on his lips. His skin felt warm and my hands went to his face.

"Now, food." He returned my hands to my lap. "I'm starved."

He abruptly stood and I watched as he poured water into the basin on the dresser. Washing his hands and face, Samuel seemed suddenly unaware of my presence.

Mrs. Adams was waiting for us in the kitchen. Spread out on the square wooden table was a yellow crocheted cloth. On top of that was a platter of cold beef and bread. "Sit," was the only signal she gave that she knew we had been watching her pour coffee into chipped cups. "It's simple but goot." A hint of a German accent slipped out.

"Thank you," I said and sat down.

"Yes, thank you," Charles and Samuel repeated, seating themselves.

"We certainly hope this doesn't inconvenience you too much," Charles added.

"No trouble." Mrs. Adams dished out boiled potatoes and green beans onto our plates.

The meat was tasteless but I was grateful for the nourishment. My fork was bent and caught on my bottom lip as I ate. The three of us sat in silence and chewed our dinner while Mrs. Adams stood in a corner by the stove with her back to us. Fearing it would be impolite to speak without including her in our conversation, I remained silent. Through nods and wiggling of eyebrows, we managed to signal our likes and dislikes to one another during the meal.

When our eating slowed down, Mrs. Adams turned and asked if we would care for more coffee. I had barely managed to gag down the first cup of bitterness but did not want to offend her by refusing.

After she had filled our cups and cleared away the dishes, Mrs. Adams told us we had to share dessert with her. If the finale to our meal was anything like the beginning and middle had been, I thought it best to decline.

"Oh, I'm really quite full. Everything was . . ."

"Plain. I am not a cook. Necessity has made every meal a chore. No joy. But baking of the desserts is for pleasure. At that, I am very goot."

She turned and disappeared into a large pantry. When she returned, her hands were gripped around ornate handles of a beautiful silver platter. In the middle of the platter was a three-layered cake shimmering with white icing. Red berries were evenly placed around the bottom and piled artfully along the sides. A red jelly had been spooned over the top making it look like an intricate piece of tatting.

Our delight was evident.

"It looks like a birthday cake," Samuel said. "Are you sure you weren't saving this for someone special?"

"It is for my own anniversary. I had plans to eat it tonight when I was alone. But now I want to share."

"Anniversary? What about your husband?" Charles asked.

Mrs. Adams looked at my brother. "Ach, no. My husband is dead, killed by the Indians three years ago. That isn't the anniversary I speak of. Tonight marks two years I have been here in my house." She placed the cake in the middle of the table.

The woman stood a moment, studying her masterpiece. Then she turned and went into the adjoining room we could see through the open door of the kitchen. She carefully removed four plates from a large china cabinet. Returning, she set our places with great care. Turning the plates until the cottage painted on each surface faced us at the just the perfect angle, she went back to the cabinet and removed four wine glasses. The care she took with these equaled the preciseness she had displayed placing the dessert plates. After slicing and serving four equal portions of the cake, she poured wine from a crystal decanter into each goblet. Lighting two candles on a sideboard, Mrs. Adams finally sat down with us.

"To my return to civilization." Coral Adams raised her glass, offering us a toast.

We lifted our goblets. "To civilization," I said.

She took a long drink before returning the glass to the table. Her right index finger circled the middle of her chin. "You think to be civilized means a wooden house?"

At first I thought the question was of a rhetorical nature. But Mrs. Adams stared at me until I finally offered an opinion.

"Yes. I think being civilized means to live properly."

Charles and Samuel had started eating their cake and seemed oblivious to the staring match Coral Adams now waged against me. It was I who finally looked away.

"Do you suppose that what is 'proper' for you is the same 'proper' for me?" Again she waited for my answer.

"I suppose so; I guess I've never given it much thought."

"I have." The woman rubbed her forehead. "I have thought of this question for two years."

CHAPTER SEVENTEEN

As I opened my eyes to the first day in our Iowa home, my senses were immediately insulted. Morning sun made the surroundings appear even uglier than they had the night before. I wondered, as I rolled over on the lumpy bedding, if Mrs. Adams was color-blind or merely cursed with bad taste. Blues and reds dyed into the single set of curtains were oppressive and I hoped she would not be offended if I offered to replace them.

Inhaling deeply, my nose caught the odor of burnt bread mingled with wet animals. I could hear horses outside as well as voices throughout the house. A baby cried from somewhere not too far and a cat sounded as though he was sitting outside my door. I reluctantly sat up, realizing even one minute more of sleep was impossible in the middle of such tumult.

Using all ten fingers as a comb, I tried detangling my long hair. Often I had been complimented on its golden color but more often I had cursed the fineness of each strand. Tracing my mouth with the tip of my tongue I could still taste the grime from the road. Both actions made me feel in need of a good scrubbing.

The large bureau occupying the wall directly across from my bed was nicked and missing several drawer handles. One leg seemed to have been chewed in spots. But in spite of its bad condition, the surface shined, the result of heavy polishing followed by a daily dusting.

I wondered again at the strange Mrs. Adams. Over dessert

the night before, she had thrown out questions I had never before considered. Each time I hesitated, no matter the reason, she would answer herself, as if my voice was not necessary. Was my curiosity to know her better merely fascination with this odd person or had I detected a potential friend beneath that leathery skin?

I put on my dressing gown and wondered where my husband was off to. This was a casual thought for the room being so small and our traveling the past weeks had brought me in such close proximity to both my brother and Samuel that I was enjoying having space to myself.

Searching for my brush and comb forced me to unpack the smallest of our bags. Opening a narrow door beside the bed, I found a tiny closet. After hanging up some of my things, I realized it would be a fierce battle to squeeze even half my garments inside. Samuel walked in while I was fighting with one particularly full skirt, a favorite in brown and pink.

"Good news, Abby, our things have arrived! Right on schedule. They're being unloaded now."

I continued fighting with my surroundings; my struggle went unnoticed.

"I thought that would cheer you. Just a little? Now you may feel a little less alienated. I know how important it is for you to have your things close by."

"Close by? More than likely they will end up on top of me, burying me alive. Look at this!" I stepped away from the closet and stood in the middle of the room. My arms folded themselves tightly across my chest, my fists clenched like two rocks. "This place is ugly and noisy and cramped."

I truly believe I expected Samuel to rush to my side and apologize for all of it. For the inconvenience, for never considering my feelings the entire duration of our marriage, for forcing me to come to this horrible house. But as I stood there, barefooted, angry and aching from holding myself so tightly, he never made one move to comfort me. I look back at that moment and see now that it was a turning point in not only our relationship but in the making of my childhood friend turned husband, into a man. This is not to say I enjoyed any of it, simply to relate that I took note.

"You promised you would give it a week's worth of chance. You are a fair and honest woman and I expect you to live up to your word."

I stared at the dark brown hair curling along his stiff collar, then made my way up his large jaw to those blue eyes. At one time I had thought them the color of the sky but now they seemed the cold gray of a February sea.

I contemplated throwing myself across the bed, refusing to move from that room. There was no denying the fact that Samuel was right. I had promised. But I wasn't going to let him know I was aware of the soundness of his logic. Not just yet.

"Would you mind leaving me so I might dress in peace?"

There did not have to be a vocal judgment made for Samuel to know he had won this bout. If my turning away from him made him angry, he never said a word. Neither did he choose to grab my shoulders, firmly, with both hands, and turn me around to face him and the situation.

I wished he had.

We had both been raised to be polite, gentle people . . . to each other, to our family, to strangers. And this politeness now dictated my husband ignore my anger. It held his annoyance in check and made me ashamed each time I expressed displeasure.

"Hurry then. You'll want to have breakfast before helping us inspect the crates for damage." Samuel softly kissed the back of my head and left the room.

CHAPTER EIGHTEEN

Pinks and yellows, red-tipped whites and purples overflowed in vases, milk cans, bowls and pitchers scattered throughout the hallway and what little I could see of the front rooms. Flowers were everywhere. As I stopped in the dining room, I noticed how the blossoms even seemed to sprout right up through the center of the large oval table. Circling the room, I touched soft blossoms that had been strewn across the buffet and tucked behind picture frames.

"The others have finished." A young girl of perhaps twelve or thirteen announced as she entered from the kitchen. "I can make you some eggs."

My surprise at not finding Samuel or Charles waiting for me must have been apparent.

"You are Mrs. Gray, aren't you? Arrived last night?"

"Yes. Sorry, I didn't mean to cause any inconvenience."

"No trouble at all. I'm Jane. Sit yourself and I'll be back with coffee."

I pulled out a rickety chair. "Could I have a cup of tea, please, and just a piece of fruit or bread?"

"We have strawberry preserves. I could toast you some bread to put them on. The tea's no problem. Cream and sugar's on the table." Having finished, her lips jumped into a sudden smile and she hurried out of the room.

Infernal politeness forced a "Thank you" out of me that was left hanging in the breeze she left behind.

While I waited for breakfast, I marveled at how my arrival

must have somehow startled the house and its occupants into silence. Spreading my hands in front of me, I played with sunshine flickering through the windows. The white light shot the glass sugar bowl and creamer full of yellow and green. Fragrance from the assorted flowers set off memories of home and I missed sitting at my own table in my own dining room. How long would this sense of tentativeness last? I wondered. And why should I be so tired of it when we had just begun?

Jane returned with my plate and a large steaming cup. "There now. Will you be needin' anything else?" She was a mousy girl but her ableness and delightful Irish accent made a lasting impression on me.

My head nodded no, that I required nothing further, while my mouth opened to ask for information of Samuel's whereabouts. But before I could verbalize my question, she was gone, back to the kitchen.

I ate slowly that morning. There seemed no need for hurrying. The room was cheerful; the air serene. But after finishing my meal, I left the table and went in search of my family.

I had checked Charles' room before coming downstairs so I started my hunt on the first floor. When that proved fruitless, I retraced my steps down the hallway and continued out the front door.

A porch swing covered with an old quilt, more full of holes than design, was suspended to my left. Still unable to locate my husband and brother, I sat on the swing wondering what I should do next. The chains supporting my weight were rusted in places and creaked a comforting creak as I swung back and forth.

The house faced east and I was bathed in yellow daylight. The sun felt wonderful on my face; I lifted my head to take full advantage of its warmth. This was the mildest day I could remember in months. Two dogwood trees stood like sentinels on either side of the house. I had not noticed their purple blossoms last evening nor the tulips planted in alternating rows of red and yellow, four deep, flanking the front of the house. Circling a willow in the middle of the yard, there were daffodils. It appeared that outside, Mrs. Adams had arranged colorful boundaries between her possessions and those of her guests.

On the other side of the large yard, man-made chaos, rather than this living order, took control. A broken wagon wheel, crates of all sizes, barrels and scraps of canvas gave the footage nearest the road a disheveled appearance.

The neighboring house was surrounded by a cornfield, its calico scarecrow waved at me with each gust of the early wind. Beyond that were bluffs covered with green and purple vegetation.

My shoes scuffed the porch, making a comforting swish as I took in my surroundings.

"There you are!" Charles shouted as he came around the house from somewhere out back. His hair was windblown, causing the dark locks to shadowbox his delicate face. His shirt was opened at the collar and the sleeves had been rolled up. He brushed his dirty hands across the legs of his dark pants.

"Good morning," I said. "You look well."

Manual labor seemed to agree with my brother. Without his cravat or topcoat, he appeared plain and happy.

"I feel wonderful. Deciding to make this trip will prove to be my salvation. I'm sure of it."

"We'll see." I stopped the swing with my feet. "Where is Samuel?"

"He was offered a ride into town and said he couldn't wait any longer for you. There's a lot to be done, you know."

"But he said he wanted me to check over our things, that they had arrived this morning."

"I've already done that. I've been up since dawn." It was obvious he was very proud of himself.

I pushed my feet into the floor and the swing creaked into motion again. "But it's only our first day here. I would have thought . . ."

"Spring's come early this year, Abby. Don't you know what that means for us? We'll be able to leave sooner than planned. We have to move quickly now. There's no looking back. Only forward."

As he started back to whatever work he had been occupied with, I asked, "What am I supposed to do now? I have no friends here, no one to talk to. I am not familiar with the area."

He stopped moving forward and turned to glare at me. "You've made it very clear that you never wanted to make this trip. You've never done one thing to make it easy on any of us, so why don't you simply enjoy the day and do what you've done for months . . . nothing."

"You are not my husband nor are you my father!" I shouted to his back as he walked away. "How dare you judge my behavior!" He was gone and still I shouted. "I fought to bring you along on this trip. If it wasn't for me, you would still be in Maryland." Fury forced me from my seat, from the porch and in the opposite direction my brother had walked.

I don't know how long she had been there on her knees, but I stumbled into Mrs. Adams and nearly knocked us both over.

"I'm so sorry, I didn't know there was a garden here . . ."

"The beginnings of a garden. For now just some holes."

"Forgive me," I apologized again. "I didn't see you."

"And if you had, would you have spoken to your brother in such a tone?"

Embarrassment burned my cheeks. "Certainly not."

"Then I am glad you were unaware. In this world you must speak your mind. A temper is only harmful when it is misdirected."

She kept her face turned toward the ground. From where I stood I could only see the green and white checks of her blouse and hair tied into a fat bun at the nape of her neck. Coral Adams continued digging and I remained standing.

The distance between her ear and my mouth remained constant and yet I lowered my voice. "In my house it was considered bad manners to raise our voices. My mother almost considered it a personal affront if my brothers and I argued. She taught us that there was always to be a level of decorum . . ."

"Ach, my mama taught us the same. But, you are not in your mother's house today." Her words were simple and the logic infallible.

"No, I am not."

"Nor will you be tomorrow or the day after or the month to follow."

I knelt closer to her. "No, I won't be in my house for a long time."

"Then," she looked up at me, "you learn a new way to talk."

CHAPTER NINETEEN

Our accidental meeting led to conversation, which led to us settling into the dry grass bordering the side of the house. My skirt spread full around me, I noticed Mrs. Adams had hers gathered and cinched at her waist, making her look as though she wore pantaloons. I tried not to stare at the black markings on her chin but Mrs. Adams caught me.

"They held me down, it took four of them. I know, you look at me and think, she is a big woman. But they were strong young men and I put up quite a fight. It took all their strength, I could tell it. Go ahead, you can touch." Instead of feeling shame, she was proud of her unusual face.

Running north to south, there were four lines between her bottom lip and chin. I ran my fingertips across her skin. The ridges were smooth in spots and raised in others.

"After making the lines, they rubbed ashes from the fire into the wounds."

I was appalled. "Why would they do such a thing?"

"All their women had markings. Most had them also on their arms."

"But you weren't one of their women."

She laughed a little. "Ach, after they killed my husband and cut the throats of the other men in our camp, I guess they thought I was their property. And after they kidnapped me and my sister, I knew I was."

I was frightened now, thinking what lay ahead for me. "How could such a thing happen? I've heard there are laws,

102

that each day it is safer . . ."

"Oh, mein God, we were stupid. It was three years ago, and I have had too many days to think about how sinful we were. God wants his children to be humble. This is the truth. We were greedy. Free land. Everything cheap and for the taking. We thought it all belonged to us.

"My husband, he did not want to stay with the other wagons, he knew a better way, faster. Such a hurry to get there first. So we leave the others. Three families, including us, headed off with such confidence and a map that was no goot."

I swatted at a gnat flitting in front of my eyes and thought how much set me apart from this strange woman. Education, background, and yet I could feel her anguish. "Were there other women, besides you and your sister?"

"No. Women are not plentiful on the trail. It was just me and Pearl, my older sister by three years. I bet you think I be the oldest. I am younger than you think. The sun and wind and dirt, they age a woman before her time. No, I am only twenty-eight."

She could see my surprise as I calculated the eight-year difference in our ages. But she was gracious and chose to ignore my startled look. And I never told her that I had thought she surely had to be close to her fortieth birthday.

"Just my sister and me, dragged screaming from our wagon. At first we demanded they release us. Shouted and ordered them. But the further into the wild we go, we grew hoarse and tried coaxing them to take us to a town. We promised we would never tell the soldiers. But once we were in their village, there was nothing left to do but live our life."

"I would suspect you tried to escape?"

"Oh, Pearl did, many times. But I feel security in the sameness of the days. It comforted me."

"You said last night you had been home two years. If this all took place three years ago, that means you spent an entire year with those savages."

"Only a year. It would have been more if I had not listened to my sister. I should have remembered that we were never the same in our thinking."

Again, this woman surprised me but this time I took no care to hide my amazement. "You wished to remain with your captors? How can you say such a thing? If I had been kidnapped, I would have fought continually, searched for a way back home, I would have . . . ."

"But you forget . . . I, like you, had no home to return to."

"Like me?" I stood up. "I have a home, in Baltimore."

Coral Adams stood to face me. "Can you go back there? Now? This very minute?"

"No," I said.

"Are you staying in my house, in Council Bluffs, because you wish to be here?"

"I am here only because my husband insisted."

"And now that you are here, you wish to be back in Baltimore. You were safe there, no one hurt you, you knew what each day would bring. Am I not right?"

"Yes."

"But once you climb into your hard, dirty wagon, you will wish to be back here. Because the next few weeks will bring you comfort; you will wake each morning in the same bed and learn what every creak in this old house means."

"I suppose so."

"How surprised you will be then when you reach Oregon only to find you long to be back in that wagon you hated so much. For there you were safe. It was your familiar place."

She brushed the grass and soil from her skirt, shook it out. I couldn't think of a thing to say.

104

"I have not meant to anger you, Mrs. Gray, only to point out how similar we are—you and I."

I looked at this ugly woman and didn't want to be compared to anything about her. And yet, everything she said was true. We were alike.

"Oh no, Mrs. Adams, I'm not angry. If I have given such an impression, then I am truly sorry. You have been very kind to me. Taking me into your confidence, sharing your thoughts." I smiled to emphasize my words.

We walked back to a small shed where Mrs. Adams arranged her rake and hoe. There seemed to be too much silence between us now and I feared I was the cause of her feeling uncomfortable. Our visit had been enlightening and I wanted the time spent under her roof to be congenial for us both. I felt more effort was required of me and said, "After hearing all you endured, I am so thankful you found your way back to civilization and claimed your freedom or we would have never met."

She sounded sad now. "Pearl escaped; I helped her. She was so miserable, all the time crying. But when soldiers come from the fort, the soldiers that had helped Pearl, they make me leave. How I cursed them. I could not make them understand that I was . . . happy."

"But how could you live the rest of your life as a prisoner?"

"You speak of freedom as if it were something to purchase, to wrap in paper and tuck away. No, freedom, security, these are fragile things, like wings on a bird."

As if by design a large crow swooped past us.

Mrs. Adams turned from the shed and watched. "See? That fat body of his is graceful only because of his wings. They lift him up. Let him fly. And yet, if those feathers are broken, the poor thing is a prisoner on the ground. He is only as free as he is strong. Do you understand?"

A feeling of harmony came over me. "Yes, I do see."

"Goot!" She held the front door open for me. "Then go. Find *your* freedom on the strength of your wings."

CHAPTER TWENTY

We had been with Mrs. Adams for some two weeks when Sarah Franklin arrived. Not in the house itself, but right in the middle of town.

It was her coat that first caught my attention. Even as temperatures continued to rise and our winter garments were daily being substituted for lighter fabrics, she stood in the middle of the general store wrapped in that black satin coat of hers. When I pointed her out to Samuel, I remember he commented how she reminded him of the raven in Mr. Poe's poem. We had saved a copy when it was published in the *Evening Mirror* and recited it to each other frequently.

"I half expect her to say, 'Nevermore,' " Samuel joked.

Only her head, covered with a black cloche, moved, as she looked over her surroundings. Samuel and I watched, too stunned to approach. Before we could overcome our confusion, however, and move to extend a proper greeting, Charles walked in, having just returned from the barber next door. His surprise was evident as she threw her arms around him.

"Charles! Charles Belshaw! At last a friendly face, the first I've seen in months." When she realized she had taken my brother unawares, she released him from her hug. "Oh, dear, I do hope you remember me. I'd hate to have you think some stranger was throwing herself at you."

I held Samuel back a minute, to enjoy what I expected would be my brother's embarrassment. Instead, he smiled a most charming smile at the older woman and said, "Of

107

course, I remember you, Miss Franklin. Or do you now have a married name I might address you by?"

"No, it's still Franklin. And you? Are you accompanied by a wife?"

"No, just a sister and brother-in-law. In fact, they should be here somewhere."

It seemed a perfect time to make our presence known and I held my husband's arm as we proceeded to the other side of the store.

"Why, Miss Franklin," I put on my best surprised look, "what on earth are you doing out here?"

"I've stopped to see you, Mrs. Gray, and," she nodded to Samuel and Charles, "your husband and brother as well."

"All the way out here? Just to see us?" Charles seemed flattered and I thought it a strange reaction.

"Stopped?" Samuel asked. "On your way to where, Miss Franklin?"

"On my way to Oregon," she announced proudly. "I've come to help you fulfill Nathan's dream. That is, if you don't mind my company?"

My immediate emotion was elation. Somehow, I was convinced, Uncle Nathan had sent this angel to help us. To help me. Someone to share my thoughts with, my fears. A gentle soul to understand me. But common sense rose above the frivolous and I wondered if this stranger meant to actually move into our cramped life. Was she planning to share expenses? Or did she think we would take her with us as a favor? Cascading, like droplets in a waterfall, thoughts flooded my brain. Physically, all I was able to do was pretend to listen as Miss Franklin chattered to my husband.

"It came to me, after we spoke that evening at your home. If Nathan were alive, I would have followed him out west. I know I would have. So, why shouldn't I help his family, the

108

people he loved most in the world, with this dream of his?"

Charles spoke up, "I thought you were engaged to be married, Miss Franklin."

"Oh, that was never meant to be. It took me some time, but I finally realized the truth."

"Which was?" I asked.

"It was Nathan I wanted. Only he. Everywhere I looked, he was there. My poor fiancé could never have been the husband I desired. Nor could he compete with Nathan's memory, he shouldn't have had to. I never really loved the poor man. Once that was decided, the rest fell into place."

There was a pause that the three of us didn't know how to fill so Miss Franklin continued.

"I have some money saved plus what Nathan left me." This was the first I had heard of any money left to Miss Franklin and as she spoke, I stared up at Samuel, hurt, feeling left out. "And I don't expect to be a burden but an asset. From listening to your uncle go on about this trip, I remembered there were to be several wagons. I won't take up that much room; I've only packed two trunks. Two small trunks. I sold everything else. So, you see, I won't require much. And I will be able to help with cooking and washing. It works out better for everyone this way."

Sarah Franklin had solved each problem in a logical and practical manner. I acknowledged this in her character and admired her for it. But, she had failed to take into consideration the emotional side of it. The past year had taught me well that emotions were nothing to be discounted. Before I could express my doubts or applaud her courage, Charles spoke.

"Where are you staying?"

"Oh, I have a room reserved across the street. The River House. Now all I need to make my day perfect, is to get my bags and myself situated over there."

Charles tried acting casual, but I detected the eagerness in my little brother's voice. "I would be happy to assist you, Miss Franklin. In fact, we could get you registered and then share dinner in the hotel dining room. I've eaten there several times. I can recommend the sirloin." Then to Samuel and me he said, "I'll see you both later." That said, he turned toward Miss Franklin's bags which were stacked near the door.

"I had no idea your brother was such a gentleman, Mrs. Gray. It looks as though my first night in Council Bluffs has been decided. I will talk more with you both tomorrow. Good night." Her coat swished as she followed Charles outside.

Once again I was left standing, trying to keep my jaw from falling wide open. My husband, on the other hand, seemed to have no problem finding his tongue.

"Guess there's nothing to discuss until we meet with Miss Franklin tomorrow. Would you like to dine out this evening as well?"

"Nothing to discuss?" I looked up at him incredulously. "Why didn't you tell me Nathan had left something to that woman?"

"You didn't want to know any of it, Abby. And it was only two hundred dollars. A token really. Besides, I thought you liked Miss Franklin."

"You're right, I didn't want to know. Not then. But I want to know now and from here on out. You're also right, I did like Miss Franklin, what little I knew of her. But I will have to get to know her a lot better before I gladly share my living quarters with her, let alone my brother and my entire life for the next few months."

Samuel guided me around a large woman scooping hard candy into a brown bag while her four children pushed and jumped in the aisle to get their share of the sweets. We were out the front door and strolling toward the Iowa House before I stopped expressing my doubts regarding this woman.

"First she's in love with your Nathan, a considerably older man, then she's engaged to a doctor. Now she's alone and wanting to fulfill the dream of her dead lover. Don't you find any of this peculiar?"

"Of course I do. All of it. But I especially do not care for the fact that she expects to disrupt my plans. Every pot and bag, every trunk and piece of wood has been figured."

"What about the effect she has on Charles?" I was glad we were agreeing on this subject. It comforted me to have someone feeling what I was feeling at the same time and place.

Samuel smiled. "That may be the one good thing to come out if this. Charles needs to take care of someone for a change instead of being the one in need of care. It will be good for him."

My husband's sentiments were not my own but they were heartfelt. I could not argue.

I smoothed my skirt beneath me as the waiter pushed in my chair. My corset cut into my ribs, causing me to sit straight at the table. Tugging my stiff jacket, I unfastened the bottom button. Relaxing a little, I mused, "I had thought my life would be empty out here. All the talk of wide-open prairies, the isolation. Leaving Mother and Robert . . . all of them, behind. I had thought I would have fewer people in my life. But it keeps filling up."

"Is this a good thing or are you unhappy?" Samuel asked.

"I'm not sure."

The waiter brought us dinner at our small table for two. It had been so long since I had enjoyed an intimate meal with Samuel. For too many days now there had either been my brother or as many as ten boarders joining us, chewing and chattering at the same time.

111

"You look beautiful tonight, Abby," Samuel said.

My hand went to a long curl draping down my right shoulder. Twisting it around a finger, I suddenly felt very shy. "Thank you."

Candlelight enhanced the moment and I tried ignoring a voice, nagging, way in the back of my head. It said that Sarah Franklin had brought trouble with her.

CHAPTER TWENTY-ONE

I had meant what I'd said the night before. I did indeed want to know every detail of Samuel's plan. His purchases, bank balances, our exact route—every stream and hill we would cross along the way. Being armed with this knowledge could only be to my advantage, I reasoned. It would certainly give more credence to my opinions. Hopefully it would eliminate some of the anger blinding me at times. My Bible lessons taught, "A soft answer turneth away wrath," and I was determined to arm myself with answers. Most important of all, if I knew how to get to Oregon from Baltimore, I would most certainly know how to return to Baltimore from Oregon.

When Samuel mentioned a meeting the travelers assigned to our train would be having with the assistant wagon master, I told my husband I wanted to attend. This pleased him greatly. After I finished dressing, he even knelt before me to button my shoes and then sat patiently while I fastened my brooch.

"Have you decided what to do about Miss Franklin?" I asked as we started down the stairs toward the dining room and our morning meal.

"I thought we might stop by The River House, take her to see Mr. Hain. If, after listening to him and meeting some of the others, she still wants to make the trip, we'll talk more."

"That sounds fair."

Our feet had no sooner touched the threshold when Charles pushed us into the parlor, away from the other tenants.

"Don't say anything about her appearance. It took all my coaxing to get her here and I wouldn't want her to feel self-conscious."

"Whose appearance? What are you talking about?" I asked.

"Sarah. I convinced her to dine with us. She had a bad night. After you left us, we reminisced about Mr. Miller. Such memories brought tears to her eyes and I could not talk her out of her gloom. Maybe she'll find comfort in the company of another woman. Abby, please, be especially kind."

As my brother squeezed my arms I could see concern in his eyes such as I've never witnessed before. My heart was truly touched.

"Of course, Charles."

Samuel patted my brother's back. "We'll all be gracious to Miss Franklin . . ."

"Sarah." Charles turned to look at Samuel. "She wants us all to call her Sarah."

"I think we can do that easily enough. Now, can we have our breakfast, please?" I smiled to lessen his apprehension.

"Of course. It's just that I want her to be happy."

Before we went to sit with our guest, Charles took great care to dust his lapels and smooth the back of his hair. It was too obvious that my brother was becoming infatuated with this older woman. I wondered if Samuel noticed. But then it had been my experience that most men never took note of such subtleties. Oh, if lightning struck right in front of their feet, they would naturally see the charred ground before them. But, the glint of a warning in the sky behind a cloud? That faint light would never catch their eye let alone cause much concern.

Sarah Franklin stood and came around the large table to embrace me. "Abigail, you look lovely this morning. Rose is definitely your color. And Samuel," she kissed his cheek, "you look fit. I remember Nathan telling me, many times, how soundly you slept, no matter what the temperature or time of day."

Before either one of us could respond, Charles escorted her back to her chair, and my husband was seating me across from Miss Franklin.

For as many days as we had stayed in this house we had never settled into the same chair for two meals in a row. There was always an inconsistent number at any given meal. This morning only three people, a woman and her two children, sat at the other end of the long table. Laughing together, they barely took notice of our entrance.

"You look well this morning also, Miss Franklin—" Samuel started.

"Sarah. You must all call me Sarah. After all, we will be traveling and living together. Won't it be fun? I was telling Charlie how sincerely I am looking forward to the adventure."

Charlie? When my brother had turned thirteen years of age, he forbade any family member or friend to refer to him by such a childish name. It had taken awhile. Robert still used the nickname when he wanted to get a rise out of his baby brother. But, for more than five years, I had thought of my brother as Charles. And yet, each time Sarah referred to him as "Charlie," I saw his delight.

For the next hour, the three of us listened to Sarah laugh and talk and carry on. When he at last found a space, Samuel slipped in a few words about the meeting. By the time we finished eating, there was time enough left to leisurely walk a half mile to the Good Shepherd Baptist Church.

There were hundreds of us. All sorts. The building was too

small to accommodate the crowd so we gathered outside in a field adjacent to the church. Milling around, unsure of where to stand, we settled into a grand circle when a bulky man stepped in the center. Carrying a large crate, he stood on top of it, which elevated him at least three feet above the rest of us. He was clad in work pants and a white shirt soiled from perspiration. His suspenders were black leather, wide and worn along the edges. The soft felt hat was a brown color, either from design or dirt, and his initials had been stitched into the band with what looked like red beads. I estimated his age somewhere between thirty and thirty-five. A black mustache sat on his top lip, bushy, almost covering his bottom lip when his mouth was closed. I expected a low, booming voice to come from such a form but when he spoke, it was in a gentle tone.

"We can't hear you!" a man in the back shouted.

He raised his pitch. "Then listen more closely! It will be crucial that you all listen and follow my instructions as well as those of Wagon Master Chapman. We are the commanding officers now. You—" he rotated and pointed his finger straight ahead as he turned. When he faced me, I could see the pistol tucked in his waistband. "—every single one of you—are the army. You will follow our lead, never questioning. Your only job will be to listen and follow. I will be passing around a document to sign. It will be compared to the one most of you signed when arriving in Council Bluffs. Mr. Chapman and I will compare the two. Those of you whose name appears on both sheets, who have lasted the weeks or months necessary to ready yourselves, will be given agreements to sign."

I surveyed the faces of those around me. I could smell lilacs on the breeze and wondered at the expectations and dreams of my fellow travelers. There were more of them than

I had imagined and I wondered how many more were in hotels or boardinghouses, being represented by one person this day.

A group of young girls laughed and pulled each other's hair. They ignored the directions, confident, I supposed, that their parents would get them safely out west. They had no fear or concern on any part of their faces. I had once felt such confidence in my elders to deliver me from evil and sadness. Unfortunately, the past few years had made me cautious and frightened.

A woman stood directly in front of me. She had the longest hair I had ever seen. It hung loose, touching the back of her dress far below the waist. I wondered how she could sit comfortably without pulling strands from her head. She held a small child and one more gripped onto her skirt while sucking his thumb. When she turned I noticed she was pregnant.

The majority of the bodies in the circle, however, seemed to be male. They stood, most of them, with their mouths and ears open as Mr. Hain spoke of provisions.

I had been hearing the same list of flour, bacon, coffee, sugar and salt for months. Samuel had talked of nothing else and I had grudgingly helped take inventory of kitchen utensils, rice, tea and beans. They had all been dry goods and supplies we would have normally purchased at home, except now we were buying one hundred fifty pounds of bacon instead of one. But when Mr. Hain spoke of rifles and powder, lead and shot, I was suddenly jolted out of further comparisons I would make of life in Maryland.

Samuel misread my concern and whispered, "Don't worry. I've purchased three rifles. One for each of us."

"But, I don't know . . . I can't . . ."

"We'll practice tomorrow. You'll get the hang of it."

The journey we had talked about and planned for was, at

last, about to happen. It was a dangerous endeavor. Lives could be lost. I didn't want to practice shooting a weapon; I never wanted to get used to handling any type of rifle. I looked at the little boy next to me and wondered if he would make it to Oregon. Would the baby being rocked by her mother grow stronger each day of our travels or weaker?

A small hand waved at me from across the field. I recognized Decatur, the boy who had first greeted us when we arrived in town all those weeks ago. I waved back. My feet ached from standing so long. I longed for something cool to drink.

Sarah seemed beyond discomfort. Every so often I noticed she would smile or nod to my brother. I could not hear what she said when she leaned toward him. They had chosen to stand on the other side of Samuel. But their expressions gave away their excitement.

Mr. Hain was finishing his speech. "The Wagon Master, Mr. Chapman, arrives next week, Thursday. After he rests up a few days, we'll be on our way. If all goes well, we'll be moving out of town the following Monday."

The men cheered, women clapped and the children mimicked both the men and women. Mr. Hain jumped down from his crate, happy that he had left so many so well informed. As he walked toward the road he shook hands of those in his way.

"Twelve days, Abby. Twelve more days of waiting. Can you believe it?" Samuel was angry, anxious to get started.

"No," I answered slowly, "I can't believe it." I was suddenly very sad at the realization that only twelve days remained. Twelve days. Less than two weeks before everything would change forever . . . again.

CHAPTER TWENTY-TWO

The meeting had only served to fuel Sarah Franklin's determination to travel with us. Using Samuel's list as a guide, she set about purchasing her share of food and supplies. Samuel offered to instruct her, along with me, in the loading and firing of firearms. But Sarah explained how her father had taught her alongside her five brothers. Through all of it, the three of us listened and watched, Charles being particularly supportive. But when she announced her intention to procure a small farm wagon, my husband objected.

I sat in on the conversation as Samuel explained that the wagons had to be constructed of aged hardwood. This was necessary because of the extreme temperatures and rough terrain we were going to encounter. A mere wagon would never hold up. It was also noted, by Charles, that neither one of the women in our group was capable of managing the team or the wagons. Since we had only two men, it followed that we could manage only two wagons. The addition to our party had, unfortunately, Charles lamented, not come in the form of muscles but rather soft weight. I noticed how Sarah did not argue about this. I had expected, after her impressive display with the rifle, that she would also announce her competence maneuvering a team. But when she saw my husband was becoming agitated with her conflicting opinions, she stopped.

"I am sure you are only considering my safety and I will abide by any decision you make." She smiled up at Samuel and I saw her transform, before my eyes, from a capable woman into a fragile creature in need of protection. I found this change very interesting and was intrigued by my husband's and brother's reaction.

"I do apologize if I have spoiled your excitement, Sarah. I have firm plans and it is my job to keep us safe."

"Of course, Samuel. Whatever you say. I was letting my enthusiasm cloud my good sense. And again, let me thank all of you for allowing me to come along on this expedition. I know Nathan would have heartily approved."

Then she did something, a small thing, I wonder why it has even stayed with me this long. When she thanked us, she touched Samuel on the shoulder. I had been standing at my husband's side and as she moved from Samuel to hug Charles, she swept her shawl over a shoulder and it brushed my cheek. I know she saw the fringe hit my face but she said nothing. She never came back to make any sort of contact with me.

From that day on, Sarah Franklin was accepted as the second woman in our party and the original plan prevailed. We would take two wagons. One would be loaded with provisions and allow sleeping space for Samuel and myself. The other would carry our belongings and afford one person a small area to recline. Initially, this second wagon was to have been for Charles' use exclusively. During the day he would manage the team; at night he would sleep inside. Now, Sarah would add her two trunks to the load and she would sleep inside. Charles would manage his night's rest on a blanket beneath the wagon. When the matter of money was brought up, it was decided that we were all responsible for our own accounts—Samuel and I having one between us.

Within a week's time Sarah had practically walked a rut between her hotel and Mrs. Adams' front door with all her questions and announcements. Her face became more familiar to our landlady each day, and as she began eating more often at our table, Mrs. Adams asked that we pay for our guest.

"It is not fair to the others," she told me. "She cannot come into this place and treat me like I am her maid. This is my house, you know. I own it. I choose who will stay under my roof." How clearly I remember the exact place I stood and chore I was attending to as Mrs. Adams complained. It had suddenly turned cold that afternoon, and I was back in the shed we rented. I was dirty and depressed. Samuel had told me the night before, that even though our wagon would be somewhat wider than most, there was still too much space wasted inside. I was to unpack the china and try fitting the pieces in a smaller box. Straw was strewn around me, the afternoon offered limited light and everything I touched seemed to slide out of my hand and land on the muddy floor. When Mrs. Adams came to me with her complaint, I was not in any mood to hear her.

"Well, she'll be gone, like the rest of us, in just a few more days."

Coral handed me the gravy boat. "She stares at me, I see it." She pointed to a corner where the china would fit. "There, the perfect place."

It was true, Sarah did stare and when we were alone, she asked questions about Mrs. Adams incessantly. I, too, found the poor woman's story fascinating, and I would have expected that she would surely have been used to people staring at her face after all this time.

The handle of a teacup came off in my hand. I threw the delicate piece against the rough wall. "I'm sorry. I'll speak to her about reimbursing you. And until we leave, I'll see that she eats all her meals in her hotel. Will that be fair?"

Slumping down onto an old bench, I tried holding my skirt out of the mud but it was impossible.

Coral Adams stared at me for a minute and then slowly seated herself next to me. "I am the sorry one. I have been blaming everyone—anyone—for months now. I am very confused." Tears welled in her large eyes and overflowed into small wrinkles fanning out onto her cheeks. The sight of those tears caused my own sadness to manifest itself. At first we both tried holding back our despair, embarrassed, but once she reached out to comfort me, I was lost to the pain. My heart ached for her as well as myself and I cried.

"You were right, that morning in the garden. I'm afraid to leave this place. And yet," I cried, "I don't want to stay."

"I know," she said, swallowing a sob, "I don't want to stay, either."

She caught me by surprise. After drying my eyes, I questioned her. "What do you mean? This is your home. You have a business, a life . . ."

"I want none of this." She waved her hands like she was swatting a swarm of flies.

"But you said you were rescued and came here . . ."

"I was taken away from a life I loved. Then I was left here because I refused to go further with my brave heroes. Oh such great men. They rode into that village and fired upon innocents. How were they any different from the men they called savages. I ask you that?"

"I don't know." Again she was forcing questions upon me to consider that I was not prepared for.

"Oh, Pearl ran home, could not get back to her little life fast enough. She did not learn one thing from our husbands." Mrs. Adams shook her head while biting her bottom lip.

"The men who left the wagon train? What did you expect her to learn from them?"

"No!" She was hysterical now and stood up. "Our Indian husbands."

"But, I thought . . ."

"Pearl's husband was named Brave Swimmer; mine was called Wounded Hawk because of his arm. It was crooked; he could not raise it very high. But he was strong and kind. They believe, the Indians do, that people and earth should live together. Wounded Hawk taught me how to listen and see. And he loved me. When the others came to the tent at night, when they humiliated my sister and me, Wounded Hawk would stay outside.

"Pearl and I often whispered that we were luckier than most that we had been married and knew the ways of husbands. Ach, the cruelty, the outbursts . . . all men are the same."

I listened, saddened and shocked to hear of the terrible treatment this poor woman had received throughout her life.

"But when the mean ones learn we would not cry or beg, when they brand us and see that we do not shed one tear, they respect us. They even give us chores and let us walk around their camp without suspicions. I start to feel happy."

"I can't even begin to tell you I understand your fear or torment."

"And sadly, I know you cannot begin to understand my contentment. Wounded Hawk protected me. He would make sure my sister and I were well. As we cooked or worked on the hides with the other women, he would teach us a few of their words. He had more patience in him than any other person I have ever known. And, believe this if you will," now she smiled and I saw her teeth were almost as weathered as her skin, "he thought me beautiful."

"And you married him?" I tried imagining a ceremony of some sort but could not.

"Not like the way we do it. He came one night and took me to his tent. I lived there with him. And the other men treated me differently, the women were a little kinder. I was content . . . until my sister caused trouble."

"But she had a husband, too. Didn't she want to stay with him?"

"I never understood what my sister wanted. And now, I do not even consider her needs; we have not spoken or seen one another in over two years."

"How sad." Tears resurfaced and I could feel my throat tightening.

Her wailing began so abruptly it startled me. "I am discontent with everything. I do not belong anywhere."

I rose just in time to allow her to collapse into my arms. As we stood in the dreary shed, I tried comforting this strange woman but with my face buried in her collar, I wondered who was comforting who. My stomach ached from the desperate isolation clutching my insides.

Samuel was happier than I had ever seen him. Charles and Sarah shared my husband's dream. But no matter how I tried, I did not feel a part of any of it. How very disheartened I felt as I slowly realized that the one person I felt closest to now was Mrs. Adams. And that the strongest bond we had between us was this horrible desolation.

CHAPTER TWENTY-THREE

I thought my brother was dead. When Mrs. Adams woke me that morning, pounding on our door, screaming something about Charles, I ran from my room with no thought of appearances. My nightgown must have looked like a flag unfurling as I raced across the hall. I can't remember where Samuel was. He might have been in bed beside me. But my concern at that moment was solely for my brother.

"I send Jane up to call him for breakfast. He never misses his first meal. The others were asking for him; he always is so cheerful." Mrs. Adams spoke so quickly; I could hardly catch the words as she went on. "When she hear him moan, Jane come for me. We find him. Here. Just like this." She finally slowed down and I was able to ask for her help.

"We must make sure he's breathing. Get the mirror from my dresser." As Mrs. Adams ran, I put my ear to Charles' chest and held my own breath, listening for his heartbeat. There was a slow rhythm beneath his bedclothes. "Charles?" I touched his brow and could feel the warmth. "Can you hear me?"

"Here." Mrs. Adams shoved the mirror at me.

I held the glass beneath his nose and saw the blessed fog spread across its surface. "Charles!" I gently shook my brother. "Wake up!"

His eyes flickered open and I could see the green flecks that usually sparkled like emeralds seemed now to have melted into the amber leaving almost a muddy appearance.

"What's happened?" Samuel appeared at the door; I felt

immense relief at the sight of him.

"I think it's the consumption," I said.

"He hasn't been coughing as much lately," Samuel commented. "He's been so well. I almost forgot about his illness."

I imagine our calm demeanor reassured Mrs. Adams for she seemed suddenly to have collected herself. "They can go long times without being sick. I had a cousin, such a puny boy, always coughing and wheezing. But when he grew up, he got strong."

Charles slowly lifted his head and in a weak voice said, "I think it's influenza. Don't worry; I'll be fine."

"Ach, let's hope so. Maybe a vapor bath will help. Jane and I will bring the tub up and fill it with steaming water. Then we will put strong sticks across it and you will sit. You must cover yourself in a blanket and breathe deeply the steam. It will make you better. And a little brandy before bed will make you goot as new." She smiled at Charles and left the room.

I was touched by my brother's determination. "I don't think you will have recuperated by tomorrow, dear."

"Oh, now, he has a whole week to rest," Samuel comforted. He sat on the bed near my brother's feet. "Don't worry, Charlie, dear," he grinned, "we'd never leave you behind."

"There's always another group leaving another day." I was glad for my husband's understanding nature.

"Oh, we're leaving on schedule, even if we have to tie this one down with the baggage." Samuel laughed and I started to tell him how awfully selfish I thought he was when my brother spoke.

"Please, just let me rest. I'll be fine." And he fell back onto his pillow.

Samuel ushered me out of the room. "He's right. Come on, we have chores, let's get to them."

I was in the kitchen making a pot of soup from Mother's recipe that gave Charles strength when he fell ill at home. Mrs. Adams had kindly gathered the ingredients as I told her what was needed. I was chopping a carrot when she told me a letter had arrived for me earlier that morning. All the excitement had caused her to neglect mentioning it.

Letters from home had turned out to be my most valued possessions in Iowa. As much as the women in my family loved writing pages, I loved reading their thoughts and words even more. I would usually make an effort to answer within a day's time but there always seemed to be so much to do. I seemed to either be working, sleeping or eating. How basic life can be sometimes.

My first impulse was to rush to the small table in the front hall where Mrs. Adams left the mail, and grab what was mine. But Charles had to be tended to and so I continued chopping vegetables with the large knife. But as I dropped the carrot into the black pot and started peeling a large onion, I savored the anticipation. It was almost sinful how, as my brother lay ailing upstairs, I felt such joy at the thought of a letter.

Sometimes, when I was sure no one could see, I would smell the paper that had been touched by my mother. I would imagine that if I ran my fingers across her inked strokes, somehow I was touching her, that we were connected. Even her stationery was special. Usually decorated with watercolor designs, she would make even the paper uniquely her own.

When at last the large pot had been filled with herbs and the water added, I set it on the stove. Wiping my hands, I forced my feet to move slowly, enjoying the excitement as I walked toward the hall. I passed Mrs. Adams in one of the back bedrooms as she changed sheets. Jane was dusting the parlor. An elderly gentleman sat at one end of the dining room table, eating the remains of his eggs. Finally, I saw the single envelope addressed to me. Grabbing it tightly, I ran up the stairs to read my mail in the privacy of my room.

It was a large gray envelope, embossed on the back flap with my father's initials in black script. This was only the second message I had received from him since my departure but I was well acquainted with his writing style from years of separation during my childhood. While his letters were sporadic in arriving, they always were the fattest I received. But as dearly as I loved my father, he did have a tendency to elaborate upon events pertaining to his life alone: business abroad, international politics, the weather in his neighborhood. Short on questions and long on lectures, my family often joked that my father should have been a teacher. His enthusiasm, however, more than made up for the tediousness. He was a man who loved what he did so much that he expected everyone else to find great pleasure in just hearing about all of it. And any news was welcomed then.

I ran my nail under the seal and eagerly opened the letter that had originated in England. It began:

My Dearest Daughter,

I think of you daily and hope you are well. It is still difficult for me to believe you are a married woman, away from home, with a husband to look after. How easily I lapse into memories of you playing with your dolls. I especially remember the one I bought you from Ireland, the one with the tiny dress of plaid. How you loved her. And the great talks we would have when you were filled with such serious questions. Afterwards, I wondered who had learned more. You were always such a wise child with a unique outlook. It was because of that viewpoint that I always felt you would be fine at whatever you attempted to do. Of my three children, you were the one who caused the least concern.

But recent news from your mother has left me distraught. She writes that you are unhappy. That you are constantly in a bad humor and complain about Samuel. She is worried and at a loss how to console you. Your poor mother asks me to write you and gently reason, so as not to upset you further.

I gave this matter a few days to settle and came to the conclusion that you have had too much gentleness in your life. Too much sheltering. Too much protection. Your recent behavior has angered me greatly. I am saddened to think I raised such an ungrateful child. You have what every woman wants. An industrious husband who is only trying to make a better life for you. To provide security to the children you will one day have. A man who I have seen grow from a frightened boy to an intelligent man. A man I am proud to call my son.

It is your duty now to obey him. Support his decisions and make his life easier with your gratefulness instead of difficult with your complaining. Prospects for a business in Oregon are unlimited. It is up to you to make a home for him, raise his children and . . .

I stopped reading the letter. Angered at how a middle-aged man could even begin to understand what "every woman wants." How could this man who lived as he chose, where he chose, begin to understand my dilemma?

Such arrogance!

Turning the envelope over I noticed, for the first time, that it had been addressed to "Mrs. Samuel Gray." Not "Abigail

Gray," not even "Mrs. Abigail Gray." Searching the pages of his letter I could not find my name mentioned once. "Abigail" seemed to no longer exist on her own for my father.

That "bad humor" nipped at my stomach again. I quickly pinned my hair up and arranged a plain hat on my head. Grabbing my bag, I decided to walk off the anger.

CHAPTER TWENTY-FOUR

I had to force my way along the walk bordering storefronts, the bank and post office. Initially I had thought of stopping to see Sarah, but as I got closer to her hotel, a great throng of people, all moving in conflicting directions, pushed me right through the heart of town. Commotion had seemed to increase each day since our arrival; more pioneers flowed in to fill spots left by those departing on a regular basis, but that was the busiest I had ever seen this community. Thank goodness I was not hungry and aromas coming from the bakery did not tempt me, for I could not have stopped even if I had wanted to. I knew then how a salmon felt being pushed upstream surrounded by other anxious, single-minded bodies.

By the time my anger and the crowd had dissipated, I was on the outskirts. Grassy patches now grew in what had been mud holes when we first crossed the city limits. I was only familiar with my surroundings enough to recognize the yellow banner draped across the front of an abandoned house which declared: WELCOME TRAVELERS! That very same weathered piece of material had once waved a greeting to us when we rode into town from St. Louis. Wondering how long it had been there, I ventured past it, straight into unknown territory.

The smell of animals grew more pungent and I saw a fenced in field where a dozen or so black horses nibbled at a large bale of hay. In a small pen, a few feet from the large animals, were pigs, and running around the open space in-between the two breeds was a duck that squawked angrily as I walked by. The horses, disinterested, continued eating. On the other side of the road was another field dotted with cows. I remember thinking how lucky we were, my small family and I, not to be traveling west in hopes of farming, not having to worry about the safety of livestock while fearing for our own. We planned to travel light, needing only our team to pull the wagons. And when we safely reached our destination, they would be sold.

Past all the activity and animals there was another field. Running wild with flowers, it was the most idyllic spot I had seen—aside from those depicted in paintings. Sunlight streamed through a break in the low clouds as if pointing a shimmering finger to God's perfect place. The grass appeared soft from where I stood, like the fine hair on a child's arm. An orchard was further down the road and trees stood in rows, decorated with springtime pinks and creamy whites. My feet gripped themselves to that spot; my eyes took in those delicate pastels.

As a breeze ruffled my hair, animal smells, once responsible for insulting my senses, suddenly mingled with flowers and grass, producing the sweetest fragrance. Had I been able to bottle it, I would have made that earthy essence my own and freely sprinkled it daily in my hair.

After carefully checking all directions, I still hesitated to wander into the field. Ownership was everything out here, back then. Every bean, each pan, every inch of rope, they all determined survival. I had heard the story of a man from Alabama who had hanged his best friend, Dooley, for stealing. The two had been outfitting a wagon. Then little items, insignificant things, things the man would never have bothered with under more normal circumstances, started to vanish. The man questioned his friend. Of course Dooley denied taking the nails or tin of beans in question. But no matter how much he protested, his friend knew something had taken hold of the man he thought he knew almost as well as himself. Maybe it was fear, maybe greediness. But it was finally discovered that Dooley had been hoarding a little bit extra for himself each night, rearranging boxes and trunks to cover his deeds.

I wondered, quite frequently, if we had been told that story to discourage even a thought of touching anything not belonging to us. To teach us a lesson, or did it serve more as a warning that soon, we also would be capable of killing anyone who threatened our survival.

Either way, I knew my companions and I were honest. I also knew we were better educated and therefore, better equipped to overcome hardship than most. But that piece of rope, the one used to hang poor Dooley, still dangled from a tree limb not far from the banner where new arrivals would be sure to see it. The story was told hundreds of times; its moral learned immediately. So it was perfectly understandable why I climbed with such trepidation over the low fence. Unable to stop myself, I wandered into the field.

It was still too early for most insects except tiny gnats that buzzed around my face. I held my dress up with one hand and swatted the insects with the other. When I had crossed half the field, I was confident that no one had seen me nor did anyone care. After all, there was nothing to be taken from this area except the joy and I was sure no one would begrudge me that.

Like a bee, flitting from flower to flower, I touched first a red and then a purple blossom. Bending to run the velvet petals between my fingers, I walked and stopped, hesitated and hurried, until I was almost to the back fence near the largest of the apple trees. I slowly wandered toward shade, planning to sit and relax. Such a simple plan and yet most times it seems the simpler the wish, the more difficult is its procurement. For suddenly my peace was interrupted by voices.

First a man spoke. He said something in a soft tone. And then a woman laughed. I was startled, frozen in my tracks. Feeling like something wild, I was caught, not sure whether I had been seen, not sure if I should run or remain still. Holding my breath, I searched the long grass for a sign of where the couple might be.

"Oh Amos!" Another giggle and then she was standing right in front of me, no more than eight feet away. A few more steps and I might have trampled them. And then, to my amazement, I recognized her. My mouth was surely open; it had to be. Dropping the hem of my dress to the grass, I covered my surprise with both hands.

"Abigail?" Sarah Franklin's shock was as great as my own.

"Sarah, I didn't know you were . . . I was walking and saw the flowers . . . I didn't mean to . . ."

A man stirred in the green wave of long grass and stood. He looked like Neptune rising from the sea. He wore brown trousers; his belt and shirt were missing. His gray streaked hair was strewn with little pink flowers and bits of grass.

Sarah lifted the shoulder of her dress. She patted her hair into place as she spoke. "You startled me." A smile played across her lips instead of the embarrassment I expected to find there.

Her companion put on then buttoned his shirt as he introduced himself. "Glad to make your acquaintance, Abigail, is it?" He looked to Sarah who nodded. "My name is Amos Fell. Sarah's told me all about you and your family. She's very excited about traveling with—"

Sarah interrupted him. "Abigail knows all that, Amos . . . dear."

As they gathered the blanket, we all started back toward the road. I did not want to walk with them but the magic of the field had suddenly disappeared. All I wanted to do was run . . . away from that place, away from those people.

"Why are you out so early today?" Sarah asked as we walked past that angry duck.

"Charles is ill. I had intended to stop by your hotel and ask you to visit him."

"Well this certainly does not look like The River House." Sarah laughed at me.

"I changed my mind and decided to walk." I stammered to explain, all the while scolding myself, silently, for feeling it necessary to do so. I, after all, had not been discovered cavorting out in the open with a strange man. I was not the one who held the affection of an eighteen-year-old boy in such little regard. My respect for this woman diminished as we walked but, God help me, my curiosity increased. Part of me could not wait to tell my husband about this hussy and, at the same time, another part of me wanted to protect this woman who I had begun thinking of as a friend. And then there was Charles. I knew him to be a strong, intelligent man. Mentally, that was. But physically, he was weak, my little brother, who needed my protection.

After fifteen minutes of walking in a horrible silence, we at last came to the hotel. It was Mr. Fell who spoke first.

"Would you allow me to buy you ladies lunch?"

"Thank you, no." I tried being polite but the words did not come out that way.

Sarah smiled at the man who looked more like her father than a suitor. "Amos, I think Abigail and I have some matters to discuss, and I want to look in on Charles. You know how fond I am of the boy."

"Of course." He dropped both hands into the pockets of

his overcoat. "Another time."

As he turned to cross the street, I started back toward the boardinghouse offering not one single word to Sarah. But she would not accept my scorn and hurried to catch me.

Then in a calm, even voice, she said to my back, "How dare you."

CHAPTER TWENTY-FIVE

I feigned deafness. Marching with more deliberation than a military band, I walked away from her.

But she followed.

I heard her running to match my strides and it made me happy she was finding it difficult to catch up. When I was sure we were past curious ears and eyes, I turned around, so quickly that several tresses shook loose from their pins and slapped my cheek.

Then I growled, "I? How dare I?"

"You heard me correctly, Abigail." Sarah Franklin stood in front of me, defiant, making it obvious she wanted a confrontation at that precise moment, on that precise spot.

"Well, I suppose if I had been caught rolling around in the grass, no better than a dumb animal, I, too, would be a tiny bit embarrassed. But, Sarah . . . dear . . . I did not seek you out nor did I intend to cause you any humiliation. That, sweet Sarah, you brought upon yourself."

"How on earth were you to know we were even there? I would have to be a most unreasonable person to be upset with you for that." Her face flushed and the elaborate hat that had been hastily pinned atop her head slipped forward a little, giving her a strange look. In fact, I suspected the thing might have been on backwards for the pink grosgrain bow which matched the trim of her jacket, was in the center of the front. "What I am upset about is your judgment of me."

"My what?"

"It was in your eyes. After *your* embarrassment faded. You questioned, accused, and condemned me within a moment's time without so much as one word. How dare you judge me so harshly in such an unkind manner."

I protested. "I think I know a little about life. I am not a child, I know . . ."

"But in many ways, you are a child. Do you think life and romance, in particular, are played out like a Brontë novel? Are you that naive? I think you are." Her hat slipped a little more but she ignored it, instead she angrily brushed blades of grass from her bag and the blanket folded over her left arm.

Having heard enough of her insults, I turned my back on her once again, and was mid-way down a rickety stairway leading from the boardwalk to the street, when she caught my arm and pulled me up to her level. As I felt myself being yanked backwards, I chose to go with the movement so as not to get tangled in my hem. Besides, how would I have lived with the gossip should word spread that Sarah Franklin and I—supposed friends—had made a spectacle of ourselves in broad daylight? In the middle of town? Luckily, the crowd I had encountered earlier had thinned out, luckier still there seemed no one around who gave us much notice. Still, I went with the movement and made it look as though my friend was merely helping me back up the step.

"I have never been anything but kind to you, Abigail Gray. I have never judged you nor thought you dull, in spite of all the outward signs of it being so. I have respected you as Samuel's wife and Nathan's niece."

I crossed my arms, anxious for the scene to be over. But Sarah continued in a calm and low voice.

"I am not a married woman. I am single and, as such, free to see whomever I choose. And my choice of companion is no concern of yours."

"No concern? Have you forgotten that one of your 'secret affairs' involved a member of my own family? That your 'association' with him is the only reason you are here now? Right in the middle of my very own life?"

"I was wondering why it took you so long to bring up my relationship with Nathan. Need I remind you that Nathan Miller was a mature man? He knew all too well what he was entering into when he invited me to his home after I was engaged. Besides, did my affair with Nathan have any undesirable effect on either you or Samuel? Did I harm any of you?"

I had to admit she had not.

"And as for Charles, I have been kind to your brother for only one reason . . . I like him. If he is inclined to misinterpret my kindness, if my friendship is causing him any problems at all, I will take up the matter with him. He is a sweet boy, but, as you have guessed, I appreciate older men. They have more to offer . . ."

"Please," I held up my hand, "I do not care to discuss your preferences where men are . . ."

Her hat finally slipped all the way past her forehead and then completely off. Without hesitation, I reached out and caught it deftly with both hands.

We didn't laugh then. Maybe we should have. But the sudden movement of both the hat and my hands stopped our conversation abruptly. We stood for a moment, just looking stupidly at the straw and floral creation. Then, simultaneously, Sarah reached out for her hat and I pushed it toward her.

"Thank you." She pulled the long hatpin from the band and stared at it for a moment. "I got this in Boston; I was about your age. I thought it was the prettiest thing ever made."

She held it out for my examination and I took it from her.

It was about six inches long and had a pair of delicately carved lovebirds perched on one end. They appeared to be made of ivory.

"It's very nice." I handed it back to her.

"You see," she said, "I was like you once. I believed in purity. I recited Browning and waited."

"For what?" I watched as she replaced her hat and, this time, carefully pinned it in place.

"For genuine love." She smiled, and linked her arm through mine. "But you see, a strange thing happened. One day I realized that while I waited, I should be living an interesting life. And I have." We descended the stairs together and started back toward Mrs. Adams' house.

"Weren't you married once? I remember you saying you were widowed when you met Nathan."

She looked puzzled. "I was."

"It's just that when you spoke of love, I remembered you said you had been married and . . ."

"See what I mean?" She gently patted my hand. "You are still child-like in many ways. Marriage—love. One does not necessarily have anything to do with the other." That's when Sarah Franklin laughed. And it startled me. "Oh Abby, we are going to have such a good time getting to know one another."

It seemed such an odd reaction at the time, but I was suddenly happy.

"Now let's have a look at Charles," she said. "We must fuss over him and show concern for every tiny discomfort."

"It's nothing serious," I assured her.

"Oh, I knew that. If there was concern I'm quite sure you wouldn't have had time to beat the grass for wild animals."

I laughed then, and it didn't startle Sarah one bit.

Coral Adams came running out through the front door

like her dress was on fire. I had never seen the woman move so fast. As she ran she rubbed her large hands together.

"Now there goes one of the truly strange ones," Sarah said as we stopped to watch Mrs. Adams.

"Maybe Charles has taken a bad turn." I ran to meet the frantic woman. As I got closer, however, I could see that she was smiling and my heart felt some relief.

When she saw Sarah, Mrs. Adams pulled me off the path, making it clear that what she had to say was strictly between the two of us.

"Is my brother all right?"

"Oh, ya, he had his bath and is sleeping. Not to worry." She shifted her weight from one foot to another and continually rubbed her hands together in such a fashion as to make me most uncomfortable.

"Then what is it? You seem so agitated."

All movement stopped then and she clasped my shoulders. "I have decided. For months and months I have been wondering and hoping for a sign, something . . . I do not know. But today, I knew, it came to me when I wasn't trying so hard. I am such a dumkauf." She gently knocked her head with a fist.

Sarah was standing behind Mrs. Adams by then and I said to her, "You can go in ahead without me. Maybe Jane will bring you some coffee?" I looked to Mrs. Adams for approval of this idea.

"Oh sure, sure," she said, shooing my visitor away.

After watching Sarah enter the house, Mrs. Adams leaned a little closer and said, "I don't like that woman. Something about her. She likes the men too much."

"You were telling me about a decision?" I wanted to return to our original conversation.

"Oh," her face broke into such a smile as to make her almost attractive. "I am selling my house, the papers are to be signed tomorrow."

"But . . . where will you . . . ?"

"I'm going on the wagon train. Your wagon train. Won't it be wonderful?"

CHAPTER TWENTY-SIX

It was seven o'clock in the morning, May tenth, eighteen hundred and forty-eight, when we rolled out of Council Bluffs, Iowa. Chill laced the air, grass and flowers were bumpy with dew and fog rose from the ground as if from a great mouth that was trying to tell us something. It would have been quite peaceful had it not been for the thunder made by hundreds of wheels and thousands of hoofs beating into the dirt road. The tinkle of teacups and jars rattled inside their boxes from under quilts and old newspapers like so many tiny bells. Children laughed and waved at anyone, anything they passed. Men shouted and concentrated on the job of getting their teams and families aimed in the same direction. But the women did only one thing. They cried.

I sat next to Samuel, high on that narrow, overloaded wagon. It was all I could do not to jump and run. But instead I silently cursed the ignorance that had brought me to this place. Samuel smiled and talked as if I could understand what he said above the commotion. He never noticed my tears.

How smug I had been in the knowledge that I was born wise. I assumed my gift would always be at my very core. It wasn't until the day of our departure that I became aware my wisdom had been depleted. I felt desperately empty, unprepared and afraid. I sorely missed that satisfying feeling usually running over into every space of me. But I had my family and friends around me. Maybe that would be enough.

★ ★ ★ ★ ★

Charles had recovered from his influenza nicely. I don't know if it was his healthy attitude or determination but he looked to me to be fitter than ever.

Coral—she insisted we all call her by her given name since we would be traveling together—had no problem selling her house. A wealthy man, a past acquaintance of mine, Amos Fell, had been coaxing Coral, on a regular basis, to sell. With westward travel becoming more popular and the news of gold mines and rich land, Council Bluffs generated more revenue by the minute.

Our original two-wagon plan remained the same. After learning that Coral suffered from insomnia, Samuel became convinced her condition would force her to nap throughout the day thus freeing the wagon for us to sleep in during the night. Having made the trip once, she knew what was needed and brought her few belonging and supplies loaded onto a small wagon which Samuel agreed could easily be pulled behind our own. And the fact that she planned to leave us at Fort Bridger, somewhere in Wyoming, and make her way back to the crippled arms of Wounded Hawk by herself, made her presence less of a concern.

Sarah remained her kind, elegant self. Our encounter in the field that afternoon had left our friendship unchanged. If there was any uneasiness, it was wholly on my part. I never felt obligated to tell Samuel or Charles or Coral any of it.

Riding in the middle of the long train of wagons I had not been able to estimate our length. But as we came to a hill and the procession rose before me, I could see canvas flapping, like sails, in a sea of green and yellow.

Coral walked alongside the wagon, saying she would ride when she got tired but was too excited to sit still just yet.

Charles and Sarah rode up on the other wagon and waved to everyone including themselves and us.

I had heard Samuel say that there were sixty-two wagons in our party and a population contained therein of approximately one hundred and thirty. We left town that day with five of those people, four oxen, five horses, two prairie schooners and one small wagon trailing behind.

PART THREE

CHAPTER TWENTY-SEVEN

How I resisted facing forward! I kept looking back, staring at the buildings of Council Bluffs. I thought if I memorized the exact location of each shop, recalled my days and weeks there, I could slow down our departure. Somehow put off my anxiety.

Samuel urged me to look ahead. "The sky is clear; we have a beautiful day. Enjoy the scenery. The Colonel's taking it easy on us our first day. From here on out we'll be getting started before six o'clock each morning."

But I couldn't bear to let security trickle from my life so easily.

Soon the town was out of sight and with it any familiarity that might have offered me some sort of comfort. Even sooner, we were traveling over unfamiliar terrain without so much as a church steeple on the horizon.

Stories of savagery, murder and starvation had circulated around me for months. I had eventually grown indifferent. Each person was unique, I reasoned, and therefore reacted uniquely to any given situation. I chose not to dwell on fearsome scenarios but instead concerned myself with my priority: hold on tight. Which was more difficult than I had imagined for everything seemed out of proportion.

The wagon was high and my seat narrow. Maybe my husband hadn't allowed for layers of clothing bunched beneath me. Even as we got into the rhythm of the team, I could feel myself being pushed forward and feared I would topple right off. The oxen seemed huge. In the streets, where I had seen them for the first time being herded through town, I was impressed by their size. Pointed, curved horns spanned the width of my outstretched arms. But their soft brown eyes fringed with delicate lashes gave them a gentle appearance. On that day, just starting out, I could not see their faces from my place next to Samuel and the animals appeared fearless, intimidating.

To make matters worse, all of us, every child and grown-up, looked smaller. Contrasted against the great expanse, my traveling companions seemed like insects on the hide of some tremendous beast. And we were all the more tiny and helpless.

The lap quilt I had brought from home, my Baltimore home, warmed my legs. I poked my finger through the beginning of a hole in a flowered square near the middle and wondered. Would I ever feel completely safe again?

Suddenly our wheel hit a rut and my shoulder bumped into Samuel. The movement shook me from my thoughts and into the present. Lifting my head slowly, I focused my eyes ahead.

Then we stopped.

"What's happening?"

"Don't look so frightened, Abigail. We have to cross the Missouri."

"So soon?" Before I could ask what I should do, Samuel jumped down from his seat and went to speak with a man in the wagon in front of us.

About ten minutes passed before Alvin Hain came riding alongside our wagon and shouted, "Stay in single file. When you reach the front, be prepared to remove the wheels from your wagons. Then we'll load your belongings and wagons onto flatbeds."

"How long will it take?" Charles shouted.

The Assistant Wagon Master answered calmly, "The rest of the day." Then he galloped off, shouting the same instructions to wagons behind us.

We had finally, after a year's worth of planning and working, gotten started. At long last we were packed. And now we were expected to undo everything that had taken months of work to do.

"Why must the wheels come off?" I asked, stupefied.

"Because that's the safest way. The way it's done." Charles was standing next to our wagon and held up his hand to help me down. "That's what the rubber sheets are for. We have to cover all our things so they don't get water-logged."

"Lots of working and waiting," Coral said as she sat down on the grass.

When Sarah joined us, she seemed as mystified as I was. "I can't believe it! There has to be a faster way to do this."

"If you can think of one why don't you go tell the Colonel?" Samuel had returned and seemed annoyed.

Sarah just ignored my husband and turned her back. From the small bag looped around her arm, she removed a fan. The air was quite cool and she never unfolded it but slapped it against her palm.

I sat down next to Coral.

"Busy yourself." The large woman opened a tattered carpetbag she had removed from her small wagon. She withdrew a partially darned stocking. I watched her callused fingers swiftly stitch the cotton together.

Sarah joined us reluctantly. Fussing with the bustle of her dress, she asked in a most annoying tone, "What do we do now?"

Coral regarded the woman with disgust and continued her sewing.

"Don't look at me like that. It took days to get everything

in place. Just so. Now we have to take it all apart?"

"Many times," Coral said. "Apart—together—apart, and together again."

"I never thought of that. I just assumed once things were in place, they'd stay there."

Charles came to offer comfort to Sarah. "Look at it this way, we're not in any danger, we've plenty of food and a beautiful day. We'll count this day as one of the easiest."

"I suppose," Sarah conceded.

"Ach!" Coral dropped her sewing, excited. "This is the perfect time!" She quickly stood up, packed her sewing away and hurried to her wagon. I watched her rummage around, rearrange a few things before removing a red hatbox. Carefully setting in on the ground, she searched inside again and this time came away with a tablecloth draped over one arm.

While the others talked, I continued watching as Coral walked quickly to where I sat.

After motioning for my assistance, she placed the velvet box into my hands. Unfurling the cloth first skyward, she then spread it over the matted grass. I remember the pattern around the edge was a continuous trail of red and blue bows. Still not having uttered one word, she reached for the hatbox then placed it squarely in the center of the ornate cloth. Untying the black cord at the top, Coral Adams smiled. Sarah stopped complaining to watch and Samuel moved closer.

"Come. Sit." Coral commanded and everyone obeyed without one protest.

We watched her like children, all of us. Anxious for a surprise, wondering what she had to show. Almost as soon as the high, chocolate cake was revealed, a slight shift in the wind decorated the swirled top with fine grit.

"To celebrate our trip."

Sarah ignored Coral's pride and complained. "It's too

early in the day for chocolate. And how are we to eat it without utensils or plates?"

Samuel reminded me of the way he had looked when we were children: eager and happy. "It seems the perfect time for such a treat," he said.

"I agree." Charles took out the knife attached in a sheath at his waist. "I'll carve." And without consulting any of us, he laughed and cut across the dessert, dividing it into pieces small enough for us to manage with our fingers.

I reached for my slice. "What a nice thought, Coral, thank you." Biting into the soft sweetness, a few grains of dirt crunched against my back teeth. But the extra ingredient couldn't spoil the rich flavor.

"Sarah?" Charles offered her a piece of the confection.

Replacing her fan, she removed a handkerchief. Wrapping the lacy material around her fingers she accepted what Charles offered. Biting into the cake she neither smiled nor frowned.

Coral didn't seem to mind.

CHAPTER TWENTY-EIGHT

That first day has remained in my memory as one overrun with loudness and yellow brightness. The sun glared down at us as we stood. It seeped through the canvas when I tried resting. And it followed me wherever I walked.

Children, of which I later found out accounted for forty-eight of our population, were merely set loose. Left to express their pleasure or displeasure vocally, unrelentingly. Starting off as soft laughter, working up to a whine, finally graduating into high-pitched squeals. Like a serpent trying to shed its skin, the small ones crawled under wagons, rubbed in-between legs of adults, rolled across the grass. All the while shouting or crying.

Middle-sized ones, possessing more patience, played games alone or with each other. When that became unsatisfactory, they taunted the little ones. This produced not only ear-splitting shouts from parents, but more crying from those being pushed and bullied.

The adolescents seemed to pair off. Girls would seek shade and giggle with a best friend or sister of similar age. The boys sat sullenly, pointing at the girls or huddled together telling secrets. Then, as if bitten by something, they would suddenly cheer or whoop.

My head throbbed from it all.

Around noon of that day, I stood, shading my eyes, and tried to estimate how much longer it would be until we reached the spot where we could dismantle. Hunger grumbled in my stomach. Coral had made a picnic lunch for us and I thought it about time we spread out the food. Before I could move, however, someone tapped my shoulder. Turning, I found Sarah, accompanied by a man I had never seen before.

"Abigail, I want you to meet our . . . neighbor . . . so to speak," Sarah giggled. "This is Mr. Griesinger." She turned to face the man and smiled. "I hope I pronounced it correctly."

"Fine. You did fine."

He offered no smile, in fact, he seemed a little sad. Maybe it was his dark clothing that gave him such a severe appearance. Except for a white collar, he was fully clad in black. My first impression was that he certainly must be a churchman. But upon closer inspection, I saw his clothes were a mixture of styles, some new garments, some frayed and worn.

"Pleased to make your acquaintance," I said as I hunched my shoulders just a bit. Mr. Griesinger was noticeably shorter than I, and it had been my experience that men sometimes found women of taller stature offensive.

"Likewise," he said.

"Mr. Griesinger is all alone. Can you believe that? Coming on this journey not knowing one single person?" Sarah pursed her bottom lip as proof of her concern. "I found him, about three wagons behind us, without anyone to talk to."

"Griesinger. That's an interesting name." I tried offering friendship rather than pity as Sarah seemed to be doing.

"My family comes from Bottingen, in Wurttemburg."

I smiled. "I'm sorry but I'm unfamiliar with that part of the world."

"Oh, I would have been most surprised if you had heard of it." He seemed such a timid gentleman.

"A friend who is traveling with us, Mrs. Adams, may be better educated regarding your country. You might enjoy

155

meeting her." We had never discussed Coral's ancestry, but I assumed, if only from her accent, that she was of German descent.

"Oh, yes," Sarah seemed suddenly annoyed. "You'll definitely have to meet our . . . friend."

"The pleasure will be mine." He tilted his head forward, ever so slightly, in a most kindly manner.

"I've invited Mr. Griesinger to share our picnic," Sarah announced. "It will be nice for him to become acquainted with Samuel and Charles."

I wasn't sure if the basket in Coral's wagon had enough provisions to feed an extra person. But in spite of the commotion my stomach seemed to be making, the waiting had caused me to feel anxious. I knew I would not be able to eat even half of my share.

"Allow me to make something special for you." He seemed to be studying my face.

"For me? Why?"

I saw his lips relax a little, then his wrinkled face fell into soft drapes. "Because you have an aching in your head."

"How did you know?"

"One has only to look closely."

Before I could comment, he turned and walked back to his wagon.

"Isn't he mysterious?" Sarah asked as we watched the man leave.

Coral seemed taken with Mr. Griesinger also. "Ah, Wurttemburg! I have never been. But how often I hear the stories of your beautiful Black Forest. I have family, near there, in Bavaria."

As Coral spoke and passed our guest a sandwich piled with ham, I noticed the colored stones hanging from his belt. I was feeling remarkably better after having sipped the sage tea he had brewed for me. The vapors were calming and when I thanked him, he said I was too formal and asked me, all of us actually, to call him by his given name of Andrew.

Samuel ate, only glancing at Andrew Griesinger occasionally, out of the corner of his eye. I also noticed Charles' lack of enthusiasm or curiosity upon meeting this strange man.

As we ate, Andrew grew more comfortable and started asking questions about us. When we came to the subject of our hometown he grew very excited. "Are you acquainted with the Fox Sisters?" He spoke their names as if they were sacred.

"Are you referring to the girls from Hydesville? New York?" Charles asked.

Samuel looked up, unbelieving. "The lunatics who say they can communicate with the dead?"

"Spiritualists," Andrew corrected. "They have been blessed."

"They're girls!" Samuel almost shouted. "Silly little girls playing a game. I can't believe anyone would be gullible enough to give credence to their stories."

I stopped eating, surprised at how agitated my husband became.

"What stories?" Sarah asked, intrigued.

"They supposedly hear thumping noises. Which their mother, level-headed woman that I'm sure she is," Samuel calmed down a little and snickered, "convinced her daughters were caused by a ghost."

Charles could not let Samuel have all the fun and continued the report. "So they decided to communicate with the spirit by a most unique method. By clapping their hands. Now I ask you," my brother looked at the amazed Sarah, "wouldn't ink and paper have been more effective?" And with

157

that question, he and Samuel grabbed each other, laughing.

"Did the spirits answer?" Coral asked seriously.

Our guest seemed oblivious to his hosts' rudeness. "They devised a way of asking questions using so many claps for yes or no and for letters in the alphabet. And because of their great patience, the spirit told them his name was Charles Rosa, violently murdered, killed by a man who had lived in that very house."

I had heard the story, in fragments, over the past few weeks. Even if my sensibilities told me that ghosts were imaginary, I was glad for the diversion.

"But if I remember correctly," I said, "the girls are eleven and fourteen years of age. Hardly trustworthy witnesses."

Andrew explained, "They were convincing enough that the cellar was searched. The spot where the spirit victim claimed to have been buried was dug up."

"What did they find?" Coral seemed afraid.

Charles told her, "Just a few bones, some hair . . ."

"And human teeth," Andrew said.

"Were the bones in the spot the girls mentioned?" I asked.

"The precise spot."

After no one had spoken for a few moments, Samuel broke the silence. "You can't honestly tell me you believe any of this."

Our guest responded, "I have lived too many years, Mr. Gray, seen too much, to dismiss anything."

"There are more things in heaven and earth, dear Samuel, than are dreamt of in your philosophy," Sarah said.

"We're only speculating," I said to Samuel. "Don't you find the issue even a bit interesting?"

"No! It's blasphemy."

I could see that Charles was as surprised as I was at Samuel's outburst. As I watched the anger cause the corners of his eyes to tighten, I realized Samuel and I had never spoken of such topics before.

Mr. Griesinger stood. "I am sorry, Mr. Gray, to have upset you." Dusting off his dark pants, he looked at me. "Thank you for your hospitality." Then he left.

When she was sure our visitor was far enough away, Sarah said, "Well, what do you make of that?"

"I think he's unstable. Did you see how excited he became when he thought we might actually know those girls?" Samuel asked then finished the cider in his cup. "I think we should all stay away from the man. Especially you, Abigail."

"Why me?"

"He seems to have taken special notice of you."

"Just because he brought tea for my headache?"

"No. I get a most odd feeling just from looking at him." Samuel handed me his plate.

We didn't see any more of Andrew Griesinger that day. After cleaning away our dishes and the remains of our lunch, we resumed our slow creep forward. For the rest of the day I tried to occupy my mind but the tedium wove itself into everything I did.

My dress became increasingly more uncomfortable and my feet felt ready to burst from inside my boots. I mentally went through my trunk, trying to assemble a more suitable wardrobe for the next day.

The sun was setting when we finally reached the river. The air blew cool and campfires were being lit on both sides of the water. Our party and those wagons behind us would have to wait to cross in the morning.

My heart sank.

We began the job of unpacking what would be needed for our first night on the trail. Cooking pots were set up. Later, bedding was located and laid out.

As I worked, I didn't know then whom I felt more sorry for. Those already across the river, dry, packed together again, anxious to leave. Their job, at least for the moment, done. How frustrated they must be to have to wait for us. Or our group on the wrong side of the river, envious of those finished with the job we still had ahead.

CHAPTER TWENTY-NINE

Not all at once, but slowly, throughout the course of the next day, I began to realize how unprepared we all were. And as our ineptness revealed itself to me, I had to believe the others chose to ignore this fact, it being so blindingly true, for they never said a word. Maybe the problem was that we were all too human. Each of us too concerned with, at least in the beginning, our own comforts.

The special adjustments Samuel had specified during the building of our wagon had made good sense—on paper. Certain sections of our schooner were designed to disconnect and be reassembled in several different manners. The custom-forged hinges had been attached with common nails but required custom-built tools to engage their mechanism. I found out later that Samuel had failed to pack those tools. At the time, however, I was unaware of what was causing our delay.

While he tried to release a sideboard, I made trip after trip, inside and out of the wagon. Up and down, over and over again. Several times I carelessly dropped an item and as I frantically scooped, my belonging would come up with a handful of sand mixed with wet pebbles.

On one such hasty trip out of the wagon with three small boxes piled in my hands and held firmly under my chin, I heard Samuel curse. I could see he had cut his hands in his frustration to get us moving forward.

"Why don't you calm down?" I suggested in a hushed

tone. "Stop making such a scene and ask some of the other men to help. I'm sure they would . . ."

"Just do your job and I'll do mine." He was seething.

Without offering any suggestions, but merely his manpower, Charles removed his jacket and vest then rolled up his sleeves. He held the back axle while Samuel tried prying the wheel loose. I feared for my brother's health as the early morning was still quite chilly and I did not want his fever to return.

I could do nothing that day to satisfy Samuel. As he worked, loudly blaming his own stupidity for creating our situation, he told me to get down from the wagon for my own safety. Then in the next breath he would tell me to stop wasting time and unload the wagon.

Two young men offered the use of a sledge hammer, suggesting in a gentle humor that we simply smash the wheels off.

While things had moved so slowly just the day before, now suddenly we were in a mad dash. The river, in spite of being congested with horses, cattle and people, swept by with furious speed. And as if trying to keep up to nature's relentless tempo, we hurried.

Four cherry wood chairs along with their matching table were dug into the sand. Their owner, a frail looking, gray-haired woman, scurried to find coverings to protect them. A few feet from the furniture, barrels of dry goods and farming implements were being loaded onto a flat boat by one man while a woman cried that he was doing it all wrong and if they lost her mother's china he would have to walk to Oregon.

Between the wagons, human bodies and animals, it seemed as if I could just walk across the water using shoulders, saddles and canvas tops as my stepping stones.

While I unpacked and the men worked, Coral wrapped her

162

few belongings in India covers. It had been decided she would cross first because there was no need to dismantle her small wagon. I was on my third attempt to roll our bedding into a small enough bundle so as to fit into a trunk when I spotted Coral, standing ankle-deep in the water.

A thick rope had been strung across the river. On our side, the end of the rope was held by one large man with a tattoo on his chest. A younger man stood alongside him and held the section of rope where the boat had been attached. While Coral worked to load her things onto the flat bed, Sarah stood by chatting with the tattooed worker. I could not catch her words but saw her pointing toward the opposite bank. All those around her were dirty and wet but Sarah remained unsoiled.

Suddenly, Coral was shouting and above the splashing and animal noises, I heard her screaming, "Come back here!"

I had looked away for one moment and in that time, Sarah Franklin had been lifted onto the raft. When I looked up again, she was being pulled, along with Coral's belongings, across the river, pretty as you please, while Coral was left on the shore.

It would have been a humorous scene had not the danger been so great. Women and children had been instructed to cross last. But obviously, Sarah Franklin thought herself exempt from the rules, smiling and waving to those she passed as if on a pleasure cruise.

Then the line caught; there was a momentary snag and I thought for sure my friend would be lost. But she remained seated on the bottom of the raft, holding tightly to Coral's wagon.

And would you believe her gall? When she got to the other side, she shouted across for us to please hurry.

Samuel looked up from his work. "What is all the commotion?"

Before I could answer, Coral marched over to us, furious. "That woman is from the devil! I will not have anything more to do with her!" She shrieked at the river, sending forth words, the meanings of which I could only have imagined.

I kept my head down, afraid to meet her furious eyes. Samuel and Charles had managed to remove one wheel and were starting work on another. They offered no comments.

When Coral had calmed down a bit, she saw the trouble we were in. Heaving one long sigh, she then tied her skirt between her legs and squatted down to assist the men.

After working on our wagon for most of the morning, it was at last decided that it would be set on a large raft and the remaining wheels, the rear two, blocked. Samuel grew more aggravated as the oxen were unhitched. I tried telling him that many of the items inside were not secured, but he told me to leave them, we had to get moving. Besides, once we got to Oregon, he would buy me new things.

It had been overcast all morning. After breakfast I became aware that the sun was hidden by several dark clouds but had no time to take further notice. As Samuel climbed onto the raft and it was pushed into the water, the clouds gushed. A heavy downpour right from the onset.

Charles' wagon was the ordinary variety purchased from a builder, easily disassembled. It was the model against which we would test Nathan's original design and Samuel's modifications. My brother finished covering our supplies, readying himself for his turn on the raft.

But I could not turn my eyes from my husband. It was as if I was willing that unsteady square of wood to the other side. It did, after all, carry what meant the most to me in life. I was well aware we were all in a hurry, but for the life of me, I will never understand why they continued to move over that ugly river under such horrendous conditions. I could only hope that Colonel Chapman was on the other side, overseeing our activities, for I had never made his acquaintance nor caught sight of him since our departure.

Coral came up beside me. Grabbing an extra sheet, she held it over both of us. When she spoke, she stood so close I could feel her breath in my ear. "This is not goot."

No sooner had the words left her mouth then I heard a scream. A figure swept past us, struggling against the river's pull. The sky grew darker the more I strained to make out what was happening.

"Grab him! For God's sake grab him!"

Before Coral or I could react, Charles came running.

"Take these!" He hurled his boots toward me. Then my brother, without a moment's thought, jumped into the current.

A thunder bolt came as if from God himself and struck a tree. A giant oak that looked to have been rooted there for decades.

"Get out of the there!" I screamed at my brother. "Come back!"

But he had vanished.

The minutest details of that moment remain fixed in my memory. The smell of that rubber sheet hanging over my head, the sound of each raindrop slapping the leather of my shoes. A large branch followed in Charles' brisk departure and yet it seemed to be moving at a leisurely speed. I could clearly see two leaves attached to one of the offshoots. My sight seemed to have been enhanced like my other senses and I could see veins running through the leaves, the edges curled, from the sun. My very breath seemed to have slowed, sweeping through my body like wind in a tunnel.

Then the scream again, closer.

I could see Samuel heard the commotion. I raced to wave to him, catch his attention. "Charles!" I shouted then pointed. "He went to help!"

Samuel cupped his hands around his mouth. "I don't see him!"

I motioned that I didn't know his location either and then expressed my fear. "He can't swim very well!"

The men pulling the rope attached to Samuel's boat stopped to look in the direction of the screaming. I watched in fear as my husband threw off his coat then his shoes. Sitting down, he lowered himself into the water. I could tell from his reaction it was very cold.

Coral had run downstream with the crowd. Keeping Samuel in my vision, I ran to them. Frantic.

"What happened?" I asked.

"Some youngin' got away from his Maw. A man jumped right in after him. Then some fool crossin' over jumped in after him."

Coral stood in a small circle of children and women. I ran over to them, recognizing the person in the center as Velina Brown, the woman we had met our first day in town.

"My baby! I have to help my boy!" She struggled against the hands that restrained her.

"My brother and husband went after him. They'll get him back," I said. But she was so lost in her terror that my words offered no comfort.

All at once there was a swarm of men in the water and just as suddenly as the rain had started . . . it stopped. Black clouds passed over the sun leaving a blinding light.

Then Charles walked out of the water, dripping, grit in his hair, mud streaking his shirt . . . and a child in his arms.

CHAPTER THIRTY

Words can never convey my shock at recognizing that little face, blue from the cold.

As Charles gently laid the boy out on a blanket, it was obvious the child was dead. Disbelief held all our tongues . . . except for Velina's. She screamed with a voice deep inside, wild, like an animal. I leaned forward to touch her shoulder but was pushed aside when a man came from behind.

"How is he?" The man was thin which made the trembling coursing through his body more evident. "What have you done to my boy?"

At first I assumed he was addressing fate but then saw him grab Velina. As he shouted, he shook her, violently. "I asked you woman, what have you done with my son?"

"Leave her be!" A woman with long braids pulled the man away. "Tend to your child."

The man stood for a minute, dazed. Then he collapsed, weeping uncontrollably.

Above heads of those bent over the small body, I saw Samuel emerging from the water onto the muddy shore, his dark hair wrapped around his head like a pile of seaweed. We never made eye contact, too involved with what was happening on the ground in front of us.

The majority of our party finished crossing the wide, dreary river that afternoon, but not the Brown family. There was even some question as to whether or not they would continue with us at all. It was rumored Velina had wrapped the body of her son, Decatur, in a baby quilt, not allowing anyone to touch him. I could hear her sobbing that night, clear across the river, from our camp on the opposite bank.

Charles was the most affected by the death and became very sullen. Oblivious, he let us dry him off, change his clothing, and lay him in my bed. Sleep would not come for me that night, my fear too great he would develop a fever. Coral and I spent our time watching over my dear brother who slept soundly in the wagon while Samuel made his bed outside.

The tragedy had also caused an indifference to settle between Coral and Sarah. Anger was suddenly inappropriate. Sarah hid herself and her emotions in the second wagon. Coral expressed her frustration, mumbling and wringing her hands. "That poor woman, that poor, poor woman." She went on and on, pacing all the while. I wondered how she had survived her kidnapping ordeal without suffering some sort of attack from either nerves or her heart.

I was too overwhelmed to be weary or sad or even frightened. But after tucking Charles into bed, I silently made myself a promise. When I was safe in Oregon, I would set those horrible wagons on fire. And while the flames rose skyward, feeding on themselves, I would add my tears to the pyre.

Midway through the following day, there was great commotion. After swimming their cattle and horses across, Velina's husband came over. He then stood, waving his arms, shouting orders for the last flat boat to be loaded with the Brown women and children. Colonel Chapman was pointed out to me as the man who approached the frantic Mr. Brown. And a few minutes later, it was Colonel Chapman who mounted a beautiful chestnut and crossed back over to the Brown camp.

He wasn't the imposing figure I had imagined, but rather ordinary. The only distinguishing feature about him, in fact, was the sparse hair growing from his chin and trailing down the front of his shirt. Such a poor excuse for a beard. The hair on his head, what I could see of it, was the same wheat color, pale, with gray mixed in causing it to sometimes glisten, sometimes almost disappear in the sunlight. Swallowing up most of his head was a large, shapeless hat, apparently the victim of too many wagon wheels and storms. I don't know why I had imagined our Wagon Master would be larger, but I had, and upon seeing him, was disappointed.

Having spent the better part of the day putting our wagons back in order, unpacking things we had packed up only the day before, folding away sheets for use next time, there was nothing left to do but wait.

"We can't stay here forever," Samuel complained.

"How can you be so heartless?" Coral asked. "It was a child that was lost, not a dumb animal. A little boy."

An hour must have passed before we heard shouts. "Pull us over! Pull!"

I could see a raft. Colonel Chapman sat squarely in the middle and looked to be comforting Velina Brown, who sat to his right. Laid across their laps was a bundle. I assumed it was the body of poor Decatur.

When the men gave the first pull, the raft jerked forward and Velina grabbed the Colonel. We could hear her startled scream.

We didn't know how to treat her.

I found myself looking away as the Colonel and Velina walked passed us. And in so doing, my cheeks burned with shame. Certainly that woman deserved some acknowledgment of her sorrow. But fear of having my stare mistaken for pity forced my head and eyes downward.

"There's to be a burial. The Colonel convinced Mrs. Brown to put her poor child to rest. Hallelujah."

I don't know where the information came from for I continued concentrating on a tiny frog hopping across the rocks around my foot. But I did manage to whisper to the air. "When?"

"Now. Over the hill by those pine trees."

Then we were moving.

Coral had been wearing the same woolen dress for days. I watched her from behind; her hair pulled back in such a tight bun it looked painful. She had wrapped a shawl, made of the same drab wool as her dress, around her shoulders.

Sarah was walking beside me, I don't remember where she came from, or who told her what was happening, but she fidgeted with the veil of her small black hat as we became part of the crowd.

Samuel was at my side and held my hand. Patting it, I wondered who he was comforting and which one of us needed comforting the most.

As much as I've tried, I can't remember how Charles got so far ahead of us. I held onto Samuel's arm, struggling up that slippery hill, and there he was, my brother, in his best suit, looking more like an undertaker than one of his muddy companions.

When everyone had at last stopped and we were all standing together in the same spot, I noticed the empty grave. A small hole that must have been dug while Velina was on the raft, or perhaps the night before.

It looked too small to accommodate the seven-year-old. The moist ground was a deep mahogany and a few rocks had fallen loose from the sides where a shovel had sliced the soil. Velina started moaning in that horrible way she had the day before. While she cried, she rocked herself and her child.

The woman with the braids tried taking the boy from his mother, but Velina would not give him up.

A man pushed through the crowd then. He was short and fat and, except for two hairs sprouting from the very center of his head, bald. His white collar was soiled from what looked to be perspiration. Around his neck hung a large wooden cross. His complexion was the pink of cherry blossoms. "Please, Mrs. Brown. No need to worry; Decatur is with the Lord now. No harm can come to him."

"Wolves!" Velina shouted. "They'll git him! Or savages will dig him up. I know it!"

"Cain't no one hurt our baby now." Mr. Brown offered some comfort and I was surprised at the tenderness in his voice.

All that grief must have been so taxing. After being assured that her son would be buried deep and with God's blessing, Velina Brown gave up. Relinquishing the body of her son, she collapsed against her husband.

The minister read from his Bible. "The waters have overwhelmed us, the stream has gone over our soul. But Decatur Brown's soul has escaped as a bird."

I felt genuinely sorry for the poor mother who was being comforted by strangers who had never known her little boy.

The more the minister spoke, the more he perspired.

When Decatur Brown was at last placed into the grave, his mother gently knelt to place a small wooden horse beside him.

We all waited until Mr. Brown led his frail wife back to their wagon. Then we each passed by to leave our respects. Some tossed in flowers, some mumbled a prayer.

How many times throughout my life had I mourned the passing of someone close or distant and sighed with relief that

God's grace had spared me? But the day of little Decatur's funeral, I knew that relief had been expressed and not truly felt.

For those who had died before me were nothing like me. How could I have possibly understood their lives let alone what brought them to their ends? And had we been granted more time together, we still would not have shared as much as I had shared with those people on that hillside in just a few days' time. I didn't have to be an old man or a mother with three children to understand them. We were all the same.

CHAPTER THIRTY-ONE

By the time we finally got under way, it was with relief in my heart and not fear that I sat next to Samuel. Mrs. Brown's crying could be heard in spite of her wagon being situated five behind us. Her grief seemed to have caused other noises to hush in respect. But for all the sorrow in the air, I was glad we were moving.

The weather had gone from cool to warm; I could smell spring's sweetness in the air. We were able to roll back the canvas and air out the dampness that had seeped into our wagon.

Samuel and I started the day chatting, but by mid-afternoon found ourselves with nothing more to say. The wagon moved like a cradle, rocking back and forth in ruts cut through the grass. With the sunshine on my face I felt almost happy, being rocked to sleep. But my contentment was soon shattered when a shrill, whistling sound, pierced the air.

"What's that?" Samuel asked.

"Sounds like a cat."

"No, cats have to stop for a breath now and then. This is never ending. Horrible."

I strained to listen. "A harmonica?"

"If it is an instrument, the musician seems only familiar with one note." Samuel looked more upset than the situation warranted.

"Are you feeling well?" I asked.

"No, my head is going to burst."

"When we stop tonight maybe we can find out where the noise is coming from," I suggested.

"What help does that do me now?" Samuel stopped the team and jumped down from the wagon.

Charles and Sarah were one behind us, both riding on top while Coral napped inside. Before I could slide over to look for Samuel, Sarah was standing by my side of the wagon.

"What on earth is that horrible sound?"

"I don't know. Can you see Samuel?" I asked.

"Yes, he's trying to hide his nausea, behind that tree. Charles is seeing to him."

Charles had been different after carrying Decatur Brown from the river. Older in a way. In one day's time my brother had become the caretaker instead of the cared for.

I lowered myself down to the ground, catching my skirt on a nail.

"Now look, this is the most practical dress I could find and it's ruined."

"One tiny rip? You can mend it. Besides, who will notice? We're not at a fancy ball out here."

"You're a fine one to talk! How many times have we had to wait while you take extra time with your hair and those silly hats?"

"He's got the sea sickness," Coral was standing in front of us. "It happens in the beginning. He'll get used to the wagon."

I could not believe my ears. The very thing we had hoped to avoid by traveling on land was afflicting poor Samuel.

"But I feel fine," I said. "Maybe breakfast didn't agree with him."

"I do not think pancakes would go bad in his stomach. No, it is the swaying, like a boat rolling over the waves. Some do not feel it—some do."

174

"Will he be able to drive?" Sarah asked.

"He should rest inside. We will give him a bucket so we do not have to stop."

"Can you manage the team?" I asked Coral.

"Me?" The woman looked horrified. "Oh, no . . ."

"But you made this trip before, surely you . . ."

"That was my husband's job. He and his brothers took turns. It was not my place to . . . I do not know how."

Sarah picked up her skirt and climbed into Samuel's seat. After fastening the tiny pearl buttons at the wrist of her leather gloves, she grabbed the reins. "Well, come on. We have to stop wasting so much time."

Coral offered no argument but happily went to help Samuel into our wagon and then take Sarah's seat next to Charles.

While I felt sorry Samuel was incapacitated, his absence afforded Sarah and me time alone.

We had been traveling for about ten minutes when I asked, "Where did you learn to handle a team?"

"My brothers. I've learned all the important things from men."

"What about your mother?"

"No. It was always just me and my brothers."

It seemed inconceivable to me that not one female had influenced this woman's life. "Surely you had someone show you how to dress, you're so elegant."

"Abigail, learning which fashion is flattering or how to match gloves to a dress only takes a keen sense of observation. And money. With a sizable bank account, a woman can hire someone to dress her tastefully."

What she said was logical but I was still taken aback. "Money certainly cannot buy taste, elegance or grace."

Sarah laughed, "It most certainly can."

I wondered then what profits she had made from her affair with Nathan that we had been unaware of. But I did not ask. I was far more curious to find out what "important things" she had learned from the older man. When I asked, she responded instantly.

"Forthrightness. Determination. And honesty."

"You believe women possess none of these qualities?" I was surprised at her attitude and my anger.

"Certainly they do, but their concern with politeness and appearances dilutes those admirable characteristics."

"And in turn makes them dull."

"Dull? What do you mean?" she asked, apparently not remembering.

"You said I was dull; that day, on the boardwalk."

"Not so much dull, Abby, as young . . . inexperienced . . . unworldly. But the manner you chose to confront me illustrates my point exactly. A man would have demanded I explain myself, right on the spot. You, sweet Abby, chose manners over honesty and let the remark slide by. And that action was satisfactory for you. Temporarily. But it stayed caught, didn't it? Somewhere back in your feelings. And you've been upset about it ever since."

Sarah was right. I had been fretting about her comment for days. After a moment of consideration I said, "I'll remember for next time."

"I hope not to offend you another time," Sarah said in a gracious manner.

A quiet moment passed between us. The clomping of hooves against the dry earth seemed to beat with the same regularity as my heart. For one brief span of time no human voice could be heard. I was happy in Sarah Franklin's company. Content.

Then my peace was shattered by that awful one note shrill.

"Tonight, after dinner, I'll give you a lesson in determination," Sarah said.

Samuel spent the remainder of that day and the entire evening in our bed. When I tried to comfort him he would moan. When I suggested he eat something, he clasped his hands over his mouth, shook his head violently back and forth and motioned for me to leave him alone. I wondered why the rest of us had not felt the effects of the wagon's motion and how much longer it would cause my husband such discomfort.

After our evening meal had been consumed and cleared away, Coral went to visit Mr. Griesinger. Charles had to not only do his own work but Samuel's as well. And so, while my brother tended to the horses, Sarah and I went in search of the source of that deafening sound.

Watching Sarah Franklin was quite an education. Before we left, she took great care to apply powder to her face and a clean collar to her blouse. Opening her delicate fan, she told me she was arming herself. The spoils of her war, however, would be respect and the relinquishing of one small wind instrument.

She walked with great assurance toward the section of wagons that had been in front of us during the day but now were a part of our great circle. We started with one covered in canvas dyed a peculiar shade of red.

"Pardon me." Sarah spoke sweetly to a man sitting alone in front of a fire, holding a tin cup of coffee.

"Yes ma'am?" He seemed delighted with our visit.

"I'm Miss Franklin and this is my traveling companion, Mrs. Gray. We were about five wagons behind you today . . ."

". . . And you were curious about my rig. Splendid ain't it?"

"Striking is more the word I would have chosen," Sarah said.

"Truth be known, it was all I could find, at the last minute, bein' in such a hurry you see." Then he leaned forward and spoke like he was confiding a secret. "Gotta get west fast, before all the good land gets took."

Sarah smiled a lovely smile. "You appear to be a man of action."

"Why, I do pride myself on having great vigor." The man smiled a toothy grin right back.

"I was wondering, while we were traveling today and admiring your wagon, if you heard that . . . music?"

"Music? You're indeed a gracious woman, Miss Franklin. Far kinder than I would be in describin' that atrocious noise as any form of music."

"You're right. It was awful." Sarah fanned ashes rising from the fire away from her face. She had instructed me, beforehand, not to speak but instead listen and learn from her.

"Forgive my manners." The man suddenly stood and offered his right hand. "I'm used to bein' by myself. My name's Barnhill. Mike Barnhill. Would you ladies care for a nice cup of strong coffee?"

Sarah snapped her fan closed and shook the man's hand. "Why, thank you for asking, Mr. Barnhill, but we can't stay. Another time perhaps?" Then she gave him that smile of hers that was better than money when it came to getting what she wanted. "Oh, by the way, would you happen to know where the misguided musician resides?"

"Right there." He pointed to a large man in a red and blue plaid shirt. "Name of McFarland."

After managing an inconspicuous look at the burly Scotsman, I asked, "Is he a friend of yours, Mr. Barnhill?"

"Just met today when I tried convincin' him to stop makin'

that infernal noise." Mr. Barnhill threw up his hands in a sur-rendering motion. "The man can't speak English let alone show any manners. Maybe he'll be more reasonable when he meets you lovely ladies."

We tried thanking the man for his help but he shook off our words. Said we would more than likely come back to throttle him after trying to reason with the whistling Scots-man.

"Well, Sarah," I said as we approached the neighboring wagon, "I'll be anxious to see how your manly qualities work on this one. It seems Mr. Barnhill already depleted his share."

"There's a way around everything and everyone," she re-plied.

Sarah tapped Mr. McFarland on the shoulder. When he turned around, I saw a large piece of silver protruding from his mouth, grasped tightly between his teeth. Then in a series of what sounded like Rs and Bs strung together, Sarah spoke to the man. I could never be certain of the exact translation for I was ignorant of the language as well as greatly surprised at my friend's knowledge of it.

The man removed the instrument from his mouth and ges-tured an introduction to the women in his party. It was Sa-rah's turn again and when she was finished, the man blushed. Rubbing stubble on his cheeks he seemed to be reminiscing about times and places gone by. I stood, trying to look intelli-gent but feeling very stupid.

We were only there about ten minutes when the man of-fered the harmonica to Sarah. She held it as if it were solid gold.

Then she was waving good bye and we were walking back to our fire.

"What was all that?" I asked.

"Mr. McFarland was a member of some sort of military band. He played the bagpipes; he misses them dearly as well as his home in Scotland."

"You understood all that?" I asked.

"I have a talent for languages."

"And you were honest? You told him his playing was offensive?"

"I told him we had heard the sound and wondered where it was coming from."

"And you smiled a lot. I watched you flutter your fan and look at Mr. McFarland like he was the most important person alive."

"I have a talent for that also." She giggled and I joined her.

"Why didn't he bring the bagpipes with him?"

"Oh, he did."

"And?" I wondered why she had suddenly slowed her cadence.

"They got washed away, down the river when we crossed. He and his family lost many things, family treasures from Scotland."

"And now he's afraid he'll lose that too?" I pointed to the harmonica.

"Yes."

We walked behind our wagon and took a long look at the shiny instrument. After turning it over in my hands I asked, "Why then, did he give it to you? A stranger?"

"I promised to keep it safe."

"I still don't understand why he would entrust it to you."

Sarah shrugged. "Maybe he became convinced when I told him it would bring bad luck to the rest of us. That the Indian spirits would rise up at the sound of his music."

My smile immediately vanished. "Is there such a belief?"

"I suppose there is. Among some tribe, somewhere."

"You lied to the poor man?"

"Yes, but in a manly way. With conviction and great deter-mination."

CHAPTER THIRTY-TWO

We had been on the trail for twenty-two days when my husband announced he wanted to turn back.

"This has been the biggest mistake of my life," he said. "I have been a selfish fool. How you must hate me."

I was dumbfounded. The night was chilly and I sat inside our wagon with a blanket wrapped around me. My toes clenched inside the wool socks and slippers I wore. Our single candle flickered then hissed, burning off moisture on the wick.

"Look at us. I don't know what weighs us down more, the dirt or the monotony. I can hardly straighten up. The grit gathers in my pockets, the cuffs of my pants; my scalp itches from morning to dawn. I taste it on my lips, in my mouth, my food is peppered with it."

Keeping things and ourselves clean had been more of a problem than we had anticipated. With not one proper wall or roof to shield us, dirt managed to sift into everything. As Samuel spoke I ran my hand across our bed and brushed away as much of that day's accumulation as I could.

"Most days I'm ill; I can't go out to hunt and the few times I have, my shots have missed their target. I'm inept at everything I attempt."

"You'll learn," I said. "You have never been hunting a day in your life. Did you think that once you sat atop a covered wagon you'd become Daniel Boone?"

"Certainly not! But I did expect a calm stomach. And I expected that we would not sacrifice our civilized ways to the wilderness. Look at you, Abby. You're forced to collect buffalo chips. You've been wearing the same black skirt and hideous polka dot blouse for days now."

"I hardly think anyone cares what I wear. And as for gathering chips or weeds, all the women do it. We need it for the fires; there's nothing else to be used."

"But you're my wife! It's not respectable."

The more he spoke the more agitated he became. Excitement brought up a cough he had been fighting for days.

"Lay down." I reached to comfort him. "We'll talk about this later."

He pulled his arm away from my hand as if it had been struck by lightning. "Later—sooner, it makes no difference. We'll leave the train and back track to Ft. Kearney."

"I'm sure that once you're feeling better . . ."

"We'll tell your brother tomorrow." He continued as if I hadn't spoken.

I raised my voice, hoping to catch my husband's attention and not that of anyone outside. "You are so right, Samuel. You are a selfish fool. You try blaming your discontent on me. Wanting to return to Baltimore has no more to do with me than the decision to make this trip did. I will not be pointed to as the reason we turn back."

"What does it matter what the reasons are? I can not continue."

"What does it matter? Can't you see my whole life depends on your reasons? We are married. You expect me to support your decisions yet allow me no voice. This journey was Nathan's idea. The planning was yours. I did as you wished even though it meant giving up all I knew. And now you want to forget the whole experience? Are we to return home and continue our lives as though none of this happened?"

"If all goes well, yes." Samuel crumpled onto the bed, fell back against the sheets and tucked himself beneath the quilt. "Yes, Abigail, I want to return to our lives in Maryland and try to erase this whole experience from our memories. I want us to move back into our house, have children, wear clean clothes. Is that too much to expect from my wife?"

And then he closed his eyes.

As my heart was overflowing with emotions and my head with words, Samuel lay like a cold piece of marble.

I wrapped the blanket tighter around my shoulders and leaned over him to blow out the candle. Bumping my head against the sides of our narrow bedroom, I tried crawling between the sheets without getting tangled inside my long nightgown. My hands ached from clutching the blanket, cocooning myself from the man laying beside me. I rolled on my side, the canvas wall only a few inches from my face.

Tears dampened my pillow and I swallowed down a sob. I realized how proficient I had gotten at crying without disturbing anyone.

The realization brought on more tears.

CHAPTER THIRTY-THREE

I lay awake in my bed most of that night. Samuel snored beside me and when he finally moved to sit up, it was still dark outside. I kept my back to him taking slow, even breaths, making him think I was asleep. He stumbled into his shoes, pulled up his suspenders and as he stepped from our wagon onto the ground outside, the room around me swayed as if rolled by a great wave.

Our flimsy walls and ceiling allowed me to eavesdrop. I listened as he spoke to Coral; she offered him coffee and asked how he had slept. I laid very still, waiting for him to inform her of his late night decision. But after a few more polite exchanges, he excused himself and I was no longer privy to his words.

Quickly I sat up, my head spinning from the suddenness. My shoulders and arms were stiff from the anger I had taken to bed with me the night before. I lit a candle and went to the sideboard nearest where Coral would be. I called to her. It took several times before she answered.

"Please," I whispered, "I need to speak with you, come inside."

Her weight caused the room to rock again and I held tight until she settled on the bed and I on a small stool facing her.

Frantically I told her, "Samuel wants us to go back to Maryland. He's adamant. He wants to return to Ft. Kearney immediately."

"When would he do this?" She didn't seem as surprised as I expected.

"Today. He won't be reasoned with."

She thought for a moment, rubbing her hands together as if to generate heat along with her thoughts. "And he'll be taking the wagon of course. Just the one . . ." Then she stopped to study my face. Self-conscious by her full attention, I tucked a few strands of hair back into my nightcap and pulled the long nightgown sleeves over my trembling hands.

Coral continued. "You are not happy about this change of plans? I should think it would please you to return home. To your parents. Yah?"

"At one time I would have been overjoyed. At the very beginning, when all decisions were made for me. But not now. I've finally come to terms with all of it. I have new friends. I want to take part in making what will, after all, be my future as well as my husband's."

"I understand," Coral shook her head, sadly, slowly. "Eagerly I joined my husband on that first journey. It was exciting. We worked so hard. Together."

My hands stopped shaking. "Yes. I was beginning to feel truly a wife, of the same mind as Samuel."

"But I thought *my* happiness was spoiled when the Indians came. Oh, how angry I was! Those horrible savages killed my husband, changed my life forever."

"Well, I don't think Samuel's change of mind can be compared to your tragedy but it has left me feeling lost."

"But finally, after much thinking, I stopped letting the anger speak for me. And that was when I realized, somehow, that I was happy. I felt . . . you may think this sounds crazy . . . at peace. With me, with the world. With all of it."

"I was just starting to know that peace," I told her.

"Then the rescue and . . ." She made a blowing sound from between her pursed lips. ". . . I was angry again. So angry! Peace, then fury—anger, then happiness. I know life gives us servings from both the sweet and sour bowls but I kept thinking my meal should have been served a little more slowly. It all happened too quick."

"It seems to have gone that quickly for me, also. Oh," I sighed, "to be content for a longer period of time than merely a few weeks."

Coral nodded, rubbing the tattoos on her chin. "We change. All the time we are changing. And the plans we make are forced to change along with us." She stretched her broad back and looked upward. Her face radiated with a soft glow. "But this time, I have changed from the desire to do so and not the demand for it. This time I travel for me. Coral."

At that moment I envied my strange friend. Her freedom, her wisdom. But before I could tell her any of these thoughts, Samuel opened the flap of material we laughingly called our door. He started to climb inside when he saw Coral. "Oh, excuse me, I thought Abigail was alone."

I caught sight of the sun rising behind him and knew we would be leaving soon. I waited for my husband to say something about his change of heart but instead, he smiled at me. "It's a clear morning and I feel better than I have in a month. Hurry, we have to get on the trail."

"In which direction will we be traveling?" I asked.

"Westward. Of course." He stared at me as though I had lost my wits. And then he was gone.

Coral looked from the spot where Samuel had stood and then to me. "There. No reason to upset yourself. All is well. When the body is fit, the mind is fitter. Now dress yourself; we have beans and fresh bread for breakfast."

After she left I sat alone, stupefied. Then I remembered Mother's apron.

I started rummaging through my trunk, looking for the lace apron Father had sent to Mother from France. She had never worn it herself but rather tucked it in with my things before our departure. I had been puzzled when she told me to save it for a day when I felt dispirited.

I shook out my skirt, except for the dust it was still acceptable, and I tied the pristine fabric around my waist. Shaking out my nightcap I packed away my bedclothes and thought about the women I had heard talking around the fire last night. They joked about how useless corsets were, how only a vain woman would put herself through the torture of sitting on a wagon seat days at a time constricting her breathing. I never offered the fact that beneath my clothing my corset was tightly cinched.

I fussed with buttons on my pink blouse. The straw hat Samuel had purchased for me back in Iowa had a bunch of tiny rose buds attached to the brim tinted the same pastel color. After blowing dirt from the blossoms, I pinned the hat to my hair, which I had braided.

With no mirror to inspect myself in, I could only hope I looked as fresh as I felt. My curiosity about what had led my husband to change his mind again was great. But not great enough to bring up the matter with him. Unless, of course, he broached the subject first.

CHAPTER THIRTY-FOUR

The day Chimney Rock came into view, poking up through the earth like a giant finger of God, I felt inspired.

I had seen women, even some of the men, writing entries in little books or on scraps of paper. Each had his own technique. Some would huddle by the campfire or in front of a lantern, trying to make use of what light they could find at day's end. It was a common sight to see them after an evening meal, scribbling away with pencil stubs or fancy quilled pens. Others, the more dedicated, would try writing while their wagon swayed beneath them and a partner guided the animals. This always seemed more an annoyance than a pleasure to me . . . until the day we caught sight of that wondrous rock. And then I longed for nothing more than to have Robert's last gift to me.

It was a beautiful memory book covered in sea-green leather, filled with gold edged pages. He had sent to London for it. His farewell words were rambling, forgettable, but his present was memorable. In the chaos of packing our things, however, I had left it behind. Not one day had gone by without me missing that book, not so much as a practical item but as a keepsake from my older brother.

And then suddenly, we were close enough to Chimney Rock to see the texture of the clay and soft stones making up the whole formation and hill it was situated on. That awe-filled moment pushed me to bring up the subject, quite unintentionally, that my husband and I had not discussed for days.

As Samuel directed our team nearer to the rock, we could hear other travelers shouting. Some stopped for a closer inspection; children ran to touch the imposing stone. It was a joyous day and in my excitement I said to my husband, "Now, aren't you glad we didn't turn back?"

The look he gave me made my heart sink.

"I've been waiting for that."

Quite surprised, I asked, "What do you mean?"

"I've been waiting for you to tell me how weak I am. It was a cowardly act wanting to give up. I'll wager you told all of them, especially your brother."

"Why would I ever speak against you?" I asked, hurt. "And why, in heaven's name, would you think that wanting to return home is a cowardly act?"

"You never fail to remind me how I've disrupted your life, how I forced you to leave everything behind. It is because of me and only me that you now find yourself so miserable."

My surprise kept increasing with each word from his mouth. "Have all my efforts gone unnoticed? We are making this trip together. Why wouldn't I try to support all your decisions?"

Charles was walking alongside us as we slowed our speed. Sarah had taken to driving their wagon more frequently and my brother, believing the exercise would benefit him, walked several hours of each day. Our expressions must have given away our displeasure with each other and my brother shouted up to me.

"Come, have a look, Abby. You don't seem too happy up there."

Turning to face Samuel I said, "I never told Charles any of our private discussions. Maybe it would be better if you were alone for awhile. Stop the wagon. Now!" I ordered.

I could not wait, and before Samuel had stopped the team

I jumped down from my seat. My brother caught my arm before I could fall.

"I didn't mean this very instant. Are you all right?"

"I'm fine," I insisted.

As we started walking together, my brother's enthusiasm could be restrained no longer. His words burst forth.

"Isn't it inspiring, Abby?"

He gave me no time to respond.

"Remember when we were children? How Mother would take us for walks and we would see the great ships? They were the grandest things I had ever seen or could imagine at that tender age. I used to pretend I was sailing to some exotic port of call."

I ran my fingers down the length of his stiff shirtsleeve. "And so clean and white. When the sun struck the sails they seemed more like angel's wings than mere pieces of cloth."

"Yes, wings. But as much as I wanted to, I knew I could never . . . ever . . . fly away. At least under my own power. That I would probably not live long enough to feel the wind's pull."

I stopped to study my handsome brother, turning him to face me. "No one ever told you such a thing."

"No one had to. I knew it."

We just looked at each other for a moment. I silently searched for words to comfort him. Before either one of us could speak, he grabbed my hand and pulled me after him. Then we were running the last distance to that great rock awash in pure sunlight.

And we were there.

I felt like praying. Looking upward for feet and feet as the rock narrowed to a tip so high above us. People spoke in hushed voices. A small child plopped down first on her behind and then stretched out in the warm grass to view the rock from a more comfortable position. Even the dogs, normally snapping and yelping, sat obediently, allowing their masters a moment's reflection.

We stood transfixed upon that spot until Coral shouted for us to get back on the wagon.

Charles and I smiled at each other.

"Are you aware, dear Abigail, that my first recollection is of Mother and Father with tear-filled eyes. Do you think they knew how much pity resided on their faces? How their very postures made me feel contaminated? I was too young to speak, to understand what was being said, but I could feel the sadness. It was all around me. I could sense the fear. And the very worst part of it was I felt that I had disappointed everyone. I still do."

"Oh Charles, I was only two years old when you were born but I remember the change that came over the house. You're right, it was fear. But not of you, sweet brother, never of you. We all loved you so very much. We have always been afraid of losing you."

"I've never doubted your affection. Even Robert's. Although he has always resented the attention I received. I'm sure he felt deprived in some way."

"Robert's feelings can only be maintained or altered by Robert himself." I thought how often I had tried cutting through my older brother's cold heart and wondered if Charles was right and if he was, did that resentment extend to me as well?

"You are so right, dear sister. We are all accountable for only ourselves when the truth be told. Which brings me to a subject I've been thinking about, almost exclusively for days now. And today, here, right this moment seems the best possible time to share it with you."

I smiled, grateful to be taken into his confidence. "Go on."

192

"I've been thinking about Kansas." He dropped the statement with apparent relief and I will forever carry in my mind's eye how happy he looked, with Chimney Rock behind him.

Still I was surprised. "Why Kansas?"

"I've heard that winters there are mild, the summers warm but not oppressive. The atmosphere is supposedly extraordinarily pure and clear in all seasons. And it is a very healthy state, highly favorable to consumptives. Did you know its nickname is 'The Garden of the West?'"

My stomach lurched. "But we're going to Oregon."

"That's my point, precisely, Abby. The decision to go to Oregon began with Nathan, then was passed on to Samuel and is now being carried out by us. Oh, it was my pleading that got me on this wagon train with you; I know that too well. I will always be grateful for your support when Mother and Samuel argued I was too weak. But now, well, look at me! I've never been fitter."

I had to agree. Charles looked wonderful.

"If I want to maintain my health then Kansas seems the ideal place to be."

It was a sound plan, but suddenly I was frightened that if my brother left us, I would never see him again. "When?" was all I could say.

"The day after tomorrow."

"Why so soon?"

"Everyday I continue on this trail is another day farther from my destination. Besides, there are others to consider. I'll be riding with several men I've become acquainted with. One man, only a year or so older than myself, is a real trail blazer. Mr. Hain introduced us. He travels with the wagons for short periods of time and then just takes off. He's convinced there was a better place to cross the river back at the start. Imagine, Abby, if he'd ridden that bit of trail sooner, maybe Decatur would be alive."

I trusted in my brother's choice of friends, he had always been very particular who he spent time with. However . . . "And the others? Why are they leaving?"

"Disillusionment. Fear. Surely you've noticed all the markers lining the road? Those who have died along the way, left behind by the trains gone before. We add to them every-day. So far we've lost seven."

I had noticed. How could I keep myself from noticing? It would have been impossible to ignore the groups gathered to bury a child or adult. Sideboards missing from some wagons usually meant they had been propped into the earth as make-shift headstones. And the first time our wheels hit such a plank, I was startled to learn that some of those poor souls had been buried beneath the trail itself, covered over in hopes that their body would not be dug up by a wild animal.

If, somehow, I could have closed my eyes to the markers and funerals, how could I have ever deafened my ears to Velina Brown's constant sobbing? At times I thought I grew used to it, but upon waking and hearing the poor woman ev-eryday, I thought I would go mad. How much more time would it take to heal her emotional wounds?

Before I could organize all that I was feeling into words, we were greeted by Mr. Griesinger. Not wanting to anger Samuel further, I waited until our wagon was far enough ahead before I offered my smile.

"Quite a landmark!" He rested his hands on his hips. "Marvelous."

"Yes, it makes me feel as though we've made some prog-ress," Charles said.

"Most definitely. It's one of the signs."

"Signs?" I asked.

"They're everywhere. The earth has special ways of speaking to us. Why, you should know, coming from the east. Have you been as far as Haddam, Connecticut?"

"No." My brother and I answered together.

Mr. Griesinger seemed glad for the chance to inform us. I wondered if he had ever been a teacher.

"That region was once called Morehemoodus. Its translation is: the place of noises."

"In Connecticut? You're sure of that?" Charles seemed more curious than amused.

"Positive. They say it varies from day to day. Sometimes just a throbbing here and there, in the floorboards of the homes."

My skin felt chilled in spite of the warmth of the day.

"At other times there are loud explosive sounds. They can be heard in neighboring towns, it is that loud."

"How would you know about these things?" I asked.

"I research such reports." And before we could ask anymore questions, our strange friend quickly turned on his heels. "I must leave you now." He touched his hat and walked away.

Charles squinted his eyes to watch Mr. Griesinger leave. "He's right, Abigail."

"About what?"

"Signs. I think the difficult part isn't in finding one but in knowing when, in fact, you've seen one."

We took our time then, knowing we did not have many walks together left us. Wagons rumbled past and their giant wheels stirred up the dust, reminding me of an eggbeater cutting through a bowl of flour.

"Should I take your leaving also as a sign?"

"It does signify that I'm happy. That I'm making my own way."

I held my brother closer that day than I had at any other time of his life. He smelled of youthful excitement. Sweet around the ears, starchy and clean inside his clothes. It was then, when he patted my head, that I knew there was nothing else for me to say except, "I'll miss you."

CHAPTER THIRTY-FIVE

As we crossed into Wyoming, the terrain grew uglier. It was quite disconcerting to travel for miles without glimpsing a single structure, tree, or animal. At times it seemed as though our band of travelers were the only people on earth. How vulnerable I felt.

All other times in my life I had been pushed to introduce myself for one of two reasons: common interests or mutual friends. But back then, on that trail, it was necessity that brought us closer. This need for female understanding, conversation, or simple companionship forced the women in our train to band together. Discomforts that would normally be suffered within the privacy of our homes, now were made public. People were referred to by their peculiarities, such as "the ones with fever" or "that boy with the rash."

It was this combination of illness and loss of privacy that forced Britta Selway to make our acquaintance. Quite reluctantly. I am certain, under more normal circumstances, that that woman would never have even smiled in our direction. And yet, there she was, standing on her narrow feet, toes pointed inward, addressing Sarah. I easily overheard their conversation for we were all packing the wagon after having aired out our trunks. Mold grew so quickly in the wagons.

Mrs. Selway was traveling with her family of six: a husband and five sons. She was an older woman, probably in her forties. Less willing to adapt than the rest of us, she was having a particularly bad time of it.

All of it.

"It was my eldest son, William, who noticed you," she spoke in a clipped voice. "He said you seemed to be a woman of quality and after he pointed you out to me, my husband suggested I come and introduce myself."

"How nice. I'm Sarah Franklin."

It was obvious, at least to me, that Sarah was referring to it being nice that Mrs. Selway's son and husband had noticed her, rather than to the actual meeting of the woman.

After Sarah got over feeling satisfied with herself, she introduced me and then Coral.

"I've come to ask a favor." Mrs. Selway was obviously embarrassed. "I know we have just met and all. But, well I . . . I . . . this is so humiliating." She abruptly pursed her narrow lips together. Her whole body seemed to tighten. Before we had the chance to encourage her to continue, she began again.

"If I could manage by myself I would have never bothered you ladies. But the fact is that I need your assistance in the most private of matters."

Coral had finished with her chore and was watching the woman. I still wasn't quite sure what was being asked of us but Coral knew immediately."

"Mrs. Selway, don't be upset so much. We all suffer from the illnesses of travel. Our privacy has been stripped from us like the trees from this place."

Sarah spoke up before I could voice my confusion. "What is she asking?" Sarah addressed Coral as if Mrs. Selway was not even there.

"She needs us to make a modesty curtain for her."

"A what?"

"Stop wondering and come help." Coral grabbed my arm and Sarah and Mrs. Selway followed as Coral led us as far from the wagons as we could safely go. A large rock was the only thing we could find protruding from the earth and Coral stood next to it and turned back to face the wagons. Then she grabbed either side of her full skirt. Slowly she lifted her arms upward, level with her waist, until her skirt was spread in a half circle.

"Abigail, stand beside me and do the same with your skirt."

I picked up my hem.

Without one second's worth of hesitation, not even one resentful look at being ordered about, Sarah followed Coral's instructions and fanned out her skirt.

"Now we join hands in a circle around our new friend."

Such a look of gratitude came over Mrs. Selway's narrow features as she first stood inside our circle and then squatted.

I've thought about how we looked, standing there. Coral's skirted wings a drab brown, Sarah's eyelet petticoats and my pink and white stripes unfurled. One gigantic patchwork bird with six legs and three heads.

We kept our eyes straight ahead, our arms stretched backwards. I had to admit that I felt sorry for the woman who had been forced to approach strangers for something so personal.

After a few seconds of uncomfortable silence, Sarah started talking, quickly. "Have I ever told you about the time I met Charles Dickens? It must have been five or six years ago in New York. Such a crude, vulgar man. I have never been able to read another of his books since knowing the true nature of the author."

Britta Selway straightened up. "Thank you. Thank you all so very much. If I can return the favor, please, call on me."

"Blackberries, Mrs. Selway," Coral said. "Tea made from the roots and leaves will be very goot. If you do not have any, I will be glad to bring some to you tonight."

The concern regarding her dysentery made the woman's

pinched face relax. "That would be very kind of you, Coral. Thank you again. All of you." Then as an afterthought she said, "Maybe we can dine together one evening."

Her eagerness to be done with us gave away her insincerity.

"I'd like to meet your sons," Sarah said to Britta Selway's back.

Coral did make the tea for Mrs. Selway and many cups for me as well. Charles' departure had not only brought melancholy to my heart but also marked the onset of various ailments to my body. My husband and I seemed to have suddenly reversed roles. The healthier Samuel became, the weaker I grew. He would frequently see what he thought to be fever breaking across my brow. I tried telling him it was just the heat. Summer had come upon us swiftly; we had already suffered several days when the temperature had risen above ninety degrees. But finally, even I had to admit, I needed a rest from our westering.

Sarah, being in no particular hurry to continue, with no appointments to keep, agreed readily to stay with us. Stopping seemed to suit her. Especially since Coral still refused to even try to steer the wagon and fussed at Sarah to drive her. I know she was anxious to get to her Indian and I felt badly for causing her any delay.

Samuel spoke to Colonel Chapman. He told my husband that the trail was straight and we could easily catch up should we want to stay behind for half a day. I had expected Samuel to be upset with me for holding him up and causing us to be separated from the others. But instead he reacted kindly, more concerned for my health. Since our argument at Chimney Rock, he had begged my forgiveness a hundred times. And I knew he loved me best when I needed him most.

Trying to make myself comfortable, I unfastened my corset and brushed the grit from the bed. Laying beneath the sheets comforted me while the late afternoon offered a nice breeze. Mosquitoes buzzed around my cramped room but my illness had brought on lethargy, robbing me of energy enough to swat the creatures away.

Coral unfastened the canvas from the other wagon. Several holes and tears had developed and she set to stitching them.

Sarah climbed into the wagon to check on me. "Don't be concerned now. I think it's all the worrying about your brother that has you in such a state. Believe me, Abigail, Charles has grown into a man these past few months. He'll be fine. Besides, it doesn't matter when we arrive in Oregon."

"Not a day or two, one way or the other, but we can't get so far behind that we might catch snow . . ."

"Snow? Why summer's barely begun. Calm yourself. You just need to be still. I'll leave you now and you try to sleep."

My eyes were getting heavy and her soothing voice reassured me. "I will."

She left me then and I heard her skirt swishing across the tall grass. The sweet fragrance of alfalfa warmed by the sun was stirred by her passing. I closed my eyes.

I was nearly asleep when I was roused by hushed tones. I could make out the voices of Sarah and Samuel. They seemed to be behind me somewhere. My mind immediately raced back to a lush field, in Council Bluffs. I remembered the delighted look plastered across Amos Fell's lips.

Oh, by the time we reached Wyoming, I considered Sarah Franklin my friend. But experience had taught me to never underestimate her capabilities . . . or charms. I could say it was the fever that drove me to look for them, to catch more of their conversation. But, that would be a lie. The truth may be told, I was jealous that my husband was enjoying the company of a beautiful woman. A woman who never seemed to be dirty or sick or ruffled by anything she had experienced.

I went outside, in the shade of our wagon, not wanting either one of them to see me. They were sitting, maybe twenty feet or so from the wagon, on a blanket, eating biscuits left over from our breakfast. Coral seemed unaware of them, she was surrounded by yards of canvas, muttering to herself. The breeze brought Sarah's words to me.

"Maybe it would be better if I told Abigail myself."

Samuel shook his head. "I don't know how she'll react to the news no matter what the source."

"She will no doubt be upset, at first, but I'm sure she'll accept the situation after she has had time to reflect."

Samuel looked concerned. "You're certain about this then?"

"Positive." Sarah smiled. "We can have a doctor examine her at Fort Laramie, but I'd stake my life on it. Abigail is most definitely going to have a baby."

CHAPTER THIRTY-SIX

Sarah had said the words out loud. She had, unknowingly, expressed my greatest fear.

I crawled. They still hadn't seen me, skulking around in the grass. I lifted myself into the wagon, thinking I had escaped notice. Assuming Coral was engrossed with her mending, I was surprised when I heard her voice through my canvas wall.

"You are feeling better?"

"No."

"You are upset about something?"

"Yes."

"Ach, I understand. That woman is enough to make a saint scream. But I think she is right. You will need a real doctor."

In her peculiar way, Coral was letting me know she overheard the same conversation I had.

I felt bolder not being able to see the face on the other side of the sheeting. I addressed the concern I had been carrying for several days, the same one expressed by Sarah.

"Do I look . . . pregnant to you?"

I remember so clearly how I was laying. On my left side, my legs drawn up tightly against my stomach. I had the habit of hugging my arms around myself and rocking, back and forth, when I felt anxious.

I practically whispered into the rough material as I begged for Coral's impression. "Do I?"

"I am so very ignorant about children." Her voice sounded more filled with concern and warmth than I had ever heard before. "I have cared for none; I have had none of my own. I do not even think I like them particularly well."

I had thought Coral knew about most things. Her reply surprised me.

She waited a minute for my response. When none came she spoke again.

"Nothing to be done now. When we get to the fort you will know, one way or the other. But now, there is nothing for you to do but rest."

She muttered, half to herself, half to me, as she walked back to the spot where she had been sitting.

I prayed Sarah was wrong. But down in the pit of my stomach, like cream churning into butter, I could feel my terror growing more substantial. And I knew she was right and cursed her.

Of course I cursed my husband for his part in my misery also.

We didn't reach Fort Laramie until the next evening. It was twilight and the large wooden structure was silhouetted against a turquoise and orange sky. Situated on the opposite side of the river, the road leading past it ran straight into Sioux territory.

Sarah said she was looking forward to getting herself thoroughly clean. Tubs and washing facilities were made available to us and many of the women were busy scrubbing piles of clothing when we first arrived.

After a peaceful sleep, one that could only be had from feeling safeguarded, Samuel took care of the animals and replenished our water supply. Coral set to restocking the larder. And I went to stand in a line of coughing, moaning patients.

After about an hour or so, I got close enough to have a chair in Dr. Harvey's office.

The man was obviously uncomfortable and irritated. He asked me, in the most curt manner, what my problem seemed to be. Chewing on a cigar protruding from the side of his sweaty mouth, he made me feel silly for having bothered him at all.

His assistant was an attractive Negro woman, obviously adept at following his endless instructions while simultaneously offering a smile to ease my discomfort. That woman possessed not only her fair share of compassion but the doctor's as well.

When I recounted my symptoms, Dr. Harvey shook his head. "Could be a number of things. God didn't mean for us to set across the country, exposed to the elements, nonstop. It's only natural you would be feeling wretchedly. Can't see why anyone would want to do such a thing anyway. Just be thankful you haven't been afflicted with anything worse."

And then he dismissed me . . . at least he tried.

I can't determine what gave me the courage but I said, "I know I'm going to have a baby and your saying that it isn't so does not matter to me one bit."

That made him stop shaking his head. The Negro woman bit back a smile; I could tell it was my contrary manner that made her happy.

Dr. Harvey rechecked the name I had signed in his book. "Mrs. Gray, is it?"

"Yes."

"You insist you are pregnant when I say you are not?"

"Yes."

He turned to his assistant. "Clara, please get Mrs. Gray ready for an examination."

He said it like a threat and I was glad I had interfered

with his callous routine.

"Back this way." The woman with the gentle hands and gentler eyes motioned for me to follow her.

As I waited for the doctor to make time for me, I contemplated the idea that I might be wrong and in so doing, felt a joyous sense of well being. Compared to the prospect of nurturing a new life, westering seemed an almost easy venture.

But I knew I was right. There was a new, demanding, foreign body dwelling inside me.

When Dr. Harvey finally entered the room, he made me feel ashamed that I had doubted him. He made me feel difficult and ungrateful. Grudgingly, he examined me. When he was finished he rolled down his sleeves.

I waited for him to speak.

"Well, Mrs. Gray, I must admit I was wrong. But then, we all know medicine is not an exact science and each person is unique."

"I'll try to remember that," I said.

"My first diagnosis was obviously incorrect. You are indeed pregnant, Mrs. Gray. And by my calculations, you should deliver in late winter." Then he tried being polite in lieu of apologizing. "I'm sure you must be very happy."

Rearranging my clothing, I stood to leave. As I pulled up the hem of my glove I looked that man in the eyes, determined not to leave him with the impression that he had made me happy in any way.

"I'm sure you haven't the faintest notion what would make me happy, Dr. Harvey. Remember, each person is unique. Good day."

I slammed the door on my way out. There was so much more I wanted to say to that horrible man. I wanted to tell him to take up veterinary medicine. That way his patients would never care that his hands were as cold as his heart. I wanted to tell him to stop smirking at me while he gave me the worst news I could have imagined.

But I said none of those things. Politeness dictated I take the majority of my anger with me rather than leave it back in that office. Besides, I had too much on my mind, too much draining the energy from me. I was pregnant.

CHAPTER THIRTY-SEVEN

We never made plans for the arrival of our child. Samuel chose to ignore the situation. Maybe he couldn't face the added responsibility just then. Maybe he wanted to wait until we were safe in Oregon. I had no idea what he thought for we never discussed it. And there was no urgency to press him; I was feeling fit again.

Coral would ask, periodically, after my health. I noticed her busy hands working with knitting needles on something resembling a small sweater. I never asked what she was doing.

Sarah confided in me that she had assisted in several deliveries. She told me this to alleviate any fear I might have should I need her along the way. Having offered her help, she never brought up the subject again.

I refused to even consider the possibility of giving birth on the trail. To the others, that is. But the idea that I might bleed to death or be caught alone and helpless soon became my biggest fear. Not even the Indians held as much dread for me. But then, I had never seen an Indian, in the flesh, until one day near Emigrant's Gap.

He rode up alongside the wagon, naked except for a scant piece of leather draped over his legs suggesting a pair of trousers. His hair was long and straight, the blackest black I had seen only before in the feathers of a crow. Strapped to his back were a bow and a quiver containing six arrows. Samuel was unaware of the man's presence. I tugged his sleeve.

"I think he wants us to slow down."

"Who does?" My husband looked at me and then saw the handsome brave keeping pace with us. "I think you're right, Abby." Samuel pulled in the reins.

Sarah kept her wagon ahead of us and was oblivious to what was happening. Coral had been walking with several other women and was a good distance behind.

At first the three of us stared at one another. Then Coral came hurrying up to the Indian, winded from her run. She waved her arms and spoke in what I can only term as gibberish. The Indian looked as confused as Samuel and I did.

Shrugging, then completely ignoring Coral's attempt to communicate, the Indian turned back toward us and smiled, ever so slightly.

"Do you speak English?" Samuel asked.

The Indian shook his head no.

"Can we," I pointed to Samuel and myself, "help you." I then pointed to the Indian.

It was quite clear the strange man was still confused. He made no further attempt to speak to us directly but was ever watchful, his eyes constantly searched for something. There was even a frightening moment when he suddenly leaned so close I thought he meant to harm me. But he looked past me, into our wagon.

He must have felt safe enough that finally he whistled a loud signal. Sitting astride a great spotted horse, a squaw came charging toward her companion.

She had her hair pulled severely back, fastened with a strip of leather behind her right ear. Her manner of dress lacked almost as much substance as the man's. She abruptly pulled her horse to a stop and, seeing us, bared her teeth. Had she been a dog, I would have expected her to growl. But I knew she meant to communicate a smile.

A circular to the Oregon emigrants from Governor George

Abernethy had instructed us to treat the Indians with kindness. He warned they were inclined to steal. Small parties had often been stripped of property. We were told to keep our word if striking any sort of trade or the next group of travelers would suffer. I considered all of this while trying to understand what the couple wanted.

The woman had a satchel strapped to her back and she reached inside, withdrawing a pair of moccasins trimmed with blue and white beads. She offered the shoes to me and without hesitation I reached for them. They were very soft in my hand. I could imagine how comforting they would feel to my feet, which had recently started swelling in the heat of the day.

"Look, Samuel, aren't they pretty?"

"They want to make a trade," Coral said. She studied the two natives as if they were playing a game with her, making her look foolish when, in fact, they did understand her.

"They certainly are fine pieces of craftsmanship." Samuel handled the slippers carefully, as if they were charged with explosives.

I asked Coral, "What shall we trade them?"

"I'll see what we can spare." Coral went to search her small wagon which was then tied to the back of our large one. While we waited I tried making myself understood to the solemn woman. "Do you have others?" I held up the shoes. "More?"

She understood my interest and started pulling moccasins from her bag. One was fringed with rawhide around the edges, one seemed to have bits of fur adorning it. I suddenly found myself unable to decide which pair I favored the most.

All the while the brave sat watching, never moving toward his bow, not expressing very much curiosity toward us but simply making sure his companion was unharmed.

Coral returned with her apron loaded down with two loaves of bread and one large jar of strawberry preserves. She motioned toward what she had brought and the squaw looked to the man for permission, I suppose.

Suddenly the brave seemed agitated. He grunted and shook his head violently. I must admit his anger frightened me, but I never let on.

Again Coral tried talking with them; they seemed annoyed with her efforts. Quite unexpectedly the brave guided his horse to Samuel's side of the wagon and when he came to a halt, reached for my husband's shirt.

Coral shouted, "He doesn't mean to hurt you; he's admiring your clothing."

"It's only a simple work shirt—one of the most tattered in my wardrobe." Samuel started to move, wanting to go into the wagon to fetch something finer but the Indian pushed him back into his seat.

"I think he wants that one, the very one you have on," I said.

"I agree with Abigail," Coral said.

"Do you want this shirt?" Samuel asked in a loud, slow voice.

The brave started unbuttoning Samuel's garment and I covered my face so as not to laugh at the strangeness of our situation.

"All right, all right, you can have it, just give me a minute." Samuel quickly unbuttoned the shirt, pulled it from his trousers then tore it from his body.

The Indian held up the pin-striped cloth as if it were a flag. He said something to his woman who seemed satisfied with the trade as well. Then she stuffed all the moccasins back in her bag, save the pair I had selected.

The brave dug his heels into the ribs of his horse and in a full gallop, he was off. The woman turned to follow him but first waved to me. It was a shy sort of farewell and I responded in kind.

Samuel turned to me after we were sure they would not come back. "I had no idea this journey would require the sacrificing of my clothing."

"A small price, I guess." I lowered myself down to the ground so as to be able to get Samuel something to cover himself with.

"A small price, don't you agree, Coral?" I asked.

She walked back toward her wagon, her shoulders and head sagged forward.

"I suppose." Her voice quivered; she seemed ready to cry.

CHAPTER THIRTY-EIGHT

Our wagon train was a small village, buzzing with the gossip of foreigners. That evening when we made camp, I told Sarah about our encounter. At first she was angry, thinking I was teasing. After I showed her the moccasins, she seemed envious. She was not to be satisfied.

Coral remained silent while I helped her prepare dinner. The fire blasted ashes into my face, insects snagged in my hair and my dress seemed to catch with every turn I made. Our task required countless trips in and out of the wagon. Coral made the steps but I wondered which one of us got the better deal.

Samuel went to look at an antelope one of the men had shot that afternoon. Traveling with only one other companion, the man offered to share his meat with us.

Arranging several small stools around the fire, Sarah looked at Coral periodically. "I suppose you're more anxious than ever to be done with us. Now that you've met up with some of your people."

"They were not my people," Coral snapped.

"I was not referring to your people specifically; I was speaking in generalities. One Indian is much the same as another. Sometimes you can be so disagreeable."

Coral ignored Sarah and went back to the wagon to get our plates and silverware.

"What on earth is bothering that woman now?" Sarah asked me.

I wrestled with the heavy pot. It started to slip into the flames and I jumped back, startled, as the fire was extinguished by the broth that was to be our dinner. I kicked at the mess. "Why don't you ask her yourself?"

I hadn't expected Sarah to take my advice; she never had before. The best I was hoping for was to be left in peace to rekindle the fire. Ignoring my anger, she stood for a moment and studied the bulky woman's back.

I expected Coral to comment on my ineptness when she returned with the utensils, but instead she just dropped them onto a cloth spread on the ground. They clanged together and I saw Sarah reach out for Coral's sleeve but quickly withdraw her hand.

"Are you well?"

I hadn't expected Coral to respond to Sarah and when she answered I was surprised again.

"I am so alone."

"She misses her husband, Wounded Hawk," I told Sarah.

Coral immediately corrected me. "Until this afternoon I missed him very much, but now, I do not."

"Why?" I asked. "What's caused your feelings to change?"

Sarah gracefully took her place on one of the wobbly stools. "Tell me what happened this afternoon."

"I looked at that red man today, not with fear or love." Coral paced and wrung her hands. "I welcomed him as I would any man. Blood, hair, he was just a man. And he shunned me.

"I saw his squaw. The first Indian woman I have seen in a long time. I thought we would recognize one another."

Sarah was taken aback. "You knew her?"

"Ach, no, not by name but there was a wife in each of us. She could see I had been marked. But . . . she also ignored me. She could not be bothered to even try and speak to me.

"Looking at that couple, watching them made me see my true self. I know now, after years of wondering, that I am no more than the white woman with strange scars who does not belong anywhere, not to anyone."

When she finished speaking, Coral held her hands in a most deliberate manner over her chin. She covered the tattoos that always drew attention from our fellow travelers. I had thought Coral never noticed the stares. She squatted down then, so low to the ground that if it were possible, she would have seeped into the earth and disappeared.

Sarah did not offer one word of comfort; neither did I. We could only watch the poor woman crumple in front of us.

Coral had told me she was close to my age, back in Council Bluffs when I felt alone, but I always thought of her as the older, important one, the one who held us all together with her remedies and plain food. She knew how to do everything I did not. Watching her sit like that, talk in such a way, made me feel very unprotected.

Sarah, the eldest of the three of us had always seemed the youngest. I looked to her for laughter, diversion. While Coral was sustenance, Sarah was frivolity.

I suppose I thought of myself back then as a mixture of both those women. The youngest, most inexperienced and yet probably the most formally educated with one year of college to my credit. But I could feel things changing as we watched Coral draw into herself; we all suddenly became the other.

Sarah went to Coral, knelt down and held the woman in her arms. "We all feel like that at times. You just weren't prepared for the meeting this afternoon."

"They thought I was a stupid woman. A stupid and silly woman. They gave me no respect and they could see I had been with their people."

What I heard come out of my mouth sounded so typically Sarah. "Oh, you're just tired. You barely sleep; we have to fight with you to let us help with the cooking. Why don't you go inside and rest?"

Coral reacted like a little girl. "I am not tired and the last thing I want to do is sleep." Having told me her thoughts, she began to cry. Her sobs were loud gulping noises. Her body seemed wracked with the sadness coursing through her.

Mr. Griesinger came upon us suddenly. His eyes went from my skirt splashed with soup, to Coral crying uncontrollably, to Sarah on her knees comforting the hysterical woman.

He seemed puzzled and then said to me, "You've already heard then?"

I forced my attention from the scene in front of me to him. "What? Heard what?"

He appeared unsure as to how to proceed with his next statement. After second's worth of hesitation he said, "Your husband has been wounded. I think it was a swamp rattler."

CHAPTER THIRTY-NINE

Four men carried Samuel to our wagon. A man unfamiliar to me spoke quickly; I tried understanding all that had happened and the order it had happened in.

"He was admirin' the antelope—we all was. It went down in them tall weeds yonder." He motioned with his head. "Sam bent down to help move the carcass an' before we could git a good hold, he lets out with a yelp."

They laid him on the ground that had been covered with linen for our dinner.

"Name's Levitt, ma'am." The talkative man offered his hand after releasing Samuel's legs. "Wesley Levitt. Your husband . . . I take it you're Mrs. Gray?"

I nodded.

"Your husband was with me and my cousin, Merle. We was tryin' to decide how to divide the meat up. I guess ole Sam here was just in the wrong place. There're all sorts of nasties crawlin' in them weeds. Durn rattler came from nowhere an' just SNAP! got 'em on the arm."

As I listened, my eyes looked over the group; I recognized one of the men as Colonel Chapman. It was the closest I had ever been to the bearded man. When he became aware of my glance, he picked up the story.

"I heard the commotion and ran to help. I suspected it was a snake. We got the poison out, ma'am, but his arm is going to swell up pretty bad. It's best to leave him out here where he can be tended to. Your wagon is too confining."

I managed to revive from my shock and asked, "Why is he unconscious? Is that normal?"

The Colonel looked embarrassed for my husband and stepped closer to me, speaking in almost a whisper. "He fainted dead away when he saw my knife. I had to cut the wound to make sure we could suck all the venom out. Nothing to worry about, he'll come around soon."

"Oh." I didn't know what else to say.

Andrew thanked the men. Acting as our protector, he managed to herd them away from my husband. As they filed past me, I thanked each one again. When I got to Mr. Levitt he removed his hat and with it squashed between his hands he said, "I'm awfully sorry, ma'am. I feel responsible, it bein' on account of my animal that Sam got hurt. As a gesture I'd like you to have it. The whole thing. It'd make me an' Merle feel a whole lot better."

"Thank you, Mr. Levitt."

After they left, I bent down to stroke Samuel's forehead. I could hear Coral talking.

"Andrew, stay please with Abigail while I fetch the hartshorn."

"Good thing for snakebite," he said.

Without a word Sarah began raking through the warm cow chips that had fueled our fire. She added dry ones on top of the pile. So often she had fussed about having to touch the dung, but I watched her calmly and meticulously arrange the hard clumps and then light the fire without one complaint.

Andrew bent down on the other side of Samuel, facing me. "Your husband is a strong man; things appear far worse than they actually are right now. Not to worry." After reassuring me, he ripped the shredded sleeve completely from Samuel's bloodied shirt. The movement and sound roused him from unconsciousness.

"You're fine," I told him. "Colonel Chapman got all the poison out."

Samuel didn't move his head at first but looked at the swollen arm with only the corners of his eyes. He seemed more afraid of his own flesh than the idea of being bitten by a venomous serpent.

"It hurts, Abby."

I told him how confident the Colonel had been that everything would be fine. But instead of calming him, the words only seemed to excite Samuel. Before I could finish, he pushed himself up on his elbows.

Andrew gently held Samuel down. "Stay quiet. Mrs. Adams is getting medicine for you."

"I'll get bedding to make you comfortable. Good thing it's a warm night." Trying to cheer him, I said, "I'll even sleep with you out here, beneath the stars."

"I can get into my own bed!" Samuel shouted.

Coral ran to us with a small box in her hands. Samuel continued to fuss; he wouldn't let any of us touch him. I suspected he was embarrassed from having succumbed but I never let on that I knew the true reason.

Just when I thought we were lost, Sarah came to stand by my side. She withdrew her tortoise-shell fan from one of the deep pockets of her dress. I wondered why on earth she would do such a thing. But instead of opening the device, she held it closed. And quickly, without one word of warning, she snapped it forcefully on Samuel's shoulder. Sounding like a whip striking horse hide, it startled us all.

"Now lie down. Stop being foolish and making us all work harder at getting you better. We haven't time nor energy enough to continue coddling you."

Samuel immediately fell back to the ground. Coral took the stopper from her small medicine bottle and Andrew stepped back, allowing her more room to tend to her difficult patient.

I never thanked Sarah for her quick wisdom that day. I was too engrossed in my fearful thoughts.

For years I watched other families plagued with bad fortune and always counted myself blessed. Each time I heard of a death in a friend's family, I not only gave thanks that my own had been spared, but feared tragedy had taken one step closer to me. For I knew, just as I have known so many things, that I would have to pay for those carefree years. And I also knew that once my sorrow began . . . it would linger.

CHAPTER FORTY

Samuel insisted he was able to sleep inside the wagon. He seemed more annoyed than hurt when we tried helping him to bed.

The next morning a terrible storm blew through our camp. The air suddenly turned cold and the sky went black. Assistant Wagon Master Hain rode up and down the line shouting for us to stay covered. As lightning cracked the darkness, Samuel hugged me close. The bite he had received the day before appeared not to have worsened. In fact, he seemed more robust than I had seen him in weeks.

Our wagon rocked with each powerful gust; shook when thunder bellowed. I knew then how sailors, always fearful of being capsized, felt being tossed from wave to wave in the middle of a turbulent ocean.

From the beginning, all along the way, Samuel and Charles had patched crevices in our home using tar from the bucket thumping against the side of our wagon. But now it felt as though each bit of the black sealant was being washed away. The canvas over our head had a tiny rip I had never noticed until water started, at first, to drip on us and then stream in. We had to cover ourselves with one of the rubber sheets rolled and stored between the canvas and wagon. When the hail started I thought surely our flimsy roof would be torn to pieces.

"We're a fine pair, aren't we?" Samuel shouted above a loud clap. "Huddled in bed like frightened children."

"At least we're frightened together."

My comment made him laugh. He kissed my cheek once and then added several others until he had worked his way to my mouth. Once at my lips, he kissed me deeply. I can not remember him ever having caressed me in such a passionate way.

I hugged him tightly, making him wince when I forgot and squeezed his sore arm.

"How good you feel," I told him. His neck smelled of sweet breezes and sunshine. "I love you, Samuel."

He seemed surprised. "Even after all that has happened? I wonder sometimes how you are able to feel anything for me."

"It's been difficult. I will admit, it has been most difficult."

"I'm sorry." He said it softly, lovingly into my ear. "But yesterday, when I thought I was at death's door, I realized what a fool I've been." He planted tiny kisses down my neck.

Our fingers began moving in a frenzy, pulling at buttons, peeling away layers of clothing. And in the middle of Wyoming, in a cramped wagon, on a tiny bed, we made love beneath sheets soaked with cold rain. I knew then that things would be better between us. I also knew no matter what the size of our house in Oregon, how luxurious our bed, I would never feel as much love for my husband as I did then.

The trail to Devil's Gate was a hilly one. Rains had left us soggy and we rolled back the canvas to air out. My shoes, the practical ones I had worn almost everyday, were waterlogged. I was forced to wear the moccasins I wanted to save as a keepsake. Hoping they would not be ruined, I had no choice but to watch the bead work sink, with each step, into the muck.

Rather than worry about my damp hemlines, I cut several inches from one of my clean dresses and kept telling myself I would buy pretty new things once we were through with our journey. My hair seemed to have suddenly grown wild. Heat overcame the day and with the residue moisture from the storm, I was steaming inside my clothes.

Even Sarah had to go without one of her hats and twisted her beautiful dark hair on top of her head, hoping to cool her neck. She told me she had read Nathan's literature regarding clothing for the trip. It had gone on for pages concerning what men should pack. But it only devoted one sentence to women's needs.

"Can you imagine? It said that we are supposed to make do!" She ranted at the inconsideration. "Not one word of help; not one piece of practical advice. Make due with men's clothing! That's what they tell us, this group of stodgy old men. Well I had something specially made . . . just for this trip."

While Coral and I tried helping Samuel get the small wagon out of a muddy rut, Sarah marched into what had now become her wagon. She soon returned wearing a white cotton blouse, and corded bloomers in a blue so dark they looked almost black.

I had never seen anything like them. A short skirt covered what appeared to be a pair of men's pants. They showed from the hem of the skirt to the tips of Sarah's boots. She pranced in front of us, proudly modeling her new outfit.

"Well? What do you think?"

Samuel said he was no authority on women's fashions and withheld his opinion. I admired my husband's diplomacy.

I told her it suited her. And it truly did. I had always felt more comfortable in less conspicuous attire. But Sarah seemed able to wear anything—conservative or outlandish. She was able to carry this off because of her striking figure and charismatic personality.

Coral said she liked the bloomers as well. Said they appeared to be sensible and flattering at the same time. She certainly was well versed in practicality having started the journey with only three dresses. She kept her hems short and the calico she wore that day was fringed from being trimmed so many times.

After we had all given our opinions to Sarah, Coral and I dressed Samuel's arm with clean strips. The whistle was heard and we readied ourselves to pull out onto the trail. By the time we were in line, half the day had been lost.

I tried fanning myself once we were moving, but it did no good. Mosquitoes seemed swollen with the humidity and bumped into my face several times before biting my skin. I itched all over.

Markers had become a common sight and I took to counting the graves as we slowly moved. I had gotten to twenty when I spotted a cherrywood table and four matching chairs dumped by the road. They were in poor condition compared to the last time I had seen them on the riverbank in Iowa. I thought back to the old woman who had been so concerned for the safety of her furniture. My heart sank, thinking she had been forced to leave behind possessions that had meant so much. I wondered also what had become of her and prayed she was well.

Each day the trail became more littered. There was no room for sentimentality when a choice had to be made between life and ownership. Wagons broke down, animals died; each mile was wrought with brutal challenges.

It wasn't just the women who found it difficult parting with family keepsakes, the men had their share of heartbreak. It had been four or five days before when we saw a crude rocking chair come flying from the back of one wagon. A man leapt from inside, shouting to his wife that the chair had belonged to his grandfather and, by God, he was not going to lose it now.

I couldn't see who steered their wagon but it continued forward while the woman ran after the man. They wrestled with the rocker for a few minutes until the man got a strong hold. Then firmly, he set it down and planted himself on the seat.

Samuel had thought the episode funny. But when we got nearer, I could not bring myself to look at either the man or woman. I felt such sadness for them.

I did look back a few times, once we were further along. The man remained alone, rocking. Word traveled back to us that he was spotted, late in the evening, walking back to camp. Without his chair.

I suppose we were lucky, being newlyweds. Our first year had been spent in family homes and did not afford me time enough to accumulate my own things. Yet, each time I saw a piece of wood in either the shape of a chair or a headstone, I knew it represented a loss.

"You're going to have to learn to manage the wagon," Samuel said, jolting me from my thoughts.

"I suppose so."

"I mean today."

Pulling to a halt, he rubbed his shoulder. "My arm's bothering me. It hurts more now than it did yesterday."

The moment I had dreaded was suddenly upon me. How could I take charge of animals I feared?

Baltimore was a large city and throughout my childhood I had managed on foot. When I was included in family gatherings, my brother, Robert, or Father would arrange our transportation. I remember Mother driving the buggy on several occasions.

I never told anyone how frightened I was of the horses.

How gigantic they looked to me who was then so small. Pounding their hooves into the ground; I feared they wanted to tear me to pieces each time they snapped their large teeth. And I respected them as well as my own terror by keeping my distance.

As I grew older, I was still able to get everywhere I needed to be on foot. And in my adolescence, I had Samuel to drive me in his uncle's carriage.

When Samuel purchased my horse for the trip I thought it odd he never noticed my revulsion toward the animal. But I reasoned that if he chose not to comment, I needn't explain.

The oxen hadn't frightened me as much. Maybe it was because I first saw them when I was a woman of grown-up size. They were all such sluggish, bulky creatures. But their long, curved horns made them seem dangerous. I often thought they could spear me with one shake of their head. When they stared at me, they reminded me of a horse's stare and I felt afraid.

But I never told my husband any of those thoughts when he got down from his seat and walked around to my side. I hadn't wanted to anger him; his arm seemed to be causing much pain and our lovemaking was still fresh in my mind.

"Take my seat and pick up the reins."

I did as he told me and unwrapped the leather straps from where they had been tied. The wagon leaned as he climbed back up.

"Hold your hands like this." He laced the reins between my fingers and thumb. "Tightly. Now give a jerk and . . ." the animals moved ". . . we're off."

"Are you sure you're well enough to travel?" I asked, trembling.

"Stop worrying about me." His voice grew louder and I stared straight ahead, fearing if I took my eyes from the road for one minute we would end up lost.

An hour must have passed. My hands had relaxed their grip; I was beginning to feel somewhat confident. It was a quiet afternoon; I suspected all the children must have been too hot to make noise. Samuel sat next to me, silent. We had not spoken for at least half of the hour. His head jerked forward and I thought he had fallen asleep. I started to assure him I could manage, tell him he should crawl inside and lie down. But before I could get the words out . . . he fell.

CHAPTER FORTY-ONE

Shock had overtaken me after hearing Samuel hit the ground. It sounded as though he was merely a large sack filled with hundreds of potatoes, no more than a thud.

I suppose I screamed. I remember men grabbing me, pulling the reins from my hands. Sarah was there, then Coral, and we were all screaming. They regained their composure and then it was only me again. Screaming for help, for Samuel.

Assistant Wagon Master Hain helped the other men carry my husband to a shady spot under a tree. I can still see that ugly, misshapen thing so vividly in my mind. I couldn't believe what was happening.

"No!" I shouted at them all. "It happened before. He'll be himself in a few minutes. We have to wait."

Mr. Hain told me he would get Colonel Chapman and decide what they should do since I was alone now.

Alone?

Then Andrew was standing beside me. I suppose Coral went for him, seeing the state I was in.

"Abigail," Coral's voice seemed to be coming from somewhere far removed from me. I felt her arms around my shoulders. "She's shaking, we need a blanket," she told Sarah.

My eyes wouldn't leave Samuel, I believed then that I could will him awake. Andrew knelt over him and put his head to his chest, listening for a heartbeat.

I watched, silent.

Sarah was the one to wrap me in the wool blanket. She did

not say a word. I couldn't see what her reaction was because my eyes were fixed on Samuel.

I have no idea how long we were there before I heard two horses galloping behind me. They were pulled to a stop and I recognized the Colonel's voice shouting. "Mrs. Gray! Are you all right, ma'am?"

"How do you expect her to be? Her husband's dead!" Sarah screamed.

Dead. The word hung in the air for a moment.

"It happens like that sometimes," Colonel Chapman said. "A bite can be no bigger than a pinprick. Even if we tend to it right away, the heart gives out later."

Andrew straightened up. "I'll stay with Mrs. Gray."

"As will I," Coral said.

"We all will," Sarah added.

"Suit yourselves. We have to push hard today. The late start and the prospect of rain; we just can't afford to lose more time. I'm sorry, ma'am, we can't wait for you. But I can have Alvin, here, ride behind the last wagon; he'll keep watch for your party."

Andrew reassured him, "I'll take care of her."

"My husband will take care of me." Samuel was younger than any of those men. He was healthy and would prove them all wrong. "We don't need special attention."

Then I ran to my husband and begged him to wake up. Suddenly remembering what had revived him the last time, I desperately tore at his shirt. A few drops of blood had spotted his sleeve and collar but other than that, he appeared to be sleeping. I quickly took the blanket I still clutched and rolled it up to make a pillow. Gently I lifted his head and rested it back against the wool.

"Ma'am," Mr. Hain tried getting my attention. But I had to tend to Samuel and ignored him. "I'll hang back as far as I can and if we don't catch sight of you tomorrow, I'll come lookin'."

Coral stood firm, taking charge of us. "Thank you, Mr. Hain, Colonel, but I have traveled west before. We will manage."

I looked at the men, sitting high on their mounts and thought how surprised they would be when Samuel and I caught up with them . . . together.

The Colonel touched the brim of his floppy hat in a gallant gesture. "Good luck then." And the two of them rode away.

After they were out of sight, Sarah sat down on the ground beside me. Coral hurried off in the direction of her small wagon. Andrew's wagon was pulled into the weeds; the trail separated Samuel and me from him. He started a small fire and I noticed Coral mixing something in a large metal coffeepot. I had just settled beside Samuel, when Andrew approached me, carrying a cup.

"Abigail, please, drink this, it will help you to be calm."

Sarah took the cup from him and held it to my lips like a mother would do for her child.

I drank. It tasted of mint tea.

"Why aren't you doing anything for Samuel?" I asked the man.

"I will." He opened a felt pouch hanging from his belt. Withdrawing a green stone, he rubbed it between his thumb and the fingers of his left hand.

"'That man has very peculiar ways," Sarah said as we both watched him return to his own wagon.

The sun would be setting in a few hours. I thought surely Samuel should be awake by then.

"Abigail," Sarah at last spoke, softly. "You must understand by now that Samuel is gone. Please, take advantage of this time." She touched my arm. "Use it to say good-bye to him."

Coral joined us when she saw we were conversing. "Come, I have stew. We will eat and then put Samuel to bed."

To bed! I knew he was alive—Coral knew it too. My relief brought on hunger; I told them I would take a plate near my husband.

Sarah went to get us both a portion of the dinner Coral had prepared. She also brought lace napkins I had never seen before, and we drank our coffee from china cups instead of the dented tin ones I had grown accustomed to using.

I had not responded to Sarah's advice. Unable to express my confusion, I ate in silence, watching fat white clouds edged in pink shadows. Yellow rays cut through them allowing light to stream through. Coral and Andrew sat on the other side of the road where the fire had been built. While they ate they spoke in hushed voices; I could not make out anything they said.

When we were finished, Andrew came to me. He was dressed in clean clothes, every garment dyed the black he favored. His long curly hair had been tied back and two yellow feathers were stuck into the tangle trailing down his back. I wondered what occasion had caused him to dress in such a manner.

"It's time for me to help you . . . and Samuel."

"Finally," I felt glad. "What can we do?"

He reached down to me and pulled me to my feet. "Take your blanket and cover him."

Without asking why, I took the blanket from under Samuel's head and carefully wrapped it around him. His skin felt cold through his clothing and I scolded myself for not covering him sooner.

"Come with me, Abigail," Andrew said.

I followed him to a spot behind his wagon. A slope elevated to a small hill. A clump of wild flowers poked out of a clay pot that had been half buried in the earth. In front of the vase was a large hole. I stood there a moment before realizing it was a grave.

"We have to lay Samuel to rest. There's nothing more to be done for him. He is gone from us now."

I felt betrayed. "No! You said we were going to put him to bed!"

"Yes, so that he might rest peacefully."

Coral stood by Andrew and Sarah stood beside her; they both looked at me with trepidation.

"We can't let the wolves have him. Andrew dug the hole deep. He was lucky to find such a beautiful spot." Coral seemed proud of what he had done.

"Let him go, Abigail," Sarah told me.

I turned and looked back at that horrible tree. The blanket was still exactly where I had tucked it. Samuel had not moved at all. "Can't we wait . . . ?"

"There isn't time enough," Andrew said. He stood closer to me. "Unfortunately, dear Abigail, you are here, in this wild place. There's no time to hesitate now, you will have to mourn your husband's death later. We cannot afford the luxury of waiting."

"You're all in such a hurry, go then." I almost told them all how hesitant Samuel had been. How he had once confided to me that he wanted to turn back and I was not going to leave him in that forsaken spot. But my husband had also been very proud. Turning back would have been a cowardly act to his way of thinking.

As I stood in front of that empty grave, wrestling with my loyalties, a great commotion suddenly broke out. Gunshots, shouts and the rumble of wagon wheels thundered toward us.

CHAPTER FORTY-TWO

I recognized Velina Brown. She held a rifle; her head jerked about in the most wild manner I had ever seen. She sat next to a frightened boy who looked to be no more than twelve or thirteen years of age. He held the reins leading to three scrawny horses. Even from my position, I could hear her screaming to him.

"Faster! Hurry! They're comin'!"

Andrew raced to the road, waving his arms. "Is there trouble?" he shouted. I thought he would surely be run down but the boy jerked the reins and the animals reared back then stood still.

Velina reached across the boy grabbing the reins from him. "What the hell are you doin', son?" He fell over, crying into her lap.

The three of us watched, terror-stricken, as Andrew walked closer to the woman. He tried speaking with her. She shook her head, furiously, then raised the rifle, aiming it directly at Andrew's head.

I expected fear, but instead heard rage as she shouted, "Stop . . . right . . . there."

"Mister," the boy lifted his head, "better stay back, my Mama's touched."

Coral moved; I could almost hear her making the decision to join Andrew. She had taken only two steps toward the scene when a black horse, ridden by a man I recognized as Mr. Brown, came down the trail, stopping alongside the wagon.

"Velina! What in God's name do ya think you're doin'?"

"Daddy!" the boy cried.

Velina Brown instantly turned her aim from Andrew to the man situated beside her. "Don't come near me, Roy! I told ya I'm takin' the kids an' leavin'. I cain't take it no more. None of it!"

"Mrs. Brown," Andrew said, "you don't want to do this."

I could see two small children peeking from inside the wagon.

"I most certainly do! No one's gonna stop me from keepin' my children alive," she yelled over her shoulder.

"My brother's wife passed yesterday; it was just too much for Velina," Roy Brown told Andrew. He looked sad as his wife held the rifle to his head.

"It wasn't just Lily goin' like that. What about Jessie an' Bobby an' Deke? Have you forgotten our Decatur already, Roy?"

"Course not!" the man yelled. "It's been rough on all of us, but . . ."

"No more buts or maybes. You're a grown man, Roy, ya'll can do what ya please but I'm takin' my kids an' goin' home!"

"How will you manage to get your children home safely by yourself?" Coral asked. "Crossing back over rivers and mountains. Can you care for them along the way?"

"I don't know . . . I'll try . . . at least they'll be better off than they are now."

I could bear it no longer, not one more moment of it. "Let her go!" I screamed as I ran toward my husband. "Just let her go!" I must have appeared crazier than the woman wielding a gun. Exhausted from the horrible strain of the day, I collapsed on top of Samuel. His body felt rigid, and I knew then that he was truly dead.

"What's happenin' here?" Velina seemed to have awakened.

Sarah told her, "A burial. Her husband died today."

"Oh Lord," Velina started to cry. "Lord, oh Lord, forgive me for intrudin'."

I could hear the creak of wood then the swishing of her skirt. Velina Brown stood over me. "I remember meetin' you an' your family back in Iowa."

I didn't look at her; I didn't respond in any way. That was my time to grieve and I wasn't going to let her sorrow touch mine. I wanted to be left alone.

But she persisted. "You remember my Deke? Don'cha?" She bent down, nearer to me. "Well, don'cha?"

"Go away."

"I know what you're goin' through. Believe me, I do." Without a moment's hesitation I slapped her.

She looked shocked.

I slapped her again. And again. Both hands worked separately from my brain and in a flurry, I attacked Velina.

Roy Brown ran over and grabbed at me but his wife shouted for him to leave us alone.

I struck her a few more times, on her arm and shoulder. She lay on the ground with her hands stiff at her sides, never even trying to defend herself.

"Get up! Fight! Hit me!"

"I cain't." She looked up at me with vacant eyes. "I won't."

I fell back. One hand reached out to touch Samuel, the other went to my own cheek. My skin, usually soft, felt rough. I looked down at the dirty dress bunched around me and then to my hands. The nails were broken, mud had hardened beneath them from earlier that day. I rubbed the back of my neck, it was burnt from the sun.

"Them's the lucky ones." Velina pointed to Samuel. "Out of it. Them whose hearts an' bodies cain't break no more."

What could I say to her? I had no words that would change anything for either one of us. She thought our losses and location made us the same. But I knew we were different in the most important way. She was defeated. I was not.

We buried Samuel that evening by the light of twenty-one candles, one for each year he had lived. I stuck them in the ground, making a circle around his grave. The wind even took a rest, allowing us a few peaceful moments.

My friends made a marker from one of the sideboards of our wagon. Sarah carved my husband's name, birth date, and death date near the top of the piece of wood. Coral tried rounding off the edges.

Andrew said a prayer. Never having heard it recited in church, I suspected it was of his own composition. As I listened, however, I realized the words suited me and that place better than any reading from the Scriptures. I had thought that short man, strange in the beginning, most unorthodox. I was even a little frightened by him. But as the candlelight flickered, outlining his kind face, I felt comforted.

Realizing it would be the last time we would sleep near one another, I spent that night outside. A calm overtook me; maybe Andrew was right about the earth making sounds of its own.

The next morning, while the wagons lumbered down the trail, I stayed behind, for a few minutes alone with Samuel. Using a piece of charred wood from our fire, I added words of my own to his marker:

Beloved Husband and Father

I never saw the Browns again.

PART FOUR

CHAPTER FORTY-THREE

Having had years to mentally review that journey, I can now clearly see the transformations we went through. All of us. At the time, however, none of it was clear. Like the man whose view of the forest was obstructed by too many trees, I became so obsessed with surviving a situation that I never fully understood what that situation had been.

From the beginning, there was an order to things. I was part of a family: a daughter, sister, and then a wife. Whether in a house in Maryland or covered wagon on the prairie, family had always surrounded me.

Coral and Sarah had first been acquaintances and then my friends. Without much thought, I related to them the same way I had related to any friend back home. Not ever having had to depend on any one outside of family for my very life, I treated them with courtesy and consideration, kindness and respect. And, I admit, some reserve. But there was a nice balance to it all. Every person had his accepted place in that life . . . even myself.

Suddenly Charles left. I no longer felt like a sister. At least in a way that could be experienced daily when I looked at my brother's face or heard him say my name.

Samuel's death took away my last family member as well as my wifely role. I had no idea how to be a widow. Old women were widows; women who no longer cared about life were widows. Not I.

Even my friendships, in the blink of a sad eye, were

changed. Immediately, without any conscious effort, Sarah and Coral were my family. Each became mother and sister to me, cousin and aunt. Our attachments were unexpectedly based on more than fondness; we were as vital to one another as water and air. Our conversations went from frivolous topics to issues of survival.

While all this internal change was happening between the three of us, it also became very obvious that our status within the traveling community had shifted. Women who passed time with us, gossiping or washing clothes, looked away when we approached. Maybe those who had lost husbands saw me as a reminder of their own heartache. Young girls flirting with boys available to them probably saw the three of us as rivals. To all of them, men and women alike, my traveling companions and I were now considered curiosities.

Coral with her tattoos, odd speech and insomniac tendencies had generated rumors from the start. Sarah's flirtatious ways had been tolerated while Charles was around. Surely some of our neighbors regarded my brother and Sarah as a couple, even if the exact definition of their relationship was unclear. I hadn't taken notice at the time that attitudes toward my friend changed when Charles left and intensified after Samuel passed away.

And I, once the young wife, was then thought of as the pitiful widow. "How sad," they would whisper. "She's too young to be alone, expecting a child and all. So innocent, traveling with the likes of those women."

Those women? How dare they!

But back then, so soon after Samuel's death, I was confused more than sad. Knowing things were different but not knowing why. Relationships as well as conditions so suddenly tipped off-balance. I never realized we were living in such extreme times.

First we were accepted, then rejected, constantly fatigued or unable to sleep at all. Food supplies were brimming, or meager. We were either waterlogged or bone dry.

The only constant thing was the work of traveling. And it was that struggle that saw me through.

Andrew was an enormous help. Having worked as a blacksmith and carpenter, expert at repairs of all sorts, he began checking our wagons at day's end. The first time he made such an inspection of my Conestoga, he marveled at Nathan's design. He said he had never before seen such inventive construction or the expert use of such superior materials. How fortunate one wagon required less maintenance than most. Still, there was the other to contend with and infinitely more chores now that three women were left to do jobs originally intended for five two of that number being men.

Sarah took over driving one wagon and I had no choice but to manage the other. Coral adamantly refused to take the reins but was very good about caring for the animals. Left with an extra horse, we barely had a chance to wonder what should be done when the poor creature was sucked down into a patch of quicksand near the Sweetwater River. I feared myself becoming too accustomed to death when the only thing I felt was relief that the horse was gone and no longer required consideration.

Sarah abhorred cooking. It was decided I would help Coral with that chore, but she gladly set things out for each meal and cleaned the dishes afterwards. She never minded making endless trips up and down or in and out of the wagon, saying it was good for her figure.

We all equally detested washing our clothes. Mosquitoes were fierce around the water and it was just another chore in need of doing that resulted in getting wet. Crossing the water, bathing, washing clothes or dishes, perspiring, we always seemed to be soggy or damp.

Mending was done as needed. There seemed to be one of us who never minded a task and would step in when another hated doing it. Every spare moment was precious. If it was not absolutely necessary, we skipped the doing altogether.

The road to South Pass was uphill and forced us to slow down our pace. I could hear shifting inside the wagon and had to stop several times, realizing we had not secured things as efficiently as Samuel would have.

"Too much," Coral muttered. She sat in the seat that I had once occupied when my husband steered the wagon. Now I occupied his place. Shaking her head she said, "You must go through his things, decide what to keep."

"Not today."

"Tomorrow then. But no longer a wait than one more day. The animals have a difficult time breathing up here."

I stared straight ahead. It had only been two days since Samuel's passing. I could feel her eyes on me and chose to concentrate on the scenery. The air was pure and bracing. I had never seen such lush greenness before. The mountains were thickly covered with pine, spruce, and hemlock trees of such large proportion they seemed able to touch the low clouds. Red cedars mingled with elms; the air was spiced with their fragrance.

I inhaled slowly, deeply.

"Abigail," Coral put her hand on mine, "I know what it is to lose a husband. I've survived it twice."

"But you'll be reunited with one. Soon you'll be a wife again."

"I have doubts about that."

When I turned to look at her, she removed her hand, embarrassed. I faced straight ahead again. "Doubts? Surely you weren't serious that day I traded . . ."

"Ach, I was hurt, confused a little. But no, one day hasn't made up my mind for me."

"What then?"

"Oh, knowing you better, wanting to know your baby. Losing my dear friend, Samuel. Learning to like Sarah. Missing Charles. The miles have brought more answers than I had questions. Does that make any sense?"

"Do you remember our conversation that day in your garden?" I looked at her then. "You told me to find my freedom on the strength of my own wings."

Her large, sunburned hands retied a bow under her chin. The ugly sunbonnet hid most of her face from me. "Maybe I've been flapping, flapping my wings for such a long time, Abigail, that I don't know where I want to land."

"I've been having the same thoughts, Coral. Looking at all the canvases fluttering in front of us, behind us; each wagon like some giant hawk. Before, I was swooped up, flying under Nathan's wings, then Samuel's. Now I have my own, to fly where I please. Powered by my own strength."

Coral shook her head. "If only I listened to my own advice as well as you." Then she smiled ever so slightly. "I see it now; I do not belong with the Indians."

"Are you turning back?" Fear tightened in my stomach as I asked the question.

"Are you?" she countered.

"I can't think about that now."

"When we get to Fort Bridger."

"What will happen then?" I asked.

"We will both decide which direction to fly."

CHAPTER FORTY-FOUR

Cholera morbus!

Panic took hold of our wagon train when it was rumored Colonel Chapman had contracted the disease. How devastating it was to think the single most respected man, indispensable to everyone making that long trek, suddenly became our biggest threat. The only thing I could imagine making me feel worse would have been learning my own father meant to do me harm.

I was fond of the Colonel. We all were. He had shared meals at our campfire; he had tried to save my husband. I had seen him repeatedly rescue precious lives. But when he took to his bed, everyone, myself included, tried frantically to recall each time he had physically touched one of us or even sneezed in our direction. We were terrified of the man and more ashamed of that terror than I care to remember.

In a flurry, wagons turned back, in the opposite direction, running to previously crossed territory. Some charged straight ahead, not caring if anyone led them. Stories of shortcuts circulated daily. It was common to hear talk among the women about this husband or that friend who knew of a pass that would cut considerable time off the journey. Those who thought of venturing forth with hand-drawn maps figured the time was ideal for their departure.

Assistant Wagon Master Hain tried calming folks, but even he was thought of as potentially dangerous having been in such close proximity to the Colonel all those months.

The morning after the rumor started, it was confirmed to be true. Colonel Chapman was gravely ill. Coral said we should not let panic overtake our good sense and so we continued following Mr. Hain. But the chaos around us was incredible.

One particular incident came as close as any to breaking my heart. A small child, barely able to walk, screamed as he tried running after the wagon his family was in. He waved his pudgy arms crying, "Mommy! Pick me up! Daddy!" In their haste, the parents had left behind the very reason they were running. Sarah abruptly pulled her team to a halt and picked up the little boy. I saw her running with the child in her arms, toward the family, shouting for them to stop. They hesitated just long enough to snatch the frightened child from Sarah, never bothering to thank her for her kindness.

By midday I had counted more wagons moving against us than with us. Britta Selway was one of the deserters, and I remember her waving good-bye as she sat next to a gruff looking man, I supposed to be her husband. By nightfall, Mr. Hain called us together and reported that one third of our number were gone.

Coral searched through her medicine box for the opium. She told me she had once been stricken with fever when she was a child. Since that episode, she had remained the healthiest in her family. As an adult she felt herself immune to all diseases around her. Filled with such confidence, holding that small box in her arms as carefully as she would have held a baby, she walked to the wagon ten up from us. I feared I would never see her again. But she was adamant about offering her medicine and self to doctoring the Colonel.

"If that's what she believes, then it is so," Andrew told me when I shouted for her to stop.

"The mind and body work together, Abigail, if one tells

the other it cannot do a thing—it cannot. If Coral believes she is the exception—she is. You must not doubt it. She needs only your good thoughts now."

In spite of all the prayers I offered up to God, for the safe return of both Coral Adams and Colonel Chapman, chaos and panic seemed to be the only response He gave.

Coral's absence meant more work for Sarah and me. We were well into July by then. The animals seemed to tire too easily. Severe heat and the increasing altitude had adverse effects on us all. We were told not to drink any water—whiskey was advised for everyone. Afraid to let the animals drink, but knowing they would die without water, I filled bowls for them from our own supply. I tried making the most of the bacon and stale bread we had left. Sarah could not spare daylight time to hunt down anything for our dinner; her time was spent driving the wagon and doing her share of Coral's chores as well as her own. Andrew managed to catch a few fish but thought better of eating them should they be contaminated with the disease threatening to claim us. For what seemed like a week but was actually two more days, we subsisted mainly on berries and fear.

Poor Mr. Hain made the rounds, trying to calm those of us choosing to stay with him. But he looked more fearful than any of his charges. When he tried reassuring me, I saw a quiet intensity emanating from his dark eyes and found myself patting his shoulder, telling him things would be fine. Just fine.

But I knew there was only one course left for us. And I knew it as surely as I have known anything in my life. We had to keep to the trail and make it to Fort Bridger before any more of us died.

CHAPTER FORTY-FIVE

If I didn't think about the danger in which Coral had placed herself, but instead pretended she was visiting Andrew or some other traveler, the fear knotting in my stomach would loosen a little. Sarah had grown very quiet. I assumed it was her way of dealing with the uncertainty of our situation. When the bread had given out, she never complained about my breakfast of coffee and beans. While I tried eating the burnt glob, making conversation, she silently spooned a few mouthfuls of Coral's apple preserves directly into her mouth.

The second night of Coral's absence, I suggested something that would hopefully make us both feel better.

"It's not safe," Sarah said. Her eyes were dull. It had been weeks since a pretty bow adorned her clothing. They had ripped loose while she worked, I supposed, or been shredded against our jagged scrub board.

"One swim, a quick one. I noticed the water earlier; it's calm today."

"I don't know, Abigail."

"Maybe it will help us sleep."

She thought a minute. "Maybe."

I had never known her to show such lack of enthusiasm. While I wondered how to cheer my friend, I also wondered at my desire to do so.

The moon was full that night. Big and lustrous, one gigantic pearl. Sarah looked too thin; her skin gave off almost a bluish cast in the dazzling light. Her hair, usually so lustrous, seemed as lifeless as her soul.

"Good, I'll get a clean night dress and we'll be off."

I didn't have to tell her to wait for me; she stood as if propped on sticks.

Climbing up into the wagon, I went to the largest of my trunks. Kneeling, I lifted its heavy lid. Removing the tray where my toiletries were laid out, I rummaged through clothing near the bottom. Coming across several of Samuel's dress shirts, I carefully laid them on the floor, reminding myself to repack them when I returned.

Finally, almost ready to give up, I located the cotton nightgown I had been saving. I inhaled the intermingled fragrances of lilac soap and starch clinging to its folds. It was the palest pink I had ever seen. Five celery green satin ribbons had been stitched in rows down the bodice and then left to trail freely, almost to the ankle-length hem.

How strange. I don't remember feeling any sadness at all as I held it up for inspection. Instead I was happy, thinking back to the day I had packed the gown, how excited I had been. How hopeful we all had been. I envisioned myself in a house, somewhere in Oregon, covered in the pink, clean design. Samuel would hold me, tell me how happy he was, how beautiful I was.

At that moment, it seemed as if I was reliving a memory already past instead of one not yet experienced. And I no longer needed the gown to make me feel beautiful, but knew how much Sarah needed it to feel alive. Quickly I rolled the gown and a plainer one for myself, inside a large blanket and ran outside.

She hadn't moved one muscle.

"Come on," I reached for her hand and, surprisingly, she allowed me to take it.

The water slid past us like sheets of black velvet. It was

quiet except for a single frog croaking. I walked gingerly, fearing I would step on the creature, he seemed that close. A cool breeze dried perspiration along the back of my neck as I wrapped my braid up on top of my head. I watched Sarah do the same with her hair.

"Did I ever tell you I had a Granny Sarah?" I asked, slipping my shoes off.

"No." She unbuttoned her boots.

"She was my father's mother, a beautiful woman. I think she must have been a lot like you when she was young. She made costumes for some of the most famous actors in Maryland. 'A woman of great style' my father would say."

I stepped out of my dress then tied the petticoat around my waist.

"You think of me in that way? A woman of style?" Sarah seemed surprised and stopped unfastening her blouse.

"Yes I do; I always have. How could you not know that?"

"How could I have known any such thing? I was always under the impression you found me . . . vulgar."

"Vulgar?" I felt horrible. "Outrageous, yes, at times. But vulgar? Heavens no! Your vivaciousness has . . . surprised me, your opinions have, at times, shocked me, but you have always inspired me, Sarah." I embraced her.

Her shoulders and arms tensed. She stood, stiff. "If I gave you any other impression, I apologize." As I spoke, she seemed to relax.

"I am so sorry, Sarah. Do you forgive me?"

When she finally hugged me, she started to whimper, softly, into my shoulder.

Pushing her back at arm's length, I looked into those teary eyes.

"It's not like you to be this sad. What's caused this?"

She looked at me as if I was freshly released from the asylum. "How can you of all people ask me such a thing?"

Throwing herself down, she sat on a large, mossy, rock near shore.

"I've never told you, any of you, but Nathan planned for me to accompany him on this trip. I had finally convinced him we should marry."

"But I thought you were engaged." I sat across from her.

"Oh, my heart was never in that. I think Nathan finally believed I would make him a good wife."

"And you would have."

"Well, I never got the chance to do that. But what I could do was make the trip and get acquainted with his family. Before Nathan died, I promised I'd watch out for all of you." She looked past me. "But it seems I can't even do that correctly."

"What are you talking about?"

"Just look what's happened. Charles is gone . . ."

"He left because he's healthier than he's ever been. Independent, too. You should be proud of his decision."

"I miss him." She hesitated for a minute.

I waited for her to continue.

"Now you're going to have a baby and Samuel's gone. I can't believe he'll never see his child; I've been so afraid of saying anything to you for fear of stirring up more grief but I think about it constantly. Dying. The Colonel becoming ill, Coral tending to him, I'm afraid we're going to lose them both. That odd woman has become very dear to me. You all have. Now we're stuck in the middle of the mountains. You're probably going back to your parents, Coral's going to end up with cholera, and I'm out here with no one . . ."

"It all seems so hopeless," I said, intending my words to make her see how much she was exaggerating circumstances.

"It is," she wailed.

Not knowing what else to do, I stood up. Quickly I ran, splashing into the water.

"Abigail!" Sarah shouted to me, "what are you doing?"

"There's no other way out of it."

She watched as I ran further out. It wasn't until a tree obstructed her view, causing her to lose sight of me that she moved from her spot.

As she ran, she shouted, "Don't be silly. You have so much to live for."

When Sarah reached me, the water lapped at her knees. The combination of her bewilderment and the sudden rush of cold water on her skin stopped her movement and speech abruptly.

When she was close enough, I stood up. "You're right, Sarah. We all have too much to live for."

I had been sitting on the rocky riverbed, pretending to be in depths to my neck. She looked at the water, then to me, then back to the water. Finally her eyes locked on mine.

"I know. I guess I just need to hear the words sometimes. Out loud. From someone other than myself. Even if it's a lie. Nathan would do that for me."

"Now I will," I said.

The swim had been a good idea and as we neared camp, life seemed almost hopeful . . . until we saw the destruction.

Clothes were scattered everywhere. The fire had been disturbed but still burned. Pots and jars, paper and clothing lay strewn about, broken or shredded. Before Sarah and I had time to appraise the scene, Andrew shouted, from someplace outside our vision, for us to run away. We hadn't started to move when my wagon began shaking with great force. A loud growl, sounding like thunder, rumbled.

"If only I could get to my gun," Sarah said.

Without any warning, a large grizzly bear came crawling out of the back of the wagon. Andrew shouted, and for the first time I could see the frightened man hanging from a tree limb.

Sarah and I ran to hide behind an abandoned shack, leaning against a tall pine. Andrew's shouts apparently roused some of the other men; I could hear heavy boots scraping across the rocky pass.

We dared a look from our hiding place in time to see the bear spot Andrew and rear up on his hind legs. He looked to be ten feet tall, a giant of an animal. His paws were tipped with sharp, long claws. He swiped at our friend.

A group of four men and one woman charged toward the animal. They were either the most fearless or stupidest people alive. I have never been able to figure out which. Without hesitation, they all began shooting at the beast. One man held a pistol in each hand and cursed at the bear each time he fired.

For what must have been a full thirty seconds, gunshots blasted and the grizzly roared. Several times the bear tried to charge his assailants. That would send the small group running in all directions. But when the leap ended in a retreat, the shooting resumed. I don't know how it was possible, but it seemed in all the excitement, most of the shells missed their target.

Smoke from the barrels and dying fire burned our eyes, but I could still make out traces of blood matted into the fur on the bear's hind legs. Instead of falling, however, the shots seemed to propel the huge animal. Finally, he turned and bounded away.

I ran to help Andrew, make sure he was whole. The group that had come to his assistance began slapping each other on the shoulders, congratulating themselves.

When Andrew dropped down from the tree, they looked at him, startled.

"Thought you were a goner, there, buddy," one man said through a nervous laugh.

"Are you all right?" Sarah asked.

Before Andrew could answer, the fat woman with the shotgun started chattering. "That sure was somethin'. Surely was. Why I was busier than a cranberry merchant tryin' to keep up with everythin'. Excitin' though, surely was excitin'."

Without waiting for a response from any of us, the group headed back to where they had come from re-enacting the last few minutes as they walked.

"Just what we need," Sarah said, "more excitement."

After making sure Andrew was unharmed, I stooped to pick up a monogrammed piece of cloth. I recognized it as part of Samuel's shirts. The very ones I had intended to put away later that evening.

Sarah saw what I held between my fingers. "Looks like you won't be burdened with that decision anymore," she said in a concerned tone.

"What decision is that?" Andrew asked.

"Abigail was worried about disposing of Samuel's things." She stooped to help me pick up the tattered scraps. "You know, which ones to keep."

Andrew seemed calmer than I had expected he would be. Slapping the dust from his pant legs he kept his eyes downward as he spoke. "You just have to trust your body to know what's best. Too much thinking is not good."

"Like your body told you to climb that tree?" I asked.

"Exactly. You may laugh, but if I had stood around, thinking, Should I run? Should I hide? I would have been lost. I let my legs make the decision, not my brain."

I looked down at the two piles I had made while listening

to Andrew's theory. One was burning with the wood on the fire, the other one had been neatly arranged on the ground in front of me. I supposed I meant to repack what lay there. "I think I understand," I said.

CHAPTER FORTY-SIX

Too much damage had been done to my wagon to rescue it. That grizzly had ripped the canvas beyond repair; both axles had snapped in half beneath his weight. Time and resources to do the major work required, could not be spared. With the help of another man, Andrew was able to salvage some parts left intact. I feared the misfortune we encountered daily was rendering me insensitive, for I felt neither upset nor relieved when I was forced to hitch Coral's small wagon behind the other and ride with Sarah.

Traveling had been slow since the Colonel took ill. The disease was said to be spreading. Sarah and I were fearful most of the time—about so many things. We worried for Coral's safety, about keeping the wagon repaired, maneuvering over rocks jutting from the ridges like the devil's own fingers. The whole wagon train seemed to be limping along. In three days' time, we had traveled only ten miles.

Just when I had resigned myself to moving at a tortoise's pace, we came to a complete stop.

It was well after our morning start, not quite noon yet. We had decided I would start off driving the team. Sarah sat beside me, reading from one of her poetry books. I was mentally composing my next letter to Mother. I had not let one week pass without writing her of our . . . my well being. The next thing I knew, the sky in front of us went red.

That was also about the time Coral returned to us.

When Sarah saw our bulky friend walking toward us, she shouted for me to stop. I barely had time enough to slow down before Sarah leapt from her seat. Her pantaloon dress had not worn as well as expected and I noticed the bottom portion fluttered, like a tattered flag, as she ran to embrace Coral.

I swear I never knew Coral could smile that wide. When she saw Sarah hurrying toward her like that, she opened arms, genuinely glad.

I had become an old hand at managing the animals and pulled them over. After fastening the reins, I, too, ran to greet Coral, never thinking she might be contaminated with the disease she had been exposed to. Youth, exuberance, relief, they all mingled into our joyful outburst.

"He has survived the worst of it," Coral said, when we asked about the Colonel's condition. Patting my cheek, she told me, "Not to worry."

Flames rose in orange columns, licking at the peaceful clouds. I could hear instructions being shouted down.

"What's happening up there?" I asked, pointing toward the commotion.

"Five others have perished. Three children, two men."

"How dreadful."

"More dreadful than you know." Coral turned to watch the fire. "One of the men who died was Mr. Hain."

"The Assistant Wagon Master?" Sarah asked.

"But we just saw him, not that long ago." I thought back, calculating the last time I had spoken to the man.

Sarah nodded. "Day before yesterday. We saw him that morning."

Coral continued, "The cook went to summon him just past dawn, to tell him the Colonel was greatly improved. He was dead then. Colonel Chapman gave the order to head out.

I overheard him say he would bury poor Alvin after we had put a few miles behind us. But not more than ten minutes ago, word came that a two-year-old girl had died. That was when the Colonel decided to stop."

"What about the other three who died?" Sarah asked.

"They were buried along the trail, over the past few days."

Sarah thought a moment and then in a hopeful voice asked, "Are you sure it was cholera? Maybe some of them died of other causes. Maybe Alvin had a weak heart."

"I have seen it before, so has the Colonel. It was cholera. The only thing to be done now is to purge ourselves of the infection. Burn it out."

I was having a difficult time understanding what Coral meant. "How do you do such a thing?"

"Alvin's belongings, everything of the child's and anything belonging to the other three have been loaded onto the Colonel's wagon as well as the one owned by the little girl's family." Coral squeezed my hand. "I helped the Colonel dress, Abigail, he wanted to be there when the . . . bodies . . . were laid out in the wagons. It was his hand that set the fire."

I stood stunned, trying desperately to cope with the vivid images my mind produced.

"We should be there with the rest of them now, to show our concern."

"No." Coral put her hand on Sarah's shoulder. "There is nothing we can do. Best to keep safe."

Then my voice found itself and I said, "This is happening to us all. Every one of us is affected. I agree with Sarah, we should be with the others now."

As Andrew had told me would happen, my body turned and aimed itself toward the wagon. Before I put too much thought into what I was doing, I had a black straw hat on my head, black gloves on my hands and the three of us were walking toward the front of the wagon train.

"This will be difficult," Coral warned.

It's all been difficult, I thought. It's all been so difficult.

The three of us stood back far enough so as not to intrude on familial grief, but close enough to make our presence obvious.

The heat was intense. I assumed the canvases of both wagons, as well as their contents, had been doused with kerosene when a pungent aroma violated the clean air. No one had to tell me what human flesh smelt like when ignited; I could easily distinguish it from the fuel.

Instinctively, my hand went to shield my nose from the sickening odor. But as I watched whom I supposed was the child's sister throw a rag doll into the fire, I struggled to restrain my movements. I did not want to give any sign that could be taken as disrespectful.

Knotting my fingers together so tightly that pain traveled up into my wrists, I stood straight. My eyes burned and as our entire group was enveloped in the haze, tears rolled down my cheeks. At first they flowed merely to clear my eyes from the black smoke. But later, I cried for us all.

CHAPTER FORTY-SEVEN

The seasonal cycles were accelerated in the mountains. Within the span of a few hours it might snow, or rain, or bake our skin. One spot was barren, another was greener than I had yet seen. As I watched the wagons rumbling ahead and behind me, I thought what contrast they offered against the ancient rock formations. The new, expectant, crossing the old, impassive.

The entire trip had been an exaggerated version of life, played at a strange speed. One day I would see a newborn being suckled by its mother and almost the very next, I would see that same mother weeping over a tiny grave. Experiences normally requiring years worth of momentum, suddenly needed no more than a week or month to engage.

We were a day's ride from Fort Bridger when I first spotted three Indians on horseback. The Colonel had cautioned everyone in our wagon community to show respect, not fear, to the natives on whose land we trespassed. My last experience had left me confident and the owner of the only comfortable shoes I then possessed. So when I spied the trio, I felt nothing more than curiosity.

They kept their distance, made no move that could be interpreted by any of us as threatening. All were men, appearing large, even from the stretch between us. For the better part of the day, they sat and watched.

One moment I would catch sight of the three figures on a ridge, miles ahead of us. Another moment I would see them positioned just to the left of the trail. All day long they kept pace with us.

I began feeling a bit uneasy when they were still on our horizon at day's end. The sun stayed in the sky longer those summer nights. Being in the western part of the country allowed for more daylight time and I tried diverting my mind from the unsettling situation by admiring yellow and gold streaks of sunset. They reminded me of my mother's brush strokes when she painted daffodils, the way she tried capturing the light with splashes of white.

I had gotten myself calmed when I suddenly noticed there were only two men on horseback.

Sarah drove the team that day. The wagon left to us had not been designed for comfort. Coral sat between us on the narrow, bench-like piece of wood. While this arrangement was crowded, the closeness was comforting to us.

Before I could point out that one of our watchers was missing, an Indian approached us from the right. Feathers were stuck in the wildness of his tangled hair. He wore a blue muslin shirt and dark trousers fringed with leather.

"If we just go about our business, he won't bother us," Sarah said, trying to make the oxen move faster.

The Indian came nearer; he seemed interested in getting a closer look at Coral.

"Are you two acquainted?" Sarah asked.

I could not make out how my friend was reacting to the stranger's curiosity for she kept her head tilted downward.

Unable to think of anything else, I decided I should try speaking to the man. But before I could get my words out, he spoke.

Pointing at Coral he said, "When you come, we die." He spoke the words in a plain voice, all the while studying the tattoos on her skin.

Coral looked up at the man.

I hadn't been aware of stopping, but we sat as if in a tableau for several minutes. I did not wish to antagonize the red man and feared if we tried leaving, he might pursue us. I had no idea what to say to Coral, she seemed to be struggling, inwardly. Sarah looked directly ahead as if bored with all of it.

At last Coral spoke. Looking the man squarely in the eyes she said, "I did not come to you willingly."

Another uncomfortable moment passed.

Sarah suddenly jerked the reins and our wagon heaved forward. The Indian sat still, watching us leave.

After a few minutes I could contain myself no longer. "Was that Wounded Hawk?"

"No. His people would never be in this territory."

"Why was he talking to you then?" Sarah's curiosity was obvious also.

"Because I am marked."

"He must have seen the fire, followed the trail to us. But why would he think you're responsible for the fever?" Sarah asked.

"Not just the cholera . . . all of it."

"Why would you say such a thing?" I asked.

"Look at me! I am easy to point to and blame. He can read it here." She slapped at her chin. "He looks at me and knows I have been with both the white and the red man."

"But that's so unfair," Sarah seemed insulted.

"Ach, to hell with fairness. It is the way they understand it to be."

I untied the worn ribbons from beneath my chin and tossed my hat into the wagon. "How on earth can you defend them?"

"The Indians? Or my own people? Both blame me."

"And knowing this, you now eagerly go to live with the Indians?"

"It's been just as difficult living among my own."

I knew that I had no idea what Coral endured the years since her rescue and I was not about to insult her then by telling her I understood. But I could offer my friendship. Unconditionally. "Well you're here now, with us, and we're all the people you need." I put my arm around her sagging shoulder.

"As if you have much of a choice, huh Coral?" Sarah asked.

"I guess not."

"Well, thank you so much," Sarah said, pretending to be angry.

"I didn't mean. . . ."

"I know, Coral. I was teasing." Then Sarah laughed.

My body relaxed hearing the melody of her joy.

CHAPTER FORTY-EIGHT

Fort Bridger was a square enclosure of white-washed walls. Its heavy gate looked strong enough to resist Indians yet too weak to hold back a regular army. Around its perimeter were wagons in various conditions of disrepair, abandoned by disillusioned travelers. Prices were painted on the sides of some and the asking price for the best of the bunch was fifteen dollars.

There was great commotion upon our arrival. It was impossible to get much closer than a quarter mile to the structure, there were so many travelers stopping. Sarah polished her shoes as I drove that morning. After finally stopping, Coral and I talked about walking the distance, but Sarah was too excited and mounted her horse, promising to meet us later.

As we crowded, shoulder to shoulder, through the large gate, my ears were immediately assaulted by citified sights and sounds. Voices, all talking at the same time, horses standing in a row, tied in front of the low wooden structures. I could make out strains of "Jimmy Crack Corn," played on a piano somewhere. There were lace curtains in some of the windows where, I assumed, officers and their wives lived. Now, on the inside, I could see how the outside walls of the barracks and Trading Post were also the outer walls of the fort. A large grassy area, in the middle, had been trampled in places down to the dirt.

Coral had left me once we passed through the gate, interested in seeing about replenishing our provisions. Seeing what appeared to be a small Post Office, I headed for it, anxious to mail the letters I had tucked in my bag.

As I started to enter the small building, a woman grabbed my arm. Pulling me to the side of the door, she could see she had startled me. "Don't bother," she said.

"Bother with what?" I couldn't imagine how she knew my business.

"Trying to get your letters delivered." She looked around with great suspicion.

I studied her plain face, creased with so much worry it almost frightened me. Her fingers rubbed the cameo, pinned at her throat.

"This is the post office, isn't it?"

She touched my elbow and guided me to a narrow passageway between the office and building next to it.

"They want you to think it is. All of you. But the man inside will charge twenty-five cents an envelope, promising a messenger will get each communique to a post office beyond the Missouri. But in reality, your families will never receive those letters."

Not knowing what to make of the mysterious woman, I asked, "Why would he do such a thing?"

"For the money! What other reason is there?"

She looked at me then as though I was addled.

"I have lived in this wretched place long enough to see what goes on," she continued. "Almost seven months now and none of my letters have been answered."

"Why don't you leave then, go back. . . ."

"To Indiana? Don't you think I have tried?" Again she looked at me as though she were speaking to a candidate for the asylum.

Before I could ask more about her dilemma, a handsome man in uniform spotted us standing between the buildings.

His pace quickened until he stopped, at attention, in front of the curious woman.

"Mrs. Markham? The Lieutenant has been looking for you, ma'am. Would you allow me to escort you back to your room to wait for him?"

The soldier never acknowledged me. Mrs. Markham meekly obeyed, walking in front of the man without another word to me.

It took me a moment to compose myself. Something made me believe the woman. I stepped out from the shade, looking to either side of me, trying to figure out what to do with my letters. The woman and her escort had been gobbled up by the crowd, and I could not see so much as the top of the head of either person.

Forts had been like patches of civilization in the wilderness and we flocked to them for news, food, company, encouragement. But I was suddenly surrounded by too many unfamiliar faces and decided to find Coral.

Before I could get through the door of the main building, however, she came storming outside. Empty-handed.

"Let's go back to the wagon; I am too angry to stay here."

"What happened?"

"The stores are barren. Everyone I talk to is trying to buy food from me! From me! What do I have, I ask you? Nothing. That's what I have right now. Nothing!"

I noticed unoccupied steps across the courtyard and pulled Coral toward them. Fort Bridger had been something I had looked forward to for weeks. A reason to wear a new skirt, curl my hair. For a day or so I would be able to relax. I would be allotted time to think about my lost husband with no reminders of the trail ahead. We would celebrate the recovery of our Colonel. I had even hoped to be able to make friends with some of the wives here, have a stimulating conversation. See a friendly smile. As badly as our stop was turning out, I did not want to leave so soon.

"What do we need?" I asked, trying to calm my friend.

"Everything!" She threw up her hands in disgust.

"Come now, I'm sure we have some supplies."

"Not enough to get us far."

Sarah waved and came to where we were sitting. "I can't find anything we need. What's happening here?" She stood with her hand on her hips, looking down at us.

"I was trying to make Abigail understand there is no food, not even a sack of flour. Everyone keeps asking what I have extra to sell. I'm afraid if we don't get back to our wagon soon there will be nothing left."

Sarah sat down, one step up from us. "I get the impression if we have anything of value they'd find something to trade very quickly. But you won't be needing that much, Coral. You'll be traveling by yourself the rest of the way."

"No. I go on to Oregon with the two of you."

Eagerly Sarah hugged Coral. "Really?" Then she pushed her back to arm's length. "When did you decide this? And why wasn't I let in on your plans? I am part of this little group, aren't I?"

I never expected Coral to defend herself, but she surprised me when she apologized to Sarah. "I should have told you. You're right, we are together. You and I. With a baby coming, Abigail will be turning back."

"No," I blurted out. "I'm going on."

Both women just stared at me. I could hardly believe it myself. What a strange time to be deciding our futures. There in the middle of a fort, surrounded by strangers.

"You are?" Sarah asked. "What brought you to this monumental decision?"

I plopped my bag in my lap, straightened my skirt. "Many

small decisions I've been making all along the way."

Sarah ran a finger across her forehead, sliding a piece of fringed bangs under her pink bonnet. "Tell us a few; I'm interested in hearing them."

"I am, also," Coral said, folding her hands.

I was on the spot then and could not complain for I had put myself there. "Well, I am not continuing because it was Samuel's idea. I feel no obligations whatsoever to pay homage to him in that fashion. I am not going west to give my child a better life—Baltimore would afford that. I am not returning home because I miss my family. Oh, to some degree I do, but homesickness has always seemed a waste of time to me."

When I paused to take a breath Coral nudged me. "Now, for the reasons you want to go on."

"There is really only one. I want to keep moving forward. Simple as that. I want to."

"That's it?" Sarah asked.

"That's all that matters," Coral told her.

"I've always felt obligations were more important. That the things I wanted to do were considered frivolous. But now, my desires seem worth consideration, more than reason enough for me to head west."

"To Oregon then," Coral said with a grin.

"To Oregon!" Sarah chimed in.

"To California," I said.

CHAPTER FORTY-NINE

"California?" Coral and Sarah said the word together.

Before I could explain, something heavy fell at our feet. When I looked down, I saw Mrs. Markham.

"I know you have no reason to believe me but I have to get away from here. Now!" She looked over her shoulder, frantic. "Help me . . . please." The poor woman clung to me.

Not one word passed between me and my two companions and yet, somehow, we worked together as if rehearsed for the scene. Sarah stood, putting one arm around the woman while Coral took off her yellow bonnet and pulled it down over Mrs. Markham's head. I covered the other side. With Coral walking behind, the three of us sheltered Mrs. Markham from searching eyes. Huddled around her, we walked right through the gate and never stopped until we came to my wagon.

"Now," Coral said when we were all seated together, beneath my canvas. "For some introductions."

Mrs. Markham removed the bonnet and handed it back to Coral with a smile of relief. "My name is Julia Markham. I can't tell you how grateful I am to all of you."

"I'm Sarah Franklin," Sarah spoke up for the first time since we stepped up into the wagon. "And this is Coral Adams and Abigail Gray."

"It's my pleasure, ladies."

The frail woman looked exhausted so I picked up the story while she leaned back to rest.

"I met Mrs. Markham . . ."

"Julia, dear. Call me Julia."

"All right." I studied her face for a moment and then continued. "I was going into the post office when I met Julia. She warned me not to post my letters, something about them not getting delivered."

Coral nodded. "I've heard stories of unscrupulous men promising to take the mail to big city post offices, for money of course. But they never do it."

"See?" Julia, looked at me, vindicated.

"Why don't you tell us who, exactly, you need saving from?" Sarah asked.

"Yes, tell us," Coral said, leaning in.

Julia blew out a long breath from between her dry lips. "My husband, the Army. You wouldn't believe what goes on here. I can't leave—I can't get word to my family. I'm a prisoner. Our living quarters are unbearable. I came out here by wagon and believe me, it was far superior to what I am forced to endure inside those walls."

Julia Markham was frail to the point that her shoulder bones poked through her blouse. She trembled whether she was speaking or resting. Her hair looked to be thinning, which surprised me considering she must have been no more than thirty years old. She wore her top button fastened and her sleeves cinched tightly around her wrists. Quite excessive on such a blistering day.

I couldn't tell if Coral or Sarah believed our guest. I wasn't sure that I did. Having never actually met a military wife before, she possessed none of the confidence nor poise I would have expected.

Coral finally presented the question we were all too nervous to ask. "What goes on here?"

In spite of the fact we were safe, Julia looked behind her,

then lifted herself slightly to peek through the front opening of the wagon. After convincing herself there was no one about, she spoke.

"My husband, Romer, did not come up through the ranks due to any bravery or intelligence on his part. His father was an officer as was his grandfather. Family friends, favors called in got Romer as far as Lieutenant. That manipulation has left him . . . dissatisfied. He knows the men have no respect for him. Romer says the fort is like an island inhabited by dangerous traitors waiting to do him in surrounded by infested land. He complains about it incessantly. I am at my wit's end. He's frightened to stay and even more frightened to leave."

"And he takes out his fear on you," Sarah said flatly.

Julia massaged her wrist. "Yes."

I still wasn't sure if I believed any of the accusations the woman made. Even if I did, however, her problems were between her and her husband. There was no room for interfering outsiders. And yet, her fear made me want to help in some way.

"Take me with you!" Julia threw herself into a prone position on my floor, her fingers clawed the rough wood as she tried hanging onto the flat surface.

"Indiana's in the opposite direction," I said.

Coral stroked the poor woman's hair. "That's where her husband will begin looking for her. If she comes to Oregon with us. . . ."

"No," Sarah said biting her bottom lip, concentrating. "If we continue with the others, they'll spot Julia immediately, know she doesn't belong with us. Besides, all our names are on the manifest. If someone recognized any of us at the fort, it would be easy for Lieutenant Markham to make some inquiries and track us to Colonel Chapman's group."

"What about California?" Julia sat up, hopeful. "It sounds

like a beautiful place, sunny and warm almost all year round. Romer would never even discuss living there. A party leaves in the morning."

Coral looked at me, strangely. "Abigail has always wanted to go there, also. Isn't that right, Abby?"

"Not always, just recently."

"And why, pray tell, California?" Sarah asked. "You never did explain your thinking to us."

"It would change this trip from being Samuel's idea to being mine. Because of my work and my planning, I would end up in a place of my choosing."

"Our planning," Sarah corrected. "We're all in this together now."

CHAPTER FIFTY

Julia never left my wagon once she was inside. I stayed close by while Coral went to talk with Andrew. Sarah walked back to the fort to retrieve her horse and find out what was being done to locate Mrs. Markham.

The Colonel rode through just as I was trying to make a dinner of crackers and pickles.

"We'll be pulling out in two days, Mrs. Gray. I was hoping to have a new assistant but our number has fallen to less than sixty. I figure we can manage on our own."

I debated for a minute, wondering whether or not to tell Colonel Chapman his count would soon be reduced by another three. Without consulting with Sarah and Coral, I decided against taking him into my confidence. Even if I could trust him, I was still not sure of his nature nor his circle of friends. No, I felt more bound by Julia's fear—imagined or real—than I did to the wagon master.

"We're here until Friday morning, then?" I looked up at him.

"Appears so, ma'am. We came at a bad time, but I've been assured provisions are on their way; we'll just have to stay put until then. I wouldn't think a few days off the trail would be disagreeable to anyone." He laughed in a pleasant manner.

"I'm not sure if I'll be traveling with you." Throwing out the information, I waited for his reaction.

He looked startled at first but then appeared to suddenly understand. "Of course, you'll probably be wanting to go back east, now that Mr. Gray is gone. I can arrange for you to return with the Spahr party; they're pulling out on Friday, also."

"I'm not quite sure what I want to do right now." I thought it best to give the impression I was confused.

"Will Mrs. Adams and Miss Franklin be accompanying you?"

"I don't know what their plans are."

He gave me that smile I had seen on every man's face I had ever known. The one that said he knew women should be humored, that we were all frail creatures unable to think logically. "Well, I'll need to know the exact number traveling to Oregon. If you could get that to me Thursday before supper, I'd be obliged."

"Of course."

"Nice talking with you, ma'am." He touched his hat and rode down to the next wagon.

After the Colonel was well out of sight, I checked on Julia and was immediately bombarded with questions.

"Do you think he suspected anything? If he did, would he fetch my husband? How well do you know that man?"

"There's no reason he should be suspicious of anything." Before I could continue, Coral came up behind me with Andrew at her side.

"Coral told me about your poor friend, maybe I can speak with her," he said, "calm her fears."

My first instinct was to tell him there was nothing any of us could say that would help Julia more than getting her away from that place. But of all the people I had met up to that point in my life, Andrew Griesinger was the only one who at least tried understanding. Everything. Whether it was visible with the eyes or only the heart, he expended equal thought.

I stepped aside.

Coral told me not to worry then pointed to a sack hanging over her shoulder. "Andrew's a compassionate man and generous as well. He gave us some sugar and even a few eggs. I can't imagine where he got the eggs. . . ."

"Did you tell him we're going to California?" I hated spoiling her enthusiasm but couldn't wait a minute longer.

"I told him everything." She walked toward the blanket I had spread.

Hopeful, I asked, "Is he coming with us?"

Coral carefully lowered the sack to the ground then turned to face me. Putting her hands on my shoulders, she looked me straight in the eyes. "Abigail, Andrew makes his own plans."

"I know that."

"And none of those plans have one thing to do with us."

"I am not ignorant of that fact, Coral."

"Then why should he change his because we change ours?"

I felt embarrassed and looked away from her eyes. "He makes me feel safe and I'm afraid. . . ."

"All of us are afraid—man and woman. But can't you see what you're doing?"

"What?" I pulled away from her.

"Depending."

"On what?" I heard my voice raise and felt my cheeks burn.

"Depending on others to make you feel safe."

"I think I'm entitled to feel frightened. Look around you, Coral! How can you be so callous?"

Coral looked hurt and I felt satisfied that I was not the only one upset. "Callous? No. Concerned? Yes. I try to save you from losing years of your life to confusion as I did. To show you that safety is found in here." Then she thumped my forehead.

I can't say if I intended to protect myself or hurt Coral, but before I could lay a hand on her, Sarah rode up behind us.

"What's going on?" She jumped down from her horse. "It looks as though the two of you are facing off for a fight."

"I'm just trying to explain to Abigail. . . ."

"And I was trying to make Coral understand that. . . ."

"My news can wait." Sarah plopped herself straight down. Removing the fan from her bag, she fluttered it in front of her face, enjoying herself as though she were at the opera.

Coral and I glared at each other. I knew, in her odd way, Coral was trying to help me. But at that moment I felt more in need of sympathy than lecturing.

"Continue," Sarah said.

"No." Coral sat on the blanket and looked up at me defiantly. "I'm finished talking."

I sat next to Sarah. "I'm finished, too."

Sarah eagerly began. "Well, either Lieutenant Markham isn't aware his wife is missing or she does this so regularly that he doesn't take notice of it anymore."

"Why do you say that?" I asked.

"I was reading over the notices posted outside the Trading Post, checking to see when a group leaves for California. I took my time, trying to eavesdrop on conversations around me that might refer to Julia. Suddenly I heard someone call his name and there he was. Standing right behind me."

"Who?" Coral asked.

"Lieutenant Markham, who else?" I stared at Sarah for affirmation.

"It was the lieutenant all right. Then silly me," she giggled, "I was so clumsy and stepped back on the toe of his shoe. Well I had to apologize, and that started us talking."

"What did he say?"

"Do you think he was trying to find out if you knew anything about his wife? Maybe he purposely stood behind you, waiting for you to give yourself away," I said.

Sarah snapped her fan closed and pushed it into the opening of her cloth bag. "That's what I intend to find out this evening."

Coral sat back, visibly surprised. "You are returning to the fort tonight?"

"Yes. Lieutenant Markham is sending someone to escort me to dine with him."

CHAPTER FIFTY-ONE

"I believe her," Andrew told me while Sarah went to wash and change into a clean dress. Coral busied herself making biscuits and, I suspected, avoid my company for awhile.

"You think her husband means to do her harm?"

"He already has."

I asked but did not want to hear the answer. "You saw something?"

"There are bruises, and she thinks she is in danger. Having that weigh on her mind makes the fear as real for her as the cruelty. We must help her escape, Abigail. She can contact her husband later if she wishes."

I reached for Andrew's hands. They were almost the same size as my own; he responded with a gentle squeeze of reassurance.

"You said 'we,' Andrew. That 'we' should get Julia away from here. Does that mean you'll come with us?"

In spite of the fact that he was shorter than I, Andrew Griesinger had seemed to grow taller in my eyes with each day. As I waited for him to answer, I hoped Coral had been wrong.

"No, Abigail, we say good-bye here. Having my body in a neighboring wagon would be no more beneficial to you or the others than if I were miles away. Ahh, but my prayers will guide and inspire you."

I embraced him then which was very impulsive of me.

"You'll be fine, Abigail, just fine." Andrew returned my hug.

"I don't want to be fine, Andrew, I want to be better."

Sarah's escort arrived driving a fancy buggy pulled by one white horse and one black. We were all surprised by Lieutenant Markham's nonchalant attitude concerning his wife's disappearance, but his lack of interest also left us relieved.

I never told Julia about Sarah's dinner plans; the three of us had decided to let her sleep. She seemed calmer since her visit with Andrew. It was decidedly wiser to keep Julia Markham out of sight.

Two hours passed, maybe three. Coral and I ignored our bad feelings and sat in front of the fire together. It felt good to rest. There was no packing or unpacking to be done. Our clothes would be washed the next day and dinner was finished. Until it was time to bed down, we could enjoy the crisp night air.

I could hear someone singing in the distance, a child cried that he wasn't tired and didn't need to go to bed just yet. For the first time, I realized I wanted my baby to be born a girl. And while thinking about my unborn child, I marveled at how calm I felt when I should have been anxious and nervous.

"Have you ever known you were in the perfect spot at the perfect moment?" I asked Coral.

"You mean when something lucky is getting ready to happen?"

I stroked my arm, enjoying the sensation of my own skin being touched by my own hand. "No. I mean when you aren't thinking about chores needing attention tomorrow or lamenting something you should have done yesterday. When your body is comfortable in its clothing and nothing is poking or pinching you where you sit. And the air seems to be exactly the same temperature as your skin. Not too cold—not too hot. But perfect."

Coral rubbed her stomach. "Ach, you must have thrown away your corset today."

"Quite awhile ago." What a strange thing for her to think of. I looked into her eyes reflecting the flames and knew she would always be one of my dearest, strangest friends.

Before I could expound further about my contentment, horses approached. I recognized Sarah's voice.

"Thank you again, Sergeant."

She smiled and calmly waved to the driver until the buggy turned and headed back toward the fort.

"Get up!" She urged us in a controlled growl. "Now! Follow me and don't look frightened."

We did as we were told.

Sarah led us into the wagon and as she lit a lamp, Julia woke with a start.

"What's happening? Is it Romer? Oh, God, is he here?"

I didn't know what to say and could only sit beside her, waiting for Sarah to explain.

"If Julia doesn't return by tomorrow night, he says he'll start looking for her. He vows to never let her go."

It was crowded inside the wagon and Coral looked more uncomfortable than frightened. "Why tomorrow? Why isn't he searching for his wife now?"

Sarah looked at Julia. "He told me she does this quite frequently but always returns. He talked about her like she was his pet, no better than a dog."

Julia seemed dazed. She never asked how it came about that Sarah had spoken to the lieutenant. "I tried running away twice before. Romer acts so bravely in front of his men and so charming in front of other women." She glanced at Sarah. "But he's the most horrible sort of coward. If I don't smile when he instructs me to or should I feel poorly when he orders me to be cordial, he flies into one of his rages. And when that fear and anger erupt at the same time . . . he hurts me."

I put a protective arm around Julia, feeling her trembling begin all over again. "Do you think he meant what he said?" I asked Sarah.

"When it comes to a man's pride, he means every vile word he threatens. You can take his horse, even his money, but if he thinks his pride is at jeopardy, he'll kill you and feel justified in doing so."

"I don't want to bring harm to any of you; I have to get away from here." Julia moved to leave.

"Sit down," Coral said. "You can't go out into the darkness, wandering around with no food. Don't be so silly."

Julia slumped back onto the bed.

Sarah nodded. "Coral's right; Julia can't go alone."

"The Colonel told me there's a wagon train leaving for California Friday morning." I suddenly had the solution to our problem. "What we have to do is set out tomorrow. With all the confusion around here, we'll probably not even be missed. If Mr. Markham holds to his word and starts checking the camps, we'll be gone. First thing in the morning, I'll tell the Colonel we're turning back—all of us. That way, if he's questioned, he'll throw suspicion in the opposite direction. Then all we have to do is sit tight and wait for the Friday group to catch up to us."

Having finished, I waited, expecting there to be some sort of discussion. But instead, each woman sat in silence, contemplating what I had proposed.

Sarah was the first to speak. "Perfect," was all she said.

"Yes." Coral crossed her arms and leaned back, thinking a moment longer. "It should work very well."

Julia wiped at a tear and nodded. "Perfectly well."

CHAPTER FIFTY-TWO

"Take it," Andrew Griesinger urged. "After talking with that horrible man, I have no doubt Mrs. Markham is in danger."

"We can't take your wagon, Andrew," Sarah said, trying not to offend him.

I agreed. "No, we can't."

"You need another wagon now. Am I correct?"

I stopped brushing my hair. "Yes, I was thinking that very thing while trying to sleep last night."

"If you purchase one of those outside the fort, you'll then have to get a team. Is that correct?"

"Yes, it is," Coral continued hanging her damp laundry.

"And won't all of that activity stir up questions?"

"I suppose so," Sarah said.

"Supplies have come in. I watched the wagons being unloaded myself when I was at the fort earlier. Everyone's scrambling to get his share. And while people line up and barter, load and unload, Lieutenant Markham orders them to answer questions about his wife. He detains some, women mostly, and has soldiers escort others out of the gates before they can finish their purchasing.

"I took my wagon up there. I have made camp in different spots these past days. I imagine folks don't take enough notice of me to realize when my wagon is gone."

Sarah finished buttoning her boots. "He's right. It's been nothing but chaos since we arrived; I can't keep track of things myself."

"Now is the best time to leave," Andrew concluded.

"We can't leave without supplies," Coral moved a little faster with her work.

"They're in my wagon. I bought what I thought you would need."

I was overcome. "You did that for us?"

The kind man fingered an amber stone hanging from his belt. "You'll find, Abigail, that people do what pleases them. I did this for me. How could I live happily not knowing if my dear friends were safe?"

"But what will you use for a wagon?" Coral stopped her work and came to stand next to the man I suspected she had developed special feelings for. "How will you get by?"

"I have until tomorrow to arrange something." I saw a warmth in Andrew's eyes when he spoke to Coral and knew he felt very attached to her, also.

Sarah seemed to be figuring something in her head. "We'll pay you for the wagon and team and of course, the supplies. I have . . ."

"Money would change my intentions. No." He seemed resolute. "Take what I offer as a gift, a blessing of sorts for your safe journey or else the good wishes lose their potency."

There had been many times, during long conversations with Andrew, when I had not understood the full import of his words. But this time when he spoke of the potency of wishes, I was struck with an inspired moment of clarity. "Wait here," I told him. "Don't move." And I scurried inside the wagon.

When I returned, the three of them looked as though they had taken me at my word and not moved one inch. "Here." I handed him the plans for Uncle Nathan's wagon.

"What is this?" Andrew unrolled the heavy paper.

Sarah gasped when she recognized what I had handed over to our friend. At first I thought she would snatch them away or scream at me that I was being stupid. But when I looked at her, she smiled and simply nodded.

"Those drawings were inspired by dreams for a safe and exciting future. An experiment of sorts. But I think they need some revisions, looked at with the eyes of an experienced traveler."

"That handsome wagon you and your husband and brother left Council Bluffs in?" Andrew asked. "Made from these plans?"

"Yes. A gift from my uncle."

"Surely there must have been a patent? There are many good ideas here."

"No patents," Sarah said, "just hopes."

"This is what you were to make your fortune with?" Coral looked concerned.

"Oh, no. I have my shares in the shipbuilding business back home. Mr. Laird, our foreman, is quite capable of running the outfit himself. Maybe by now he would even like to own it. I'll wire him when I get settled. No need to decide anything until then."

Andrew smiled. "I accept your gift, then, Abigail."

Coral pushed Sarah toward me and me toward Andrew. The four of us stood in a circle, our foreheads almost touching.

"We accept your generous offer and thank the good Lord for sending you to us. Don't we, ladies?" Coral spoke reverently.

Without one more word, Sarah and I joined Coral and wrapped our arms around the small man.

Things began moving very quickly.

Coral went to tell Julia we would be leaving within the hour. Half a day lead would be possible if the sunlight beat out the threatening clouds.

I twisted as much water as I could from Coral's just-washed clothing and rolled them inside a clean sheet. I ran back and forth, for what seemed a hundred trips, putting away dishes and pots, breaking up the fire, rolling up bedding. Sarah kept up with me until she suddenly stopped.

"Mr. McFarland's harmonica! Abby, I have to return it to him!"

When she ran to get her bag, I yelled after her, "Wait for me!"

I hadn't seen the McFarland family for weeks. It came as a surprise to me then how, in spite of all the confusion, Sarah was able to locate their wagon so effortlessly.

My friend greeted the large man in his own language as she had done the last time we all met. After cordialities passed between them, she produced the instrument from her bag. It was carefully wrapped in a satin handkerchief edged with forest green lace. Nodding and smiling, Sarah held it up to the big man.

I expected Mr. McFarland to be overjoyed. Relieved to have his possession back. But instead, he back-stepped, refusing to even touch it.

"What's the matter with him?" I whispered.

"He took it to heart when I told him his music brought bad luck."

Sarah slowly unwrapped the handkerchief. The small instrument had been polished. Then she smiled and tried coaxing the Scotsman to take back what belonged to him. I could tell, without being able to understand the exact words themselves, that Sarah told him it would be fine if the man played his music. Assuring him no bad luck or evil spirits would spoil his happiness.

Carefully, as if lifting a newborn baby from the arms of its mother, the man with fat, stubby fingers picked up the harmonica. Holding it to his lips, he blew so gently it almost reminded me of a kiss.

I always thought memories had a way of muting brash colors, of softening harsh realities. But I vividly remembered Mr. McFarland's ear-piercing noise. Time had not made me forget being upset and angry when hearing the shrill sound. When that red-faced man played, however, the tones were heavenly.

Sarah offered a bit of applause when he finished and I followed her lead. Mr. McFarland seemed embarrassed by the attention but bowed slightly. Then he rewrapped the harmonica with the soft handkerchief and handed it back to Sarah.

Forgetting herself, Sarah spoke in the voice I was accustomed to hearing come from her mouth. "I can't keep it for you any longer. Don't you understand?"

In what I can only describe as Mr. McFarland's American voice, he said, "I give this fer ye ter ha'e. A present fer watchin' out fer us. Ma family has had no more harm come tae them since yer last visit. Ye're a beautiful angel, that ye are."

Sarah stood, stuck to her place. Her expression went from confused to sad to excited all within the span of a moment.

"I accept your gift, Mr. McFarland, thank you. And I ask that you give your wife something from me." She opened her bag again. After putting the harmonica back inside, she withdrew her beautifully carved fan. Handing it to the man she said, "It has always brought me good luck."

CHAPTER FIFTY-THREE

Coral practically cried with relief when she saw us running toward the wagon. Then she got angry.

"Ach, I had no idea where you were; how could you both have been so cruel to me? I was thinking the soldiers dragged you to the fort. Or that horrible Lieutenant Markham knew something. How could you leave like that?" She stood with fisted hands on her hips, her feet planted firmly. But before either Sarah or I could answer, Coral grabbed my right arm, Sarah's left, and pulled us toward the wagon. "Never mind. You're back now. No time to waste standing and talking."

Andrew waited next to his wagon, motioning for us to hurry.

Sarah climbed up onto the seat of my wagon. Adjusting her skirt and hat, putting on gloves to protect her hands from the pull of the reins, she was finally ready.

Coral waved her on. Used to beginning our days on the trail walking, Coral apparently had no intention of changing her routine, even under these unusual circumstances.

I handed Andrew a letter. "If you could manage to leave this in Colonel Chapman's wagon, I'd appreciate it. Make him think I dropped by with it. It just says the three of us will not be continuing on to Oregon with his party. That should keep him from getting suspicious or looking for us."

"Of course. I'll do it today."

A commotion could be heard in the distance. I turned, pretending to be curious but actually hoping the pause would keep me from once more asking Andrew to come with us.

"Looks like that group we expected earlier, going back east from California. That should make your departure even less conspicuous."

"I'll miss you, Andrew." The words could no longer be withheld no matter how desperately I tried.

"And I'll miss you, Abigail. But you have good friends in Miss Franklin and Coral."

"I wish . . ."

"It's not my turn to make the journey with you, it's Mrs. Markham's."

He helped me up to the top of his wagon and after kissing my hand, went to pet each one of his animals good-bye.

I could see Coral urging me to follow her.

Looking back over my shoulder at Fort Bridger, I realized I was frightened to leave the humanity behind. But none of the people. As I looked forward, to where Coral walked, and my own wagon trundled toward the mysteries beyond, I felt renewed excitement.

And that excitement at last, at long last, overcame my fear and resentment.

EPILOGUE

How foolish I was to think I was born knowing. Truth is, I was born remembering.

Rocking steadily, in rhythm with the oxen and uneven ground, afforded uninterrupted time to reflect. What a shame that only came before or after the trauma and chaos. On the edge of Wyoming, colors presented themselves to me, making me, Mrs. Belshaw's practical daughter, want to set up a canvas or write a song. Poetry fluttered inside my brain and I thanked the talented, artistic women in my family for their inheritance. Until I got my journal I recited one particular verse over and over, afraid I would forever lose it.

> How heavy life,
> how burdensome dreams,
> yet we sustain them,
> on the strength of wings.